Dark Tyrants

EDITED BY JUSTIN ACHILLI

AND ROBERT HATCH

A

ANTHOLOGY

White Wolf Publishing
735 Stonegate Industrial Boulevard
Suite 128
Clarkston, Georgia 30021

World Wide Web Page: www.white-wolf.com

Table of Contents

A FOOL'S EMBRACE

WRITTEN AND ILLUSTRATED BY GUY DAVIS
AND VINCE LOCKE
LETTERED BY MATT MILBERGER

THEY ARE BUT FOOLS, ALL OF THEM. FOOLS AND CHILDREN WHO FEAR THE DARK...

...WHO FEAR THE NIGHTMARES OF DEVILS AND BEASTIES THAT BEAR THE BLAME FOR THEIR SICKNESS AND MISFORTUNE.

COWERING AMONG THEIR KINE, CLINGING TO LIVES THAT COME AND PASS AS QUICKLY AS THE DUSK TO MY IMMORTAL EYES.

OH, THEY ARE COWARDS AND CATTLE, THESE FOOLS WHO FEAR THE SHADOWS IN THE NIGHT - SHADOWS THAT LURK IN THEIR CORNERS, THAT CLAW AT THEIR THROATS.

SHADOWS THAT CARRY OFF THEIR YOUNG AND FEED UPON THEIR SOULS, MONSTERS AND DEMONS THAT EXIST ONLY TO PUNISH THEM FOR THEIR LACK OF FAITH.

FOR THESE ARE THE NIGHTMARES AND TALES THAT SEND THESE FOOLS HUDDLING IN PRAYER THROUGH THE NIGHT...

...BUT IT'S ME WHO THEY TRULY FEAR...

AND AT ME ALL THEY CAN DO IS LAUGH.

MUDDLEGUMP!

MUDDLEGUMP!

MUDDLEGUMP!

HEEEEEE!

MUDDLEGUMP!

MUDDLEGUMP!

MUDDLEGUMP!

OH, THEY DO LOVE THEIR LITTLE MUDDLEGUMP, THEIR TWISTED AND GNARLED LITTLE PLAYTHING, THEIR TORTURED MSSHAPEN FOOL.

HOW THEY HOWL AT THE MERE SIGHT OF ME. I'M A MIRROR FOR THEIR VANITY, ALTHOUGH A CRACKED ONE.

HEEE! SIT WITH YE I WILL, DINE WITH'Y I SHALL!

FOR OUR VISITING GUESTS OF SUCH HIGH REGARD I MUST MEET ON A SIMILAR FASHION!

9

WERT!

WERT!

WERT! WHERE ARE Y', YOU LAZY...IF THOSE ANIMALS AREN'T READY I'LL...

WHAT?...MY GOODS...

HUH?

THERE YOU ARE, YOU BASTARD! YOU DINNA THINK I'D HEAR YOU MOANING AWAY, YOUR BELLY FULL OF ALE PERHAPS?

UNNHHH...

YOU'RE WORTHLESS! I GAVE YOU A SIMPLE TASK AND YOU FAIL AT THAT. THROW MY GOODS IN THE YARD TO COWER IN HERE LIKE THE FOOL TOWNSFOLK TILL MORNING, DID YE? AND THEN DROWN YOUR FEARS AWAY.

UNNH... UNHMUH

I'LL QUIET THAT STOMACH OF YOURS, BOY. YOU'LL BE SCREAMING WHEN I'M DONE!

UNNH...UNHMUH

11

THIS OAF AND HIS KINE ARE NOT YOUR MASTER, NOR ARE THEY MATCH FOR ANY OF YOUR WHIMS. THEY ARE BUT CATTLE TO YOUR THIRST AND CLAY TO YOUR FOLLIES JUST AS I HAD SHAPED THIS REALM FOR AGES.

...BUT...I'M JUST A SQUIRE...A BOY. HE WAS MY TEACHER! WHAT COULD I LEARN FROM YOU?

HAHAHEEE! A SQUIRE TO A FOOL!

NO, YOU DID ALL I WOULD EVER ASK BY KILLING ONE WHO WOULD STRIKE OUT AT ME. NOW YOU MUST GO AND FIND YOUR OWN WAY, I'LL NOT BE YOUR TEACHER.

BUT WHAT WILL BECOME OF ME...WHERE DO I...

HERE, CHILDE, TAKE THESE...AND THIS...HEEE... AND WHATEVER WITS LEFT YOU.

TAKE THEM AND RUN...FAR INTO THE NIGHT AND DARKNESS.

AND THE WORLD THAT IS NOW YOUR HOME...

16

19

22

THE DARKNESS AND THE DAWN

24

Bearer of Ill News

BY RICHARD E. DANSKY

The clearing of the Black Monk was far less impressive than the villagers' tales had made it out to be. If one listened to the tales of the stable hands at the local inns, the place was guarded by gargoyles and had a pit straight to Hell at its center. When glimpsed on a rainy night, however, the place seemed to have a great many trees and a well, and not much else. I saw no hellhounds, no demons, no proof of the Black Monk's great powers. On the other hand, I had not expected such. I knew precisely the powers of darkness with which the man, one Friar Offa, had been dealing, and as such was prepared for more sensible perils.

This Offa had courage. He had taken it upon himself to save Christendom, single-handedly, from me and my kind. He had learned all he could of us, sacrificing his own faith to do so, and sent his knowledge to Rome so that the Pope himself might know what terrors haunted the European night. One of our servants (and when I say "our" servants, I mean of course one of my clan's servants—the others are inconsequential in this tale) fortunately intercepted the fatal missive and delivered it to our hands, instead of the Holy Father's, and thus was catastrophe averted.

RICHARD E. DANSKY

32

Still, it had come too close, and as such my sire was resolved to take action on the matter. And so, he bade me make a servant of this troublesome priest so that he might cease to work against us. Thus did I sojourn forth from Londinium (as my sire calls it) and travel into the teeth of the English autumn. Thus did I pack my courier's pouch with that which would bend this priest to our will, or break his will all to pieces. Most importantly, however, thus did I find myself picking my way through the thorn-riddled forests near Cheltenham in the middle of an unseasonable storm, my cloak and patience both torn to pieces. It was all so that I might visit the Black Priest in his cottage, far from prying eyes, and show him the fruits of his labors.

I tethered my steed to a branch about twenty yards from the priest's cottage, hoping that the cover of leaves would afford him some protection from the storm. A light spilled from behind a shuttered window, and smoke bubbled from the cottage's rough chimney. Off to one side of the building, a well-tended herb garden had magically transformed itself into a sizeable swamp, and on the edge of vision, a rough-hewn gray stone squatted as a monument to some corpse or other. Wishing to delay the inevitable, I sloshed my way over to the marker. The light from the window was poor, but I could still make out the legend. It read precisely as I'd expected it would, which did nothing to ease my nerves.

I had hoped, as I led my horse along the woodcutter's track we'd taken, that Offa would be in Somnus's arms when I arrived. That way, I would be able to surprise, wake and deal with him on my terms, as his mind would be muzzy with sleep and whatever preparations he'd made for defense against intruders would be unavailable. Instead, he looked to be wide awake, which meant that this duel would be on slightly more even terms. Admittedly, he'd captured and killed one of our kind only through trickery, not through main strength, but any mortal who kills a Cainite without aid earns my respect. And so I had intended to treat him with the greatest respect one can show an enemy: I had no intention of ever allowing him to act.

I considered waiting to see if the good friar would drift off to sleep on his own, but quickly discarded the idea. Tarrying would merely rob me of precious minutes before dawn, minutes which might be needed. Cursing to myself, I damned the priest for living so far from any civilized town, and for being such a thorn as to demand my personal attention. I wondered glumly if he would recognize the honor when all was said and done, and then trudged through the muck to his door.

By the time I reached the door, he'd already opened it. Silhouetted against the light inside, his figure was naught but a black shape. "It's an unfit night for man or beast," he said. "I've been expecting you; come in where it's dry."

"Expecting me?"

I paused. Boukephos had demanded that I deal with the priest personally, but he had *not* mentioned that he'd informed my host that I was coming. The notion that I had been expected was unsettling.

The monk—for he was dressed as one, and as a monk was how I thought of him—smiled ruefully, gently. "You, or someone very much like you. I have opened some doors that cannot be shut, and for these few months I have been waiting for the arm that would pull me farther into the shadows." He backed away from the door, gesturing that I should enter.

Even after all this poor fool had endured, he still looked formidable. His faith might have withered, but not his strength—the hand that gestured me to follow him had a swordsman's calluses—and he still moved like a fighting man, never quite relaxing. His sword hung on the wall, though, hovering over a large, bloodstained table half-covered in herbs and dried leaves.

With a wary eye, I stepped inside and shut the door behind me. A pair of rough wooden stools glowed dully in the firelight, and with a grunt I settled myself on the one farther from the fire. Smiling as at some private joke, my host placed himself upon the other. His calm was unnerving.

"So what brings you to Cheltenham wood on a night like this, good sir? Mind you, you're likely not to be the only visitor I receive."

"Even on a night such as this?"

He nodded. "Even so. The wilder the weather, the more of my neighbors come skulking along that path asking for healing-potions and love-philtres. They labor under the illusion that visiting me at night means that no one else in the village will see them doing so. Of course, not a one of them has realized that everyone else in Cheltenham has had the same idea, and there's a veritable Roman mob on that path out there some nights. And, if the good citizens see one another on their way to or from my little domus, instead of owning their shame at resorting to my foul wizardly arts, they blame the meeting on the damned black wizard in his cottage and curse my name." Bitterness crept into his smile. "I expect they'll be trying to burn me out shortly; I've refused two of them who would have had poison of me, and that sort of disappointment breeds revenge. But in the meantime, if they want their herbs or their healing, they find their way to me."

In the fireplace, a log snapped and a spiral of sparks flurried their way up the chimney. That seemed to shake my host from his reverie, and he regarded me with a steady eye. "So, what business does bring you here, good sir *vampyr*? Surely you didn't ride all this way to hear tales of a local herbalist's troubles with some ungrateful peasants."

"Actually, I'm here to play courier," I replied, reaching into my pouch for the papers that had sent me on this godforsaken journey. "I believe you've managed to misplace something, and it is my pleasure to return it to you." Wordlessly, he took the sheaf of papers I offered him and began rifling through them.

After a long minute, the monk looked up at me, despair in his eyes. "These are my own notes," he said quietly.

"I know, and it was judged meet that they be returned to you as expediently as possible. I'd be happy to discuss some of the inaccuracies in your findings should you w—"

"God's wounds, these are my notes! In the name of Christ and all the saints, how did you get your foul claws on these, you beast?" He stood, face flushing bright red with rage as he brandished the roll of papers like a rough club. "I was never supposed to see these again! They were to be given to the Pope, for the love of heaven, that the Church might know about your kind! These papers went to Rome, to a *priest*!"

"Yes, they did," I said quietly.

It took a moment for the implications of what I'd said to reach him. All

BEARER OF ILL NEWS

the color drained from his face, and then he collapsed on his stool like an abandoned Punch doll. "You lie," he whispered.

"I fear not, Father."

It was the worst thing I could have said. When the notion of his martyrdom is all a man has to cling to, woe betide he who tells the would-be saint that his sacrifice was pointless. Offa's head snapped up, and there was hatred in his eyes. "You lie. Damn you, you lie."

I merely shrugged.

Spittle flecked his lips as he bellowed at me. "You lie, creature of Satan! These were to be delivered to a priest. Did you divert the courier, or slay him? Did you magic these papers away with black arts? Did you bribe Bernardini's servants, or merely steal these? Answer, damn you!" He was shaking with rage, the veins throbbing in his neck and his hands clenching uncontrollably into fists. "Answer, or by God I'll treat you as I did Harald!"

Looking at him, I pitied him. Here stood a lone man in the wilderness, arraying himself against powers both secular and supernatural, the least of which could crush him with a thought. And yet, he assayed himself the equal of those powers, and dared to pit his efforts against the whole of the society of the Cainites. Here was truly a man of substance, and one who had the will and courage to be a worthy servant.

Or, should my efforts this night fail, a most dangerous enemy.

A gap of perhaps a foot separated us; I made no effort to close it. "Quiet," I said gently. "You wish to know how I obtained those papers; very well, I shall tell you. Bernardini is ours, and has been for three years. He is much esteemed by my master. He was recommended to us by a certain archbishop whose name you might well recognize, and who also has been ours for a very long time. Shall I name names of those who do us reverence, and see how many you recognize?"

Again, the bluster drained from him. "No. Not Bernardini. We fought the Saracens together. No. Not…" His voice trailed off, but I could guess his thoughts.

"No, not the Holy Father, merely some of those who serve him. Does that make you feel better?" I felt myself growing cross.

RICHARD E. DANSKY

He looked up at me, eyes bright with tears. "You are cruel," he said. "Crueler than Aelfred was."

"But more honest, which makes him more of a sinner than me. Tell me, good friar, did you shrive him before he left you? Or was his last confession not sufficiently contrite?"

He turned from me and faced into the fire. The papers slipped from his hand and spilled on the flagstone before the hearth. "No absolution was granted. Even had I wished to, I could not have given him that."

I felt my lips draw back into a smile; part of me was glad that the priest did not see it. "Then his sins be upon his head, friar. He will trouble you no more."

"Dead, then? I expected as much; there was another shape moving through the woods some weeks gone, and the animals all acted strangely."

I sketched a bow from the neck. "That would have been my lord and master, who found your account of the Cainite curse to be fascinating. It is he who requested that I return your property to you, and that I do so personally."

"These?" He kicked the pile of papers; some tumbled into the fire and began to burn. The taste of the smoke filled my mouth, mingling with the scent of the firewood. "These are now worthless. No, your master wished me to know how fruitless my efforts were. It would have been kinder simply never to have let me know that what I'd done was in vain."

I nodded. "Yes, it would have."

He turned back to me, rose from his stool. "Kindness is not something you creatures know, though, is it? I thought not." He began to pace the length of the cottage, weaving past clumsy chairs and other furnishings. "So, you have still not answered my question. Why are you here? This...humiliation could have been accomplished by a lesser servant. Why have you come, oh child of Satan?" There was mockery in the last question, but no malice. He had lost, he knew that he had lost, and now all that was left to him was pride. I had told him that those men whom he considered holier than he had been long in our service; under such circumstances, his insult lacked teeth.

"God as my witness, friar, I am here for your sake—and I prefer my Christian name to 'Child of Satan,' if calling me such would not trouble you unduly."

He turned, amazed. "Christian name? God as your witness? Well, if Bernardini can be in a monster's purse, then I suppose the monster himself can invoke God with impunity. So tell me, *Christian*, what shall I call you? Barabbas, perhaps, or do you claim a holier name?"

"Geoffrey will do."

"Geoffrey, as in the late prince? Fascinating. They accounted him a better general than Richard, you know."

I nodded, once. "I am quite aware of that." He smiled, and returned to his pacing.

"So, Geoffrey, what can you do for me? Your kind has taken from me my faith, my name and my hope. What did you wish to steal? The herbs are on the table; there's naught else here worth taking." He circled the table, gazed up. "Oh, I forgot, my sword. It's slain one of your servants and one of your own, so that must make it valuable indeed to you. Shall I wrap it in a cloth, to protect it from the weather?"

"Enough!" He stopped his rambles and froze like a hare before a snake. I stood, crossed the room to where he stood, took him by the throat—he never moved. "Enough. I have come over a hundred miles to see the brave friar my sire thought so highly of, and whom do I meet? A self-pitying, second tier village witch whose greatest sorrow is that he's likely to be burned instead of crucified. Listen to me, little monk, I have come a very long way to deliver you, and deliver you I shall, even if I needs must empty every thought from your head and fill your skull with so much fear that you'll beg my permission before pissing against the wall! Do you understand me?" I let him drop; he collapsed to the floor. I crouched down next to him and lowered my face to his. "Understand this: You are a blade, to be wielded as we see fit. Since the first word you spoke to your Aelfred, that is all you have been, nothing more. And now that your Aelfred is dead, we intend to make use of you, for you are potentially a very fine tool indeed. We have taken the temper of your steel, and found it good—and so we shall use you, for one does not throw away a good blade while there is still edge to it.

"You will leave this place and return to the monastery you left. You will find Abbot Daffyd somewhat more friendly than he had been upon your departure, and you will join him in the secret worship. You will drink from his chalice and partake of his communion, and thus will you be reconciled to your dear Bernardini, who worships likewise in Rome. As for Daffyd, his usefulness to us is near its end, and when he dies, we shall need a strong successor for him. Serve us well and that man shall be you."

I was telling him far more than was necessary, but for once he seemed frightened enough truly to heed what he heard. He had proven himself intelligent in the past; no doubt he would have uncovered all that I told him eventually in any case.

"I shall not serve." It came out as barely a whisper, so quiet that he repeated it before I was sure what I had heard. "I shall not serve thee."

"Oh, but you shall. What else shall you do? Remain here until they come for you with the torches?"

"If I must. I shall not serve."

"Listen, fool…"

There came a pounding on the door. Instinctively, we dropped to silence. From outside a voice came calling.

"Friar Offa? Friar?"

I looked at my little friar. "Do you recognize the voice?"

He nodded. "Eadmund. A noble's son. One of my regular patrons. Good-hearted, not very swift."

"Do you wish him to see dawn?"

Frightened, he attempted to rise. I held him down with the pressure of a hand, nothing more. "What do you mean?"

"I mean that if you open that door or cry out, I shall take your Eadmund and rip out his throat, and then lay the body on the doorstep of the nearest church with your name written on his forehead in blood."

"You wouldn't dare!"

"Friar? You must let me in. It's vital!"

"I've dared the grave, Offa. Tell him to go, and then quit this place."

"But if it's vital…"

BEARER OF ILL NEWS

"Not as vital as your life."

"Friar! They'll be coming for you with the morning! You have to leave this place! William and the others, they'll be coming at dawn for you! They're claiming witchcraft!"

"And I'll be here to meet them." This my little Offa said aloud, loud enough for his voice to carry through the door into the rainy night. "William's been to my door many a night, Eadmund; I've naught to fear from him."

I stared at Offa in amazement. "His blood on your head, shepherd," I said, and started for the door. In truth, what Offa had said mattered not. He'd simply given me an idea.

"But friar…" poor Eadmund sputtered, and then I swung the door wide. He gaped for a second, then scrabbled for his knife. I reached forward and snapped his neck, then left the body on the doorstep. "A tool," I said, and lifted one of Offa's knives from the tabletop. He reached for his sword, but, like his visitor, he was too late. I had him an instant before he grasped the blade. "Idiot, you do not yet understand. Your service is not requested. It is demanded." I dragged him to the fireplace, his remaining papers still scattered before it. Offa struggled, but I let the blood strengthen me and he worried me as a child might worry his father. "Tonight, the cottage of the black monk burns, and he descends to Hell—or Eboracum." Ignoring his screams, I thrust a wad of the papers into the fire, then tossed them onto the straw of his bedding. The flames shot up with gratifying speed, and I strode out into the night, dragging Offa behind me.

At the threshold, Eadmund lay dying. As an afterthought, I drove the dagger into his breast, and a great gout of blood spewed from his lips. Satisfied, I strode over to my horse and admired my handiwork. "Come morning," I said to Offa, "your villagers will come here. They will find a noble's son sacrificed and your foul seat of wizardry burned to the ground, and they will naturally draw all of the wrong conclusions. These woods—nay, the southern half of England—are no longer safe for you."

"I will throw myself on their mercy."

"They have none. You're looking for a martyr's death, that's all. But martyrs have to die for something, Offa, and you've done nothing. Nothing

RICHARD E. DANSKY

at all." Behind us, the cottage roof had begun to burn. The rain slowed the blaze, but not much. Again he tried to escape, this time seemingly with the intent of flinging himself into the flames. All the strength was out of him, though, and he struggled weakly as a kitten.

"Take my horse and go to the monastery at Eboracum. You'll find sufficient moneys in the saddlebags to last the journey and buy admittance. Now go, else I'll lay a compulsion on ye to do so."

Slowly, numbly, he untied the horse's tether and climbed into the saddle. The black shifted under his weight, no doubt unused to a living master, but seemed to take to the friar well enough; after a short minute Offa had his bearings in the saddle. He turned to me, eyes full of hatred, and then rode off. North was the direction he chose; north to Eboracum.

"And why did you not lay a compulsion on him?" came a voice from behind me. Without turning, I knew who it was.

"Had I merely compelled his will without breaking it, he would have rebelled again once my compulsion ended. This required more of an effort to begin it, but he will never question us again. I have shown him his place, as well as the consequences of leaving it. No, Friar Offa will do our will from this night forward."

My sire came gliding out of the shadows, an expression of faint approval upon his countenance. He was dressed as an Aragonese, but I knew him to be Greek, born in the days of poets and ship-kings. He seemed to move between the raindrops, so that the torrents that soaked me parted for him; I envied him that animal grace. "And the gifts of the money and the horse?"

"All that he has now came from me, and he knows it. It places him in my debt, and he knows that as well. By the old laws, I have made him my man, and he'll not counter that tradition. He is too honor-bound to steal what I have given him; they'll see him in Eboracum soon enough. He may hate me for the giving, but you see that he did not refuse the gifts."

"Still, to give away your horse when dawn is but a few hours off, and Londinium many leagues gone…"

"I felt certain, sire, that you would be watching, and had assumed that you'd brought an extra as a matter of course. I trust you did not disappoint?"

He merely laughed and then, silhouetted by the flames, bowed with exaggerated courtesy. "But of course, Sir Geoffrey. And shall I squire thee?"

"Not necessary, I think, my sire. But the road to Londinium is long…"

"Of course."

And so we traveled together back to Londinium. I turned to look back once, but the night and the trees had swallowed even the sight of the fire. All that I saw was darkness.

Boukephos, of course, felt that to be fitting.

NOT DAMNED

Not Damned

BY LAWRENCE BARKER

"Our god Dolor will not forget your betrayal." The wild-eyed Colpta, the last islander unmoved by Brother Iolo's teachings, flailed his long, spindly arms. His shrieks rose and fell, like those of the fairy women the credulous believe presage death. "Not forget and certainly not forgive."

The crowd, fish-oil lamps bobbing like tiny boats awash in the cold black Irish Sea, made its murmuring way to the barren stone beach.

"What will happen when Dolor's herrings no longer surrender to your nets? When Dolor's seals no longer yield to your bludgeons?" The cold wind whipped Colpta's unwashed black mane. "Are a few children worth risking famine's lash?"

Brother Iolo, leading the crowd, felt his fists clench in exasperation. To dispel the unwanted emotion, he silently clasped the only worldly possession he had brought to the isle of Morna, his hand-sized black stone statue of the Virgin. The touch of its smooth and comforting contours—from the rounded base to the conical headdress's sharp point—sent waves of calm through him.

Brother Iolo glanced over his shoulder, reassuring himself that his followers did not listen to Colpta.

All was as expected. Neriss—the island's stonecutter, unofficial leader, and Brother Iolo's first convert—hefted on his shoulder the cross he had carved from the island's unforgiving gray stone, his drooping mustache trembling as his muscles strained. The others, accepting Neriss's judgment, followed.

As the crowd reached the shore, the moon, a round cold coin for a dead man's eye, rose above the black waters. Dolor's stone image, its moonlit shadows dancing like poisonous spiders, crouched at the point land and sea met. A strand of wave-tossed laver, wrapped about the statue's protruding tusks, waved like a warrior's banner.

Brother Iolo glanced at the statue's outstretched flipper-hand, ready to receive its infant offering. Instinctively, he shielded his eyes and crossed himself.

"How long have these people cowered before you, demon?" he whispered, the shadow of the statue's pointed muzzle falling across him. "How many generations' firstborns have known your dark embrace?"

As if in response, a cold gray wave sprayed Brother Iolo.

Brother Iolo flung the water from his robe. "No more," he whispered. "The child you would have received, come low tide," he muttered, glancing at the infant in the arms of Nessa, Neriss's young wife, "will be no devil's fodder."

Pulling his monk's robe about himself, Brother Iolo clambered atop a gray stone outcropping. "People of Morna," he cried, voice straining to pierce the roaring wind and surf. "The riptide runs unchecked. The moon rises, full and clear. This is the time your ancestors believed this abomination," he said, gesturing at Dolor's statue, "was strongest." A babble of assent came from the crowd. "Tonight, we test its mettle."

Neriss handed the cross to his neighbors and motioned for his brother, Earn. Leathery hands gripping stonecutters' hammers, the burly pair advanced.

Colpta threw himself in front of the statue. "Your foolishness will doom us," he screamed. He glanced over his shoulder, looking out to sea. "Dolor's

NOT DAMNED

will reigns supreme." His eyes blazed with madness. "Will your White Christ shield you from the sea-god's rage?"

Brother Iolo whispered an *Ave Maria*, thanking the Virgin that only Colpta rejected the light. As always, the holy words soothed him.

"Take the poor man away," Brother Iolo intoned, "before he harms himself." The men set the cross down and dragged aside the screaming Colpta.

Brother Iolo nodded. Hammers descended.

The first blow did nothing. The second left a crack along Dolor's throat. At the third, the statue's evil head separated from its shoulders, splashing in the roiling waters.

"Let no trace of darkness remain," Brother Iolo cried. "We will plant the holy symbol," he said, gesturing toward the cross, "in the demon's place, erasing its foul memory."

Again and again, the hammers fell, smashing the statue to rubble.

Brother Iolo turned to gaze out to sea.

The eternal roaring sea, a constant reminder of God's boundless mercy.

Was it a trick of the moonlight, or did vile green eyes rise and fall with the swelling black waves? Brother Iolo clutched his statue of the Virgin to his breast.

For the first time since taking his vows, he felt no comfort at the act.

One night later: "Why is Colpta's disappearance so important?" Neriss scratched his drooping mustache. His eyes, anxiously scanning his stone dwelling, told Brother Iolo that Neriss thought the search had already lasted too long. "If he has fallen into the sea, he is dead," he shrugged.

"We must give Colpta every chance. All men deserve Our Lord's compassion."

"Would Colpta do the same for you?"

Brother Iolo sighed, wondering if planting the seeds of faith was always such a struggle. "Our Master bled to teach us to love those that love us not," he added, his exasperation beginning to show.

Neriss bowed his head. "If the Holy Brother instructs, we will search for the idolater until ice chokes the bay."

Brother Iolo's eyes fell on the moon's pale face, peeping over the horizon. Colpta had vanished shortly after the idol's destruction. The search had already cost a day's fishing.

A ringed moon, silver and glistening, said that the season of cold approached. That approach made precious every day of preparation for winter.

"Call off the search," Brother Iolo sighed. "The people must rest for tomorrow's labors." He turned and trudged away, head bowed in silent prayer.

Reaching the low door of the hut he had made his cloister, he knelt and wriggled through. He had barely entered the chamber when something moved in the darkness, telling him he was not alone. "Colpta?" he asked nervously.

"I have worn many names. Never that one." The voice was a woman's. A voice with an accent, neither of Eire nor Caledonia, nor even of the savage Northmen that sometimes raided coastal villages. "You may use the name men first gave me, Wersartel."

"Are you an angel, bearing holy tidings?" Brother Iolo asked, automatically reaching for the carved jet statue of the Virgin.

"An angel? Hardly." Wersartel stepped into the pool of moonlight streaming through the smokehole. Her hair, midnight-dark and decorated with crab-claws and starfish, hung over her shoulders. Her eyes, green like the sea-grass, green like the hills of Eire, flashed. But her most striking feature was her skin.

Black. Blacker than her hair. Not the dark brown of the Saracen or African, but the true black of ebony. Or carved jet.

Like the Virgin.

The thought struck Brother Iolo like a thunderbolt. "Lady," he stammered, falling to his knees. "How may I serve you?"

Wersartel laughed. Her laughter echoed like the sea pounding on a cold stone shore. "Serve me?" she said, her eyes glowing dimly. "You have served me ill indeed."

"Ill? Have I not been faithful to the Church?"

"As faithful to your god as the islanders once were to theirs," she replied. An expression Brother Iolo could not interpret—had she not been a Holy visitor and he sworn to the cloth, he might have identified it as lust—crossed her face. "I had thought to repay your pruning of the vineyard from which I took my wine with death," she murmured.

"My lady?" he stammered.

"Having met you, I see I was hasty." Like a shark rising from the depths, her hand clamped about Brother Iolo's head. She dragged him upright. "A dark intensity burns within you. Such severity must not be wasted," she barked.

"Mother of God," Brother Iolo gasped, clasping the statue. His lips silently implored the Blessed Virgin to spare him from this fiend he had foolishly confused with one of Her emissaries.

"Your idol will not help," Wersartel replied, taking the statue and tossing it aside. "She will revile you, as you did this island's Dolor."

"Such is beyond your power, were you Satan himself."

"I think not." Great rending fangs sprang from Wersartel's mouth, reaching down over her lips. Her eyes blazed like the fires the ignorant light atop the hills on the year's longest day.

She dragged his face to hers, breathing Hell-scented breath in his nostrils. "Has your god taught you the word 'Gangrel'?" she whispered.

Brother Iolo's eyes widened in fear. He felt his heart pounding. "The Damned," he gasped.

Her fingers ripped Brother Iolo's robes as easily as Brother Iolo himself might have shredded rotted rags. She lowered her lips to his chest. "The Damned," Wersartel snarled. She bared spear-sharp fangs.

Brother Iolo tried to scream. His voice would not sound.

"Welcome to endless night, *Brother* Iolo."

With an ice-fire touch, her curved ivory scimitars sank into his flesh.

LAWRENCE BARKER

Cold, like the Irish sea's midnight chill, took Brother Iolo. The room spun as his feet crumbled.

Brother Iolo felt darkness rise.

Just before it would have taken him, Wersartel pulled free. Her long, supple tongue darted across the wound, stopping the bleeding.

Brother Iolo moaned in agony.

"It is far from over," Wersartel replied. With her pointed fingernail, she opened her breast. "Drink," she commanded, pulling Brother Iolo's mouth against the wound.

Brother Iolo willed himself to recoil. His body refused to obey.

"Drink." Her fingers sank into his neck. "You might not remember this night, but it will haunt you through eternity." Her voice became the hiss of red-hot iron plunged into the cold dark sea. "Now drink."

Brother Iolo's tongue, moving of its own volition, touched the thick red pool.

Its taste sent a shiver of pleasure through him. Stronger than the pleasure he had once received from ice-wine. Stronger than the love of women had been before he had taken the cloth.

Perhaps—dare he think it—even stronger than the love of God that had made him take that cloth.

Unable to resist, he swallowed.

In desperation, Brother Iolo's eyes sought the Virgin's image.

The image lay at his feet.

Face turned away from him.

Brother Iolo begged the saints to grant him death while his soul was still his.

If any heard, none listened.

Four nights later: "Brother, come in from the cold," Neriss begged, pulling his woolen brat more tightly about himself. He motioned Brother Iolo toward shelter. "Surely the White Christ cannot mean you to freeze."

NOT DAMNED

Brother Iolo listened to the howling wind and the pounding surf. Holy Mother of God, what had happened? How had his robe become tattered shreds? What had scarred his chest?

He held a hazy memory of a stranger in his hut. But between passing through the door and waking up with an overpowering thirst, there was nothing.

Instinctively, Brother Iolo's tongue danced over the fangs his canines had become. The fangs that marked him as one of the Damned That Walk the Earth.

Neriss's heartbeat, pounding like a great goat-skinned drum, echoed in his ears. Brother Iolo could sense—not hear, not smell, but sense all the same—the blood in Neriss's veins.

And, try as he might, he could not exorcise the demon that whispered the dark truth that only blood could assuage his salt-dry thirst.

"If we have offended you, tell us how to make amends," Neriss pleaded.

"You have offended me in no way."

"Something troubles you."

Brother Iolo nodded. "You are correct. I am sorely vexed," he said. "I have prayed for guidance. My prayers remain unheard."

"You have told us God's answers are not always obvious."

Brother Iolo nodded. "Perhaps God's silence has answered me." He trudged to the stone cross and slung his arms about it.

"Brother, what does this mean?"

Brother Iolo stood motionless, eyes locked on the churning waves. The self-destroyer was forever separated from God. As if that mattered now.

"Brother?" Neriss repeated.

"Here I shall remain," Brother Iolo said, eyes closed, "until sunrise." His voice quavered as he, for the only time he had known these people, lied to them. "Then I will be miraculously delivered directly into God's hands."

Neriss's voice raised in alarm. "You are leaving us?"

"I must."

"But what happens when winter comes?" Neriss gestured toward the northern sky, where the ice season's orange and green dancing lights already flickered. "When the winds blow cold, the herring grow scarce, and dusk swiftly follows dawn's tail?" His hands shook with anguish. "Faith is poorly rooted here. Without your counsel, hard times might well renew Dolor's rule."

Brother Iolo felt his fangs lengthen. He prayed to the God that had abandoned him for strength. "Making certain that never happens falls to you."

"I know little of the Faith." Neriss shook his head. "The people know even less. This task exceeds my power."

At Brother Iolo's feet, churning in the surf, lay shattered pieces of Dolor's hand. The hand on which the children had lain, waiting for the sea's cold caress. Fragments, turning and tossing. Carried away by one wave, but returned by the next.

The wind bore the wail of an infant—Neriss's child, Karal—to Brother Iolo's ears. Although cold no longer bothered him, he felt a chill.

Satan must not reclaim these people, newly won for God.

A mad scheme entered his head. True, it was dangerous. True, no Abbot or Prior would ever approve.

But no Abbot or Prior was present to see what would happen to Morna's people without Brother Iolo.

Brother Iolo released the cross.

"You have decided not to leave us?" Neriss's voice trembled.

"At least not for the present." Brother Iolo felt the icy cold stones beneath his sandaled feet. "Now, before the night grows colder, call the people. I have taught them of baptism, marriage, and extreme unction. Now, I must teach them another sacrament." And pray, he silently added, that he was still the servant of God and not of the Darkness. "Of...of..." Brother Iolo struggled for the word. "Of Holy Communion. Each must bleed into a cup, as did Our Savior."

Neriss frowned.

"Have no fear," Brother Iolo continued. "No man or woman shall suffer from the few drops each surrenders. By my vows to God, this I swear."

Brother Iolo watched Neriss run to gather the people.

NOT DAMNED

"By my eternally damned soul," his grave-quiet voice whispered, "this I swear."

Fifteen years later: Karal, grown to young manhood, extended his hand above the Vessel of Holy Communion. "In the name of the Father," Brother Iolo intoned, baring the Communion Blade into which he had inscribed the Lion, Man, Bull, and Eagle of the Gospels. "The Son," he said, drawing the knife-edge across Karal's arm. "And the Holy Ghost," he added, as the blood dripped. Brother Iolo knelt before the altar he himself had consecrated, watching the holy fluid drip.

His eyes skimmed his congregation. Neriss, gray streaks having appeared in his mustache as his once-mighty arms and chest had withered, stood beside Nessa, beaming with parental pride. The other islanders, as best their untutored tongues could manage, mumbled semi-appropriate words at semi-appropriate times. And, best of all, the cross he had planted in the idol's place had been joined by dozens like it, marks of the islanders' faith.

When the chalice was half full, Brother Iolo genuflected and lifted Karal's arm to his lips. He ran his tongue across the wound, stopping the bleeding. Brother Iolo raised the chalice. "This is my body you eat," he intoned. "This is my blood you drink."

His robe's much-repaired sleeves flapping in the night air, Brother Iolo drained the chalice.

Assuaging his thirst. At least for the moment.

He stood at the altar, watching his flock silently depart. Sturdy Earn. Silent Nessa, wrapping her shawl about her son's arm. Magin, the potter who had formed the Vessel of Communion from the clay of Uisghe, the tiny uninhabited island across Morna's bay.

Brother Iolo closed his eyes, hoping the vision that had plagued him would not return.

Brother Iolo sniffed the air. His nostrils, inhumanly keen, detected the sour scent of nervous sweat. His ears recognized an anguished heart's irregular rhythm.

LAWRENCE BARKER

Brother Iolo's eyes opened. Neriss, as visible in the darkness as a man in bright sunlight would once have been, lurked in the church's shadows. "Something distresses you," Brother Iolo said.

Neriss sighed, as though suffering a deep and invisible wound. "The sea is bountiful. The children prosper. We know the Christ's blessings." He turned to go. "What could possibly trouble me?"

Brother Iolo placed his hand on Neriss's shoulder. "A wise shepherd knows his flock."

Neriss's eyes fell. "It is only superstition. A remnant of the forgotten past. I should not have disturbed you."

Brother Iolo, with his inhuman sense, felt a pungent bead of sweat roll down Neriss's side. "A burden shared is a burden lightened," he said.

Neriss shuffled his feet. "A dream, Brother. One that comes again and again."

"God sometimes speaks in dreams."

Neriss shook his head. "Not this one. I dream a corpse that is not a corpse splashes its way from the surf." He nervously tugged at the cross about his neck.

Brother Iolo shrugged. "Life is hard. It is natural to fear the death the waves can bring."

"No sooner has the corpse appeared," Neriss continued, "than a monstrous beast, cold water dripping from its black hide, follows."

Brother Iolo stiffened. "What does this beast look like?"

"Neither of earth nor sea." Neriss crossed himself. "What it walks upon are neither feet nor flippers. It lurches across the shore, fingers stretching into claws."

Brother Iolo laughed. His laughter sounded nervous and false, even to himself.

"In the dream, I try to run, but the corpse pursues me. Its fingers lock about my throat. They clasp tighter and tighter, cutting off my breath." He shivered, like a child caught in a cold swell from the sea. "It holds me down, while the beast lumbers forward."

Brother Iolo wiped his brow. True, he no longer sweated. But old habits die hard. "What does the beast do?" he asked.

NOT DAMNED

"Its jagged fangs brush my throat. Then I wake, drenched in cold sweat."

Brother Iolo trembled. In the distance, a gull's mocking cries echoed. Brother Iolo stood motionless for a moment before answering. "A warning. To beware the Deceiver's snares."

Neriss raised his face. "The dream signifies no more?"

"Is that not enough?" Brother Iolo rubbed his hands, as though he still needed to warm them.

Neriss clamped his hands about Brother Iolo's. "Thank you, Brother. You have eased my mind." With that, he turned and strode into the night.

Brother Iolo fell to his knees before the altar, begging for forgiveness.

For lying to faithful Neriss.

For continuing to exist.

Because, after each and every Holy Communion for the last year, after the congregation had filed out, a similar dream—or a vision, which is but a waking dream—had come to him.

At first he had ignored it. Then it had come more frequently. Each time more real, harder to ignore.

In this dream, a walking corpse pursued an islander, overtook him, and dragged him down. A great black beast shambled from the darkness. Its teeth—like his own—became great fangs.

The beast drank the islander's life. And then the corpse bowed down to worship the beast.

The main difference between Brother Iolo's and Neriss's dreams was in point of view. Neriss's visions painted him as the victim.

Brother Iolo's made him the beast.

❖

Six months later: "Brother, come quickly." Magin burst into Brother Iolo's chamber. "Neriss has been found."

Brother Iolo, kneeling before the altar, looked up at the frightened islander. Had the saints heard his prayers? Had Neriss, missing since Holy Communion, been found alive? "Well?" he asked.

LAWRENCE BARKER

Magin's sorrowful eyes answered him.

"Come," Magin replied, motioning for Brother Iolo.

Brother Iolo emerged into the night. The cold air carried Nessa's keening—the way the widows of Eire mourn—to his sensitive ears. As it carried the stench of death.

"I fear some devil walks among us," Magin muttered, leading Brother Iolo over the rocks.

"Some devil," Brother Iolo repeated, voice leaden-bell dull. His tongue ran over his fangs—God forgive him, God forgive the Damned—enlarging as the death-fetor grew stronger.

They rounded a boulder to find Nessa kneeling on the beach, her high-pitched wail piercing the night. Karal, choking sobs inaudible to all but Brother Iolo, comforted his mother.

Beside them lay Neriss, motionless as only the dead can be. Eyes wide and staring, moonlight reflected off his waxy gray skin. His fingers, locked in a claw-like pose by death's stiffness, contained great masses of matted black fur.

Fur like some Hell-cursed night-hunter might wear.

Magin crossed himself. "Brother, this was neither accident nor work of man."

"What do you mean?" Brother Iolo withdrew the tiny statue he had carried for so long from his pouch. He whispered a silent prayer, asking for any answer save the one he half-expected.

Magin's trembling fingers pointed to Neriss's throat. Two gaping red wounds lay above the carotid artery.

Separated by the same distance as Brother Iolo's fangs.

Brother Iolo shivered. He turned to stare out to sea.

Could it be? Mother of God, could his dark dream have come true? Could he have, at long last, surrendered to the Dark Thirst unawares?

"Well, Brother?" Magin's hand closed over Brother Iolo's shoulder. "Does a devil not walk Morna?"

Brother Iolo closed his eyes. He raised the statue of the Virgin in his hand and kissed it, as if in farewell. "I fear one does," he muttered.

NOT DAMNED

"Saints preserve us." Magin stood close to Brother Iolo, as though expecting an aura of holiness to shield him. "What can we do?"

Brother Iolo stared blankly at the cross that Magin—that all the islanders—wore and shook his head. "You? You need do nothing." He turned to stare at the weeping Nessa and the lifeless Neriss. "I, on the other hand, must act."

"Act? How?"

"I must do something that I should have done as soon as Morna could sustain the Faith without my aid."

With that, Brother Iolo turned and marched into the darkness.

Tongues of orange-red flames licked the night. Clouds of grayish smoke from burning driftwood obscured the thousand thousand stars that looked down from the island of Uisghe's inky sky. Brother Iolo, nails buried in his palms—lest he think too hard on what he must do—cautiously prodded the fire-pit with a broken oar. A shower of sparks—like a wind from the Hell where he must surely go—shot upward, tumbling into the surf with a breathy hiss.

Brother Iolo listened to the pounding waves. Their endless roar reminded him of the endless torment which must be his. He nervously glanced at the skins of fish-oil that he had gathered. Fish-oil to fuel a raging conflagration.

He picked up the skins. They lay, cold and heavy, in his hands. "Neither as cold nor heavy as my burden of guilt," he muttered.

He had been so certain he could master his stained soul. And now, he had lost control—he must have, even if he had no memory of the doleful deed—and Neriss had paid the price.

No one else would.

Brother Iolo's eyes closed. Whispering a prayer to the God from whom he was eternally sundered, he clutched both his statue of the Virgin and the fish-oil to his breast.

With a mighty act of will, Brother Iolo strode toward the flame.

LAWRENCE BARKER

He reached the fire-pit's edge, its crackle and hiss filling his ears like the blaring of the judgment trumpet. For a split second, the desire to see the ocean—one final time, before surrendering to his just and eternal punishment—overcame him.

Brother Iolo opened his eyes.

In the surf stood a man, bedraggled garments flapping like bats' wings. A black and matted beard reached the man's chest, while wild eyes stared from beneath sea-urchin prickly black eyebrows.

Brother Iolo blinked. The face, while not that of one of Morna's few score inhabitants, haunted him with its familiarity.

Recognition struck Brother Iolo like a thunderbolt. The face was one of which he had not thought in more than a decade. One that, despite the encrusted filth, had changed no more than had his own.

"Colpta," he gasped, retreating from the flames.

Colpta shook his head. "No longer." He came closer, walking to the edge of the circle of light. "I have the honor of being the most loyal servant of Dolor."

"You boast of being a demon's thrall?"

Colpta sneered. "The word, Dolor has informed me, is 'ghoul,' not 'thrall.' And should I not boast?" He gestured broadly. "Wind and weather stoop shoulders, sink eyes deep beneath brows, and make sagging wattles of well-rounded chins," he said, fingers stroking his throat. "I, Dolor's servant, remain eternally young."

"At what price?" Brother Iolo demanded.

Colpta sneered. "As the youngest seals' flesh is tenderest, so did the young best nourish Dolor. These harsh times' rougher diet has, in turn, roughened Dolor. Capturing prey is not as easy as was once the case." He ran his fingers through his beard. Almost absentmindedly, Brother Iolo noticed the bare patches there. "Let us simply say I assist in the hunt." Colpta stepped into the fire's circle of orange light, pantomiming clasping a figure from behind and dragging it down.

"Assist in the hunt," Brother Iolo repeated. His eyes locked on Colpta's beard. Like the fur clasped in Neriss's dead hands.

NOT DAMNED

Brother Iolo sniffed the air. A heavy scent—not strong, and hard to distinguish from the woodsmoke and fish oil—lay in the air.

Still, Brother Iolo could not fail to recognize the familiar scent of Neriss's blood.

"You slew Neriss?" Brother Iolo demanded.

Colpta laughed. His laughter rang like a tarnished bronze bell. "Slew? Better to say I stilled the Vessel of Holy Communion while my god drank."

Brother Iolo felt an animalistic snarl rumble in his chest. Throwing aside the skins, he stuffed the statue into his belt. "You are worse than a devil," he growled. "You had a choice, and you chose darkness."

"A choice." Colpta pulled at his beard and glanced over his shoulder, as though expecting something to emerge from the sea. "And I made the only one a wise man could."

Brother Iolo felt a howl break from his lips. He felt himself sink into a crouch. Without thought, his muscles bunched to spring.

Before he could act, a great black mass rose from the sea, water dripping from its sides like the tears of those condemned to Hell. It rose, balancing its great seal-like bulk on two flipper-like feet and flexing its long-jointed fingers.

Colpta prostrated himself, his face buried in the wet stones.

"Dolor," Brother Iolo whispered. Or something that might, once seen and half forgotten, have inspired the hideous black statue. In shock, Brother Iolo rose.

The sea-beast shambled forward, moonlight glinting on its ivory tusks. When less than twice a man's length separated its oozing bulk from Brother Iolo, it stopped, resting on the rocks.

"It has taken long enough for you to cast away the tattered remnants of your old life." Its inhuman voice reminded Brother Iolo of a sea lion, barking at the fisherman whose catch it pilfers. "Long enough for the visions I sent to bear fruit." Its great bulk shifted, coming closer. "I had feared you might taste True Death before swearing fealty to the foe of the god you once served."

Brother Iolo's eyes blazed. The statue tucked in his belt whispered the words of peace that had led him to his vows while the rage within him howled their furious negation.

"God might, in His wisdom, have condemned me," Brother Iolo growled. Were his fingers actually lengthening, forming claws? Did the itchiness on his face mean his jaw was becoming a snout, that tufts of hair were sprouting? "If that be so, I shall serve Him until Hell's gates slam behind me."

A rumbling chuckle sounded from the creature's belly. "Really? Your god wants such as you?" it said, motioning toward a tidal pool. "Look," the creature commanded.

Without thinking, Brother Iolo glanced at the still water. The sharp-snouted image in the water could not be his reflection.

He whispered a prayer to the Virgin, asking Her that what he had thought he had seen might be mere illusion.

Soft words whispered themselves in Brother Iolo's ear.

If the image is real, what of it?

Brother Iolo shook his head. The words might originate in his own mind. Some saint, or even the Virgin herself, might have spoken them.

Whatever their origin, they told the truth. Had God not become man and bled for all? Did this not show that, no matter how great the transgression, there could always be forgiveness?

Brother Iolo turned back to the hulking monstrosity. The creature's eyes reflected the moonlight. Green like the sea-grass, green like the hills of Eire.

"Wersartel," he whispered, as his nightmare's beginning returned to his memory with lightning-stroke suddenness.

"Transformed to match my one-time worshippers' expectations. Transformed by the lack of the children's succulent blood," Wersartel replied. "I have you—and others like you, in other islands—to thank for that." She ran her purple tongue along her black lips. "If draining a useless old man's watery essence is what it takes to change you as you have changed me, so be it." Brother Iolo felt a snarl cross his lips. This monstrosity had ruined his life, had slain uncounted innocents, had—from some dark need too vile for comprehension—slain Neriss.

Making certain this Hell-Minion slew no more would be his redemption.

NOT DAMNED

With a wild wolf howl, Brother Iolo sprang.

Wersartel, expecting the charge, caught Brother Iolo as easily as a man might catch a leaping child. "Good," she replied, holding the struggling Brother Iolo, his claws flashing wildly, at arms length. "Your years of denial stoke the fires of the Darkness Within. Soon you will embrace the shadows, embrace your true self."

Brother Iolo tried to answer. Only inchoate growls came. He tried to break free, to rend Wersartel's lying throat. The elder Gangrel's strength so overmatched his that, at best, his claws barely raked her dark forearms.

"Soon endless night will utterly overwhelm you," she muttered. Her green eyes turned toward the waters. "Then you and I will scour Morna, and slake our thirsts in an orgy of bloodletting."

From deep within himself, Brother Iolo felt a still, small voice—almost but not quite driven into abeyance by his righteous anger—whisper to him to him. *Opposing this Creature of Darkness with more darkness is madness. Use the gifts of God, not those of the Deceiver.*

In his mind, Brother Iolo began chanting the *Ave Maria* that had calmed his rage in the past. Focusing. Praying. Bringing all his being to a single point.

So God—and not the creature whose features he now wore—might be master.

Brother Iolo felt the dark thing sharing his very being snarl and withdraw into a dark corner of his mind. He felt the claws retract, his face's very structure shift. Brother Iolo ceased struggling, begging God to grant him the strength to carry out the act he planned.

Wersartel frowned, or at least came as close as her seal-muzzled face would allow. "What has happened?" she demanded.

Brother Iolo felt her grip loosen.

With a lightning-like motion, he pulled the statue from his belt. Gripping its base in both hands, he buried the statue's pointed headdress in Wersartel's chest.

Wersartel's mouth flew open, bloody foam dripping down her black snout. A wail, like the howl of Judas when he realized the enormity of his deeds, emerged from her lips. For an instant, Wersartel's claws scratched at the

60

statue, as though attempting to pull it free. Then she fell over and lay still.

"No," Colpta screamed. Arms flailing like an untrained swordsman's weapon, he flung himself at Brother Iolo.

Brother Iolo turned, facing Colpta. Instinctively, he crouched, a forbidding hiss on his lips.

Colpta froze, as motionless as Wersartel. Sheer terror, apparently inspired by what he had seen in Brother Iolo's eyes, painted itself across Colpta's face.

Brother Iolo felt his thirst rise. It would be so easy to wrap his hands about Colpta's throat, as Colpta's fingers had wrapped about Neriss's, and drain the murderous demonolator dry.

Kill him, a dark voice whispered. *Quench your thirst.*

"No," Brother Iolo shouted, covering his eyes.

No, he would not kill. Salvation was fragile, and any surrender to Darkness might deliver him to Hell.

But the thirst was still there.

An idea of how to satisfy it formed in Brother Iolo's mind. He knelt beside Wersartel's motionless body. He sank his fangs into her throat and drank.

A power—it must be the power of God, he told himself—flowed into him as he emptied her. He felt himself growing stronger—faster—than he had ever imagined possible.

When he had finished, he poured fish-oil over Wersartel's body and lit it with an ember. Standing at a respectful distance, he watched the orange flames dance.

"Master?" a tremulous voice sounded from behind him. Brother Iolo turned. It was Colpta. Abasing himself before Brother Iolo.

"I am not your master," Brother Iolo responded, crossing his arms.

Colpta raised his head. "A ghoul without a Gangrel is nothing," he stammered. "Less than nothing. Let me serve you as I served Dolor."

Brother Iolo spat on the ground. He drew back his hand to strike.

Colpta looked up at him. A pitiable creature, for all his evil.

If one such as Brother Iolo himself could find redemption—and, as long

NOT DAMNED

as he resisted the darkness, he surely had—could not Colpta, who was still human, do the same?

Brother Iolo's hand dropped to his side. A plan, far madder than the one that had come to him more than a decade ago, when he first realized he must slake his thirst, formed in his mind.

"How many Gangrel are there?"

Colpta scowled. "I don't know. Scores. Maybe hundreds."

"Are they all like...her?" Brother Iolo nodded toward the flames devouring Wersartel's remains.

"Some resemble wolves. Some resemble cats. Only Dolor, to my knowledge, took the seal-form."

Brother Iolo nodded. The reddening eastern horizon told him little time remained until he must have shelter. "But all were, originally, human?"

Colpta nodded.

"Then all deserve Our Savior's grace." Brother Iolo's eyes scanned the bare shore. With Colpta's help, he could hastily build a rock hut to shelter him until nightfall. "As Patrick carried the Gospel to Eire, so shall I carry the good news to the Gangrel." He took Colpta's head in his hands. "And you shall be my acolyte...I mean 'ghoul,'" he added, quickly changing to words Colpta would understand.

"Master," Colpta whimpered. "If you attempt such a thing, you will surely die."

Brother Iolo chuckled softly, feeling a sense of peace that had eluded him for more than a decade. "If offered martyrdom's crown, I will wear it with honor." He motioned toward the stones that needed moving. "Now get up. There is work to do. For us both." His eyes swept over the seas, toward Eire's mainland. "Much work indeed."

LAWRENCE BARKER

THE HAWK AND THE SLIPPER

The Hawk and the Slipper

BY JAMES S. DORR

now this: That King Roderico was betrayed by a hawk. And also a woman. I speak not of that other Rodrigo, the one of Bivar, but of the original king who had been chosen among his peers at Toledo. This king was the one who had spied the daughter of his Count Julio bathing naked in the Rio Tagus and, smitten with her charm, took her by force. And for this all Spain fell.

Ah, you say. Every child knows this. Every *niño* who studies at the priests' feet, and even the offspring of peasants as well. And also they know of the huge battle fought at Guadalete after the count had reached Gibraltar and promised the king he would send him a fine hunting hawk—an *halcon*—pretending he knew nothing of his daughter's dishonor. And how, when the Moorish hawks of El Caid Tarik flew at the count's beckoning out from Ifrikiya. the king was destroyed there.

Yes, even I know this; I, Maria Isabella Jebez y Garcia, the brat of a soldier, know these things and more. About how the king's body was not recovered, but only his horse with its buckskin saddle adorned with rubies, his cloth-of-gold mantle encrusted with pearls, and one silver slipper. And how some say even now that King Roderico was never slain but, rather, lies sleeping in a cave to the east of Seville awaiting Spain's call in its need to complete the Reconquista—the taking of its lands back from the Infidel.

So this, my story, will be about knowledge.

Know from the start that I am a bastard, born the youngest of three daughters and the only one illegitimate, some thirteen years before the great battle of Alarcos that retook for Spain the *Ciudad Real*. My father gave me his name and acceptance, but while my sisters grew up to be ladies in their mother's house in Leon, I was raised at my father's side on the bleak plains of Castile, in a series of soldiers' encampments. I learned how to ride almost before I could walk, and soon enough also to use an *espada*, the short, two-edged sword the army fought with. I grew up in harshness. And yet, for all that, I knew in my heart I was my father's favorite.

I was the darling, in fact, of the camps too. The soldiers would do anything that I asked them. And I grew up pretty, quite unlike my sisters, whom I was able to see at such times when my father would visit his family on leave. My hair, especially, was black and lustrous, my figure was slim, and my eyes— ah, my eyes!—I was told were so dark and so deeply set that men, when they gazed upon my face, felt my eyes might pierce into their very souls.

But I did not know much about souls at that time. Soldiers think not of such things. Nor of death or sickness. But when in the Year of Our Savior 1195 my father returned from the field of Alarcos, bringing a casket of booty with him, his face was strangely pale and his eyes sunken.

"Isabella," he told me once in the two years that followed before his death—he used that name for me, from Ysabel, "Consecrated to God"— "know this, that although we have claimed it a victory, at Alarcos the army was stopped. It could go no farther. The Muslims were too strong. I do not know what it was, but in the south where their cities lie there is some kind of power, dark and fearful."

I shook my head, weeping. "You will get well, father," I protested. "You will fight more battles." But as the months passed his condition worsened until word was sent to Leon to his family that he would be granted leave to go to Burgos. That there they should meet him.

And so we set off in the spring of the year with a troop of returnees, north past Toledo to Valladolid and Torquemada, and there my father died. "Isabella," he said on his deathbed, his captain as witness, "you must know the bulk of my worldly goods must be left to my wife and your elder sisters. That is what the law expects."

I nodded, weeping. "Yes, father," I answered. I held his hand within my own and only then, I think, I realized how frail he had become, how pale and bloodless.

"Isabella," he repeated, "there is one thing more, though. A thing I leave you. My sword and my harness. The favor, as best I may, of my companions. And one thing more."

He half rose from his bed and pointed, his hand shaking, to the casket he had brought back with him from Alarcos, small and decorated with gold leaf much as the reliquaries of saints are. And I remembered that never once had I seen it opened.

I nodded. "Yes, father."

And then he whispered, "You must do as your heart tells you, daughter. Remember your honor—"

And then with a groan, with a rasping final breath, he fell dead in my arms.

Shrieking, I laid him back in his bed, crossed his arms on his chest; then, tears streaming from my eyes, I clutched up the casket and fled from his tent, leaving it to the priests with their incense and books and prayers. Nobody stopped me. I ran to the quartering of the women who followed the camp, the cooks and laundresses, where my own bed was. "Leave me!" I screamed as I entered that tent and the others obeyed me. Trembling, I opened my father's gift to me.

Inside the small box, on a lining of blood-red velveteen cloth, lay a single, silver-embroidered slipper.

❖

JAMES S. DORR

That night as I slept with my father's casket beneath my pillow, I dreamed of a field filled with cast-off armor and corpses of slain men, both Christian and Muslim. I dreamed of this: Of a figure rising, tall and regal, up from this sea of gore, his mantle taken, his horse fled from him. I dreamed of him walking with only one shoe on, dazed, to the east, toward the rock and peaks of the Sierra Nevada.

I dreamed of him walking only at night, lying in hiding during the daytime.

And I knew then what this figure was: It was King Roderico and, within the casket my father gave me, it was his slipper. And so as well I knew what I must do, and it would not be to go on to Burgos to beg of my father's wife and my two stepsisters that they might take me in.

When morning came, I called one of my women-friends of the camp. "Carmelita," I called, "I want you to cut my hair. Short to the shoulders, like young soldiers wear it. And find me men's clothing—not too fancy, but as a peasant soldier might wear—from among the troop's laundry."

"Isabella, no!" my friend answered. "Your beautiful hair? I would die before cutting it!"

"Listen," I said. "I am on a mission my father gave to me. I must seek out a thing's rightful owner." I begged. I entreated. I gave my friend Carmelita the box, the gold-leaf casket, in return for her favor. But the slipper I kept myself, wrapped in its red lining-cloth, bound with my breasts beneath the man's shirt my friend finally found for me.

And yet she still protested. "Wait at least," she said as she cut my hair, "for us to meet up with a new army troop, or at least a caravan headed south, so you will not have to travel alone. Even in men's clothing there will be dangers. Shadows—*Las Sombras*—that prowl the night, and not just brigands. You've heard the stories. You know that these things are true."

I nodded. "Yes," I said. "I know the stories. But shadows or brigands, one walking alone will sometimes be overlooked, while a large caravan waits to be preyed on. And I will protect myself."

And so, in men's clothing, while Carmelita watched, I strapped my father's own sword to my belt rings. Then, waiting till after the supper hour to leave in the darkness, when guards would be sleepy, just as the king had within

THE HAWK AND THE SLIPPER

my dream, I set out alone on the dusty road south until, ten days after, my footsteps fell in with those of a priest.

❖

Know this about Castile, the land I grew up in: It is a vast, high plateau, both Old and New Castile, broken only by the Sierra de Guadarrama which I recrossed in the eighth day of my journey. I traveled swiftly, but know this also: Unlike the rich, southern lands of the Muslims, in Castile, they say, there are but two seasons, of Hell and winter. During the one the country is baked dry, and then, in the second, it freezes and cracks into canyons and fissures, caves and grottoes, as if in places the land had become a twisted forest made all of stone. And as it was with the ending of winter that we had set on our road to Burgos, so it was now as I struggled back through the jagged Sierra and down to the Tagus plain, that my descent took me into Hell.

Thus I traveled by night for the most part, just as had the king in my dream, never minding the shadows. I traveled in darkness first, lest my disguise be penetrated, but more and more to avoid the searing heat. I knew the land, where caverns could be found for shade in the daylight, the signs that showed where to look, and so it was, as I say, on the tenth morning as I descended the long rocky slope that would lead past Toledo, I entered a cave where I found a black-robed priest.

I cleared my throat, politely of course. It was a man of the cloth. As he looked up from beneath his deep cowl I inspected his face, seeing that it was as thin and as pale as my father's had been, except in this case from an ascetic's fervor. And as his eyes in turn found mine, I felt them pierce into me. I felt them pierce my very being, as men in the past had claimed that my eyes might.

Finally he spoke. "What is your name, boy?"

"T-Tomas," I answered—the name I had taken to use on my journey. He smiled when I said that, a knowing smile. And once more I felt the piercing of eyes.

"Ah, named for the Doubter," he finally said. "The beloved of Jesus but,

JAMES S. DORR

of all the Apostles, the one who insisted on actually placing his hands in Christ's wounds before he would accept His Resurrection."

"And your name, Father?" I asked in return.

"In the priesthood," he answered, "men take on more than just one name, as surely you must know. But in the south, the name the Muslims give me is El Halcon."

El Halcon. The hawk, yes. It well fit the gauntness of his appearance. "And so, do you travel south, Father?" I asked him.

He nodded. "I do, child. My road takes me there on a quest for knowledge. Moreover, as I see you travel south too, and not only that but you seem to prefer to journey in darkness, I would invite you to be my companion. That is, if you wish to."

I nodded back. Yes. After all, I thought, not even the most desperate of brigands would dare to set on a priest. Nor would even the others, the creatures of shadow that my friend Carmelita had so feared, if he be even a half part as pious as his demeanor would have suggested.

"Then it is done," he said. "Rest here beside me. Eat if you wish to—I myself crave nothing—and build your strength up. Tonight we will start on our journey together."

I fell asleep quickly after I'd finished my simple meal and I dreamed once more, for the first time since I had left Torquemada, of the Field of Blood. I dreamed of a land that was filled with corpses, some of them as gaunt and as white as my new companion. When I awoke I felt suddenly giddy. I saw I had chafed my wrist somehow, perhaps from some movement while I was sleeping. I saw my companion was deep in his prayers, so I left him alone while I washed my face, then sought bread and wine from within my pack. Then when I was filled, I saw he was ready, and helped him with his own meager belongings as we set off together into the night.

We walked a long time saying nothing until at last we stopped to rest, and then he turned to me. "Child," he said, "as we travel on, perhaps I shall instruct you in the Faith. Would you enjoy that?"

THE HAWK AND THE SLIPPER

I nodded. Yes. "Of course I would, Father."

"Good," he said. "Now tell me this first. In that you've taken the name of the Doubter, you must have an open mind. Do you accept the idea of Transubstantiation?"

"I-I don't know, Father. I-I don't know what that means. As you can see, I am only a soldier...."

"Just so," he said. I heard him chuckle as we stood up to continue our walking. "It is a new doctrine, not wholly decided yet. It was, however, noised about somewhat some eighteen years back at the Lateran Council. Perhaps at the next one...."

We walked on in silence. "Then it is important?" I finally asked him.

He turned and smiled and, in the moonlight, I saw his teeth glimmer. "Extremely," he answered. "It has to with the very center of the Mass, the words of Christ to His disciples, that 'whoso eateth My flesh, and drinketh My blood, hath eternal life; and I will raise him up at the Last Day.' You do attend Mass, Tomas?"

"Of course I do, Father," I answered. "That is, when I am able."

"Yes," he said. "I understand. You are only a soldier. But as you can see, the question is this, then, whether the bread and wine the priest raises up are only symbols, or whether they truly become Christ's substance. Is the wine truly blood?"

"I-I find it hard to believe. But...."

"Yes," he said. "Because if you taste it, if you drink it, it still seems like wine. Can one thing, therefore, be really two substances? Tell me this, though. In general, Tomas. Do you accept miracles?"

"I-I don't know," I said. "I mean, of course, the Church teaches us so. Nevertheless...."

This time the hawk-priest laughed out loud. "Nevertheless," he finished for me, "you have never seen one."

When morning came we had found an abandoned farmer's hut to use for our shelter. And this time I did not dream, or, if I did, I had no remembrance

JAMES S. DORR

of what I had dreamed of. I woke again giddy, though, weaker this time than the previous evening. I wondered if I was ill. Still, I was young and easily strong enough to continue once I had eaten.

This time El Halcon was easier on me when the time came for my instruction. At least at first. "You are but a simple soldier," he said. "I understand that now. But tell me, have you heard of Peter Abelard?"

This time I nodded. "Yes!" I nearly shouted. A soldier or not, I was a young woman, and what woman did not know Abelard's story? "I even saw a picture of him once, Father," I added. "In a real book. And of Heloise...."

"Then you must know that they cut off his genitals for his illicit love," the priest answered. He turned and glared at me, and I nearly staggered. I had not known that part. "But it is not love that we speak of tonight, but rather what came after, after he went to the monastery. Of Abelard's doctrine—it's one that you would understand, Tomas. It's of the importance of doubt to faith, because doubt leads to questioning. And it is only through that that one learns truth."

I nodded. "I think so. I think I understand so far, Father."

He nodded back. "Good. Then we shall discuss doubt. This is something, too, that I think you may understand because it comes from the land around us. What do you know of the Spanish Adoptionists?"

This time I shook my head. "N-nothing, Father."

He waited a moment, then he continued. "This comes back to our question of last night, can it be that a thing can have two natures? Can wine be also blood? In this case, the Adoptionists asked how it could be that Christ was both God and man. And do you know what they decided?"

I shook my head. "No."

"They said He could not be. A single thing cannot have two substances. They were fools, Tomas—they said instead that there were two Sons of God, one, the Christ, as divine as His Father, and the other, Jesus, a man the same as your fellow soldiers, whom God had adopted. Do you believe that?"

I shook my head, puzzled. "Isn't it true, though, that in a sense we are all the adopted sons of the Father? I mean, I think our chaplain once told us...."

El Halcon cleared his throat. Loudly. "I did not ask you what your chaplain said. I asked what you think. Could this be true, that the Son of God was only adopted? A foster Jesus? Do you believe in the depths of your heart that not even God, the maker of all things, could in his own Self become two substances?"

I shook my head again. "No," I answered.

"Good," the priest-hawk said.

The following night we were set on by brigands, despite my instructor's cloth. Yet as weak as I was, and I was weaker than the night before, I was able to use my sword in a way that belied my sex, first thrusting at one, then at another, slaying a third with a draw stroke downward. El Halcon, meanwhile, backed against a rock, striking at those that came near with his staff, but otherwise, as was to be expected of a priest, being of little help.

Nevertheless, training had it out in the end. The remaining brigands fled from us and, suddenly, a thought came to me. "What if"—the words came out unbidden—"what if, Father, I were not a soldier as you can see that I am, but something else? Let us say a woman. What if, if I were only a woman, I were still able to defeat these bandits with my sword—as you can see I have—would that then be a sort of example of what we spoke of last night? Of two substances, let us say essences, completely different, but still in one body?"

The priest looked at me in a peculiar manner, as if he had somehow expected me to say just what I had said. "In a sense, yes," he finally answered. "You are learning, Tomas. But you have been wounded. You have lost blood, I think."

I shook my head. I had not been wounded. I wore a soldier's shirt, a peasant-soldier's, yes, but still a shirt that beneath its soft leather had sewn plates of metal quite strong enough to have protected me from the weapons of mere brigands. And yet my wrist did bleed, the chafing wound I had noticed before that I had caused in my sleep. Still, I shook my head.

"As you think best, Tomas," El Halcon said. "But there is a monastery not far from here, one now deserted, left in ruins when the Muslims sacked

JAMES S. DORR

it in their first onslaught—when even Toledo had fallen before them—that could give us shelter for tomorrow. In that it wouldn't be far off our route, perhaps we will go there. And, in the meantime"—he looked at me again in that odd way—"let us discuss the beliefs of the Cathars."

"The Cathars," I said. My head was swimming. Perhaps El Halcon was right—I had lost blood. Nevertheless, I had heard of the Cathars, a heresy against the Church, from one of the soldiers in my father's company.

"The Cathars," I said again. "Yes. I know that name. It is from *cattus*, for 'cat,' is it not? They worship the Devil."

El Halcon laughed and I felt myself stagger, much as I had when he had corrected me about Abelard the night before. "No," he said, "though others have claimed that. It's from the Greek, *katharoi*, not the Latin, and it means 'the pure ones.' There is, to be sure, one branch of the Cathars that holds the Devil co-equal with God—evil equal to good—and this is important, but that's not the main belief. Rather it is this—"

I staggered again, and this time he caught me. His strength surprised me. He gave me his staff to help me support myself as we continued, now off the main road as best I could tell. My head was swimming.

"The Cathars," he droned on, "hold that in the original act of creation God formed spiritual beings only. Satan, or Satanael as they call him, whether he was a rebellious angel, as the Church also holds, or God's co-equal, made the material. Thus you and I, Tomas, could be as angels too, save that we're trapped in material bodies. And, to escape that trap...."

Once more I staggered, despite the staff I gripped. Once more the hawk-priest set me back on my feet. "Angels..." I muttered.

"I've been too greedy," I thought I heard him whisper, or perhaps what I heard was only from a dream. I could no longer tell. I staggered again, a fourth time I think, but I could no longer count. Rather, I felt myself falling in blackness.

I felt surprisingly strong arms around me.

❖

THE HAWK AND THE SLIPPER

I woke to the brightness of a hundred candles surrounding an altar. I found the light painful. I woke still dressed in my armor and weapons on the chancel floor of a ruined chapel, a rug, half-rotted with age, bunched beneath me.

I tried to sit up, but could barely do so.

"A moment," a voice said. It was El Halcon. "A moment to put out some of these candles—I know their sudden glow hurt your eyes, but it hurts mine worse. It's in my nature. Nevertheless, I had a need to see you more clearly."

"Then we're at the monastery?" I asked. My voice was a whisper. "The one you spoke of?"

The light dimmed somewhat and in a moment El Halcon was once more before me, dressed in his encompassing cowled robe and holding a chalice.

"Yes," he said. He sat on the altar steps. "You have lost much blood. More than I realized. Still, I could save you."

I shook my head, feebly. "Then do so," I whispered.

"It will be a chance that I take," he said. "Therefore there must first be more instruction"—he smiled as he said that—"to assure your loyalty. Do you agree, Tomas?"

I tried to smile back. "Realize," I said, "that I am a soldier. With a soldier's honor. I can make no promise that would compromise that. But if that is understood...."

His eyes glared suddenly, piercing within me. "Then on your soldier's honor first tell me this: Who are you really?"

"M-my name is Maria Isabella," I said in a whisper. I couldn't dissemble— even if I had wished to, I couldn't. Not while he looked on me. "I am so named for Our Savior's Mother and for Consecration, thus doubly blessed by God."

"Yes," he said. "Very good, Maria Isabella. By God consecrated—or else by Satan as some Cathars might hold—while, as for Maria, the word means 'bitterness' in Hebrew, from myrrh, the grave-spice that Jesus was given." He smiled again. "You see, I can tell when you are lying."

I nodded. "I understand."

JAMES S. DORR

"Good," he said. "Now tell me this. From our conversation of three nights back: Do you accept Transubstantiation? That is, that two substances can be in one thing? To give your own example, Maria Isabella, would it be possible that one could be a woman and soldier both?"

I wasn't sure. I shook my head. "If you put it that way, yes, of course. But...."

"In a moment," El Halcon said, "I shall allow you to ask me a question. But that time is not yet. So, to continue"—he held up the chalice he still clutched within his hand, gleaming dully in the light of the few candles that remained burning behind us—"would it be possible that a cup of blood might also be wine? A wine of curative powers, perhaps?"

"Yes," I whispered.

"But you are still not sure. Behold then!" he shouted. He ducked his head and he bit his own wrist, suddenly, savagely, tearing the skin until the blood gushed out. He held the cup to it, filling it to the brim. Miraculously, his wound was already beginning to heal of itself.

I looked at my own wrist, its own wound still oozing red, shuddering with disgust. "You did this to me, Father," I whispered.

"It's unimportant," he said, "who did what to whom." Now with his arm whole again he helped prop me up, placing the chalice to my lips. He tipped it toward me.

"Drink, Maria Isabella," he whispered in my ear.

I struggled not to, even in my weakened condition. And yet, that voice. I felt my mouth open. My lips parted, even if ever so slightly.

I felt fire within me, burning within my throat, my belly. I sank back to the floor, gasping and choking. And yet it was wine I drank—something like wine. Despite my weakness, I felt something like a new strength flow within me.

I lost track of time. I may have fainted. I may have not. It may have been a full day had passed then, or perhaps just a minute. All I knew was this:

THE HAWK AND THE SLIPPER

The voice of El Halcon, as if out of darkness, whispering within my ear, "And now my promise to you, Maria Isabella. The question you may ask me."

"Yes," I whispered. But what would I ask him? My vision came back and I saw him sitting there, as before on the steps of the altar, his monk's robe and cowl wrapped around him. The first thing that came to me:

"Are you a Cathar?"

"I go as a Cathar among the Muslims, Maria Isabella," he answered. "I often travel south, you see, just as I travel now, to increase my learning. And so I will also continue to teach you. The way of the Cathars: To free oneself of one's material body is to renounce all materialism. To be an ascetic, as you had guessed I was. The Muslims respect that. The ones in the south who still have much power are of a sect called the Almoravides, that comes from Morocco, and holds also that one must renounce earth's pleasures to concentrate on the things of the spirit. To be, as the Cathars would put it, a member of the Perfecti."

"To be as an angel," I whispered. "Is that it?"

"That is what the Cathars would say," he whispered. "But now, Maria Isabella, twice blessed of your God"—he held out a second cup.

And it was as before. I drank it, more eagerly now. And then a time passed, I do not know how long. And then a whisper:

"You have a new question?"

Again I blurted out the first thing that came into my mind: "You asked me this before, so now I ask back. Who are you, El Halcon? And where do you come from?"

"The first you shall find out," he answered softly. "All in good time, as I am your instructor. As for the second"—he smiled again as my vision cleared—"know only that I am of an ancient tribe that has many members. It has its home in a place you would not know, a region called Cappadocia."

"But now you have come to Spain," I whispered. "And others, too, of this clan of yours?"

"There are many others in Spain," he answered. "Others of all sorts, some of which you may know, but others, Assamites, others perhaps as well, especially in the south. And of my own kind, yes there are others too. Some who go back even to the time of King Roderico."

✥

And so it was. My strength was returning. And as for my knowledge

—well, I did say this was a tale about knowledge. When the third cup came, and I was to be allowed a new question, I had grown more clever. I'd realized, you see, that the first question I had asked had not been answered.

I kept this thought in my mind even as I drank. Even as I passed into darkness, and then to El Halcon's voice, knowing this time that this was a game he played. And I would win it.

"Your question, Maria Isabella?" he asked in a whisper, his voice a seduction to my hearing. I waited this time, though, before I answered.

I let my vision clear.

"Yes," I finally said. "El Halcon"—I would not say Father—"are you a Cathar? Not what you pass as. Not what you go as among the Muslims. What are you really?"

He paused a long time then. "Have you heard," he finally answered, "of an ancient sect called the Cainites? A Christian sect, mind you. But one a thousand years old and more, from the time of Christ Himself. One that the Church thought it had stamped completely out."

I shook my head. No.

"I thought not," he said. "Some of its tenets have passed to the Cathars, but in much diluted form. This, however, is what their belief is—what I believe also—that God and Satanael are one and the same thing. That God is evil. That God's creation is therefore evil too, save for one person, that person my ancestor, the hero Caine who was first to resist God. That all we can do on this earth is resist as well, wallowing in its materialism if only because it displeases the Maker, until we have achieved such a surfeit that we, at last, can hope to pass beyond it."

I spat. "You believe this? That even God, Our Creator, is evil?" I tried to cross myself, but my hand trembled. "Surely not Jesus too?"

THE HAWK AND THE SLIPPER

"Yes," he said, "and you believe it as well, Maria Isabella, in your heart of hearts or you would not have drunk my blood. But as for Jesus, ah, that is the question. Some hold that, yes, Jesus was but God's agent to spread yet more evil while others maintain that, no, through His suffering He is our true Savior. The only one who knew was Judas who either destroyed Him, as one would a serpent, or else assisted Him in His attainment. And he wrote a Gospel that since has been lost to man."

"Ah," I said. "So this knowledge you seek, this learning, this thing you go on about finding, searching for in the south, is this lost Book, then? This Gospel of Judas?"

"Yes," he said. And then I realized what, in my heart of hearts, I surely had known from the beginning.

"*Vampiro*," I said. "It is what you are, yes? Not hawk, but a vampire. Kin to these 'shadows that prowl the night' that my friend Carmelita was so much in fear of?"

He nodded. "And you are a vampire as well now, Maria Isabella. I have made you one. And I've made of you something more too. The Affirming of Blood. I have bound you, irrevocably, to me."

I sprang to my feet. My strength had returned, and more. Yet he was right. El Halcon had fucked me, not as a man as King Roderico might have taken Count Julio's daughter, but as something other, as Abelard might have. Even when Abelard had been castrated. And God—if there was a God, and He not evil—God help me, I loved him. I loved him for it even as Julio's daughter, they say, had loved Roderico after he'd had his will.

And then I knew something else. I looked into the eyes of El Halcon and realized one thing more.

"King Roderico," I whispered. "This Book, you think that he has it? He has it in his cave?"

El Halcon shrugged. "I heard it had somehow arrived in Spain, perhaps when the Muslims had first invaded. And so I have searched the whole country for it, both north and south, until at Alarcos—"

I interrupted. "Alarcos?" I whispered.

He nodded. "Yes. Two years ago on the field at Alarcos I met a soldier— a Christian soldier—who had found a small, gilded casket. I knew it contained a clue. I could feel it. And yet we were separated in battle, although not until I—"

Again I broke in. "You took his blood," I said.

"Who can remember. There were many soldiers. And there was much blood too. In any event, we were separated, and so, not knowing where I could find him, I returned south to study instead in the great Muslim library at Cordoba until I was able to discover what it was the box had within it."

I nodded. "Go on," I said.

"In a moment, Maria Isabella," he answered, "but first let me teach you a thing about magic. One of its principles: Like attracts like. You see, if an object has been separated from its owner, especially if the owner, by chance, is one like us, there remains an attraction. Both object and owner long to come together. And if, moreover, the object itself were one of a pair...."

"Like wine and blood?" I interrupted. Mockingly. Teasingly—yes, I did tease him, I didn't know quite why, except that he liked it. As he had teased me before with my questions. And that my heart said to.

"Like wine and blood," he said. "Very good. A transubstantiation of baser sort, maybe. But even more, if it were one of a pair of identical things, like a pair of slippers—"

He reached out suddenly, tearing my shirt front, tearing at the binding that held my breasts and, God help me—if there be a God, and He not evil—I let him do it. *You must do as your heart tells you, daughter,* my father had said to me as he lay dying, and I loved El Halcon. My heart said to let him.

And yet, my father had said one thing more.

He reached out again, just as quickly, but just as quickly myself I backed away, circling the altar. I laid my hand on my sword.

"You drank my father's blood," I said.

"Perhaps I did. So what?" El Halcon shouted as I drew my sword out, clattering, from the rings holding it to my belt. And I backed farther.

Remember your honor, my father had said, his final words to me. And I remembered. The love they said Count Julio's daughter had for Roderico when he stole her honor. But I, Isabella—my father had never used the name Maria when he had addressed me—was a soldier's daughter.

THE HAWK AND THE SLIPPER

"No!" I screamed. I ignored my heart's prompting. *"Por honra y castidad!"* I shouted, slashing forward now. "A woman's honor as well as a soldier's! Two things in one substance!"

His strength was surprising. He beat me back with his fists. Kicked at me with his boots under his cassock. Nevertheless, training had it out in the end. A soldier's training.

Because I was strong too. A draw stroke did it. A feint to his right side. Another to his left, pricking his shoulder. Then slash! slash! backhanded, tearing his neck open. Striking again, as if a madwoman.

Until I had cut it off—cut his head clean off. Like Abelard's man-parts.

And then—a wineskin. I dropped my sword and grubbed in my pack until I found my wineskin. I spilled out its contents, because I knew that much, that much I had learned from the legends of my friend Carmelita, and held it within the fountain of his throat, letting it fill full nearly to bursting.

And I drank it empty!

So it was. And so I then knew it would be to come. The doctrine of Transubstantiation is a true tenet—yet one greater, perhaps, than even El Halcon himself might have realized. Because I was now two, two in one body, the substance of one that had been called the Hawk before I destroyed him a portion of my own self, but a new self that was more than just an amalgam of substances and appearances—rather, a self transformed. With my consuming the last of his blood I gained power and more, the power of one that was very old, if not yet ancient—not ancient as was the king, Roderico—but also a glimmering of yet more knowledge. Of knowledge and of plans.

I burned the ruin of the monastery before I left it. That much I owed him. I placed his drained body before the altar and heaped it around with dried, rotted tapestries, crumbling timbers, everything I could find that would sustain flame. After all, for that brief time, we were lovers.

And so I took flint and steel from my pack and, donning the robes El

JAMES S. DORR

Halcon had worn, I struck spark to my handiwork. Beneath the black cowl I still wore my soldier's shirt lined with stout metal, my breasts re-bound with the slipper between them, my sword at my side within the robe's foldings, as I left the monastery forever. I looked back just once to see flames lick the hot, black, Castilian night sky, and then turned my steps southward.

And so I journeyed, using El Halcon's disguise as a Cathar to cross the frontier into Andalusia, and thence to Cordoba where once more I feasted. I feasted on blood, I, Hawk-Isabella, not on the blood of men but other vampires. Islamic vampires, grown soft in their strongholds. Yet not too greedily.

That would come after.

Because, you see, I am still a Christian. I am Isabella. I may be damned, yes, a soldier's bastard—which of us is not damned? Perhaps even God as the Cainites say is damned, although, if a Cainite, I hold with that faction which still accepts Jesus. And as for the Book, this Gospel of Judas, well, not even El Halcon knew for sure if it really existed. That more I've learned from him.

But knowledge is knowledge.

And power is power.

I had a dream after I left Cordoba, wending my way through lush, sea-moistened orchards that smelled of oranges, down the Rio Guadalquivir to the battle site of Guadalete. Wrapped in my black cowl my Cappadocian flesh can stand daylight to some small measure providing I stay for the most part in shade, and so, beneath a thick, well-leafed olive tree, I watched the sun rise as King Roderico must have that morning nearly a half millennium past. And I then found a peasant's shed where I rested.

I dreamed once again of the Field of Blood, of that figure rising, but this time the face of the figure was my own. And also I saw my estranged stepsisters leading their own lives, marrying higher with each generation, and me, a "long-lost" family member rising with them for the next century, or two, or three centuries, what did it matter—we Christians are patient— until I might find a throne.

Because I now knew what King Roderico was, even more powerful than my hawk-priest lover. And I do not love him.

THE HAWK AND THE SLIPPER

Thus when I find him, as even now I walk eastward, tugged by the silver shoe, my Castilian upbringing making me an expert on seeking caves once I come into the fastnesses of the Sierra Nevada, I can and shall drink his blood until that king is dry. I shall once more know the mystery of Transubstantiation and how then, if not a king, in time a queen may rise to complete the *Reconquista*.

These things I know, and more. These things, in time, even children shall know of.

And one more thing that I know—call it a sign, perhaps? That when I woke from my dream of battles, I took off my clothing to wash myself and, taking the slipper out, burned to try it on. Thus perhaps Peter Abelard was wrong, that it is not doubt that leads to truth but curiosity. That I do not know.

But I do know this thing: That when I placed that slipper on my foot, it fit as perfectly as if it were my own.

JAMES S. DORR

Eating Medusa

BY PATRICK HADLEY

It was cold, the night we ate Medusa.

Outside the taverna, the few ragged olive trees that clung to the rocky surface of Santorini bowed and snapped in the driving rain. Down in Akrotiri harbor, fishing boats rolled on the surging waves of the gray and gale-swept bay.

But inside the taverna, where Aguirre sat on the other side of the table from me, playing his finger through a gleaming puddle of the orange beer the Greeks called retsina, it was hot. The heat came from a hearth two bodylengths away in the center of the taverna, a brazier of coals in its belly funneling brackish smoke up a low-hanging leather chimney.

I didn't like the fire...and I knew Aguirre didn't either. But he insisted we sit near it. That was Aguirre's way: to struggle, to test, to probe for weakness, in himself if necessary, in others if possible. I had learned to expect this from him. He was Lasombra, after all, and they are a clan that feeds on weakness as eagerly as ravens batten on the corpses of the battlefield dead.

That is how it was with me and Aguirre, always. He testing, searching, probing. And I, silent, waiting, stoical. And never, ever, showing him weakness. Aguirre and I were partners, and I trusted him. But trust can only be taken so far with a Lasombra before it becomes naiveté.

I was not naive. So I sat at the table near the fat, fire-bellied hearth and pretended, like Aguirre, to drink my retsina. And pretended, also like Aguirre, not to care about the bright red heat that beat upon our skins as we talked and bickered and plotted.

I think now it was the effort of lying to Aguirre about the fire, and my fear, that made me fail to notice the Assamite until it was almost too late.

A shadow passed over our tabletop, and the heat from the hearth-fire lessened momentarily. I looked away from Aguirre's eager white face.

A boy walked past us and sat down at a table ten feet away. He was dark of hair, pale of skin, slender and somewhat effeminate. He looked like a young fisherman, bored, come to the taverna to drink the winter storm away until he could return to the sea with his boat and string nets.

There was something about the boy, something familiar....

Then I knew him. The Assamite. He had found me again.

I was not unfamiliar with this Assamite, this assassin. I thought I had succeeded in evading his pursuit three nights ago, thrown him off my trail. Obviously, I was mistaken.

He yawned and stretched his limbs. His teeth were very, very white.

"She sleeps," said Aguirre, oblivious to our peril. "That is why we need not be afraid of her."

"Aguirre—"

"She sleeps, Rollo! She sleeps! What are you afraid of?"

I turned back to Aguirre. But I was no longer paying attention to either him or the fire.

The Assamite was disguised, of course. He was not so foolish as to reveal himself openly to two elder vampires. But I had seen him for what he was. Whatever his talent for disguise, my talent for penetrating it was obviously greater.

He did not seem to be carrying weapons. But that would be part of his disguise, I knew. I wondered if he was here as a scout, if there were others behind him.

EATING MEDUSA

"I am not afraid of the Sleeper," I said to Aguirre. "I am afraid of him."

There is almost no humanity left in Aguirre—our time together has seen to that—but he retains some of the habits of his days as a mortal. And so he blinked, as if he were still capable of feeling surprise.

"The fisher boy?" he murmured. "A friend of the Turk?"

I nodded.

His hand fell to his sword, mine to my dagger.

The boy's attention was now upon us. But we needed to get him closer. To fight an Assamite at a distance is to learn very quickly how to die the Final Death.

It was time, it seemed, for another of Aguirre's tests.

I spoke in a loud voice. "That Assamite. The one Viella drank. His name was Ulic, was it not?"

Aguirre's lips curled back from his teeth. "It does not matter what that filthy Saracen's name was. What mattered was the way he screamed as Viella sucked out his soul."

We laughed lightly. At the edge of my vision, I saw the boy sit upright.

Good. Most Assamites are as cold in their hearts as Aguirre and I. But some, like the fisher boy, are as hot and quick with pride as if they were still mortal. The boy was one of these. And so he would die.

More pressure. Soon the boy would break. "The Turk was a coward," I said. "He had no honor. And he stank, did he not, Aguirre?"

Aguirre's eyes upon me, dancing. "Indeed he did. I am glad it was Viella who fed upon him. It is fitting that the Saracen heretic fell to the weakest member of our cabal." He pinched his nose with his fingers and grimaced. "Though I must say she had the strongest stomach."

The boy rose from his chair.

It was time to give Aguirre the opening to deliver the final blow. "What was it the Turk stank of, Aguirre? I am trying to remember, but…"

The boy was standing two feet away.

Aguirre: "Is it not obvious? Ulic the Turk, our Assamite friend, stank of…pork!"

The boy shouted something, and a knife appeared in his hand. Behind him, mortals cried out, backed away, stumbled and ran for the taverna doors.

We stood. Aguirre's sword was already unsheathed, shadows coiled like tendrils of night around its slender blade. My dagger was in my hand.

The boy stepped back, the hatred in his face dissipating. He knew now that he had made a mistake, had walked into our trap.

"Time to join your master Ulic in Hell," smiled Aguirre. He raised his sword.

"Greetings." A low, even voice from behind the Assamite. A woman's voice, sweet but rough, as if she had just awakened from sleep.

She stepped around the hearth. She was tall and held herself awkwardly. She wore a man's tunic of rough brown wool in the northern style. Her hair was short and midnight black, wet with rain. Her eyes were either green or blue; it was hard to tell. Her skin was pale, tinged with redness, roughened by the wind.

For some reason, the Assamite lowered his knife.

Behind the Assamite, the taverna was empty. Sounds in silence: the sharp bright hissing of coals in the hearth, the crack of the olive branches snapping in the wind.

"Girl," I said. "Go away. You do not know what you face here."

The girl shrugged, looked at the boy. Her face remained expressionless, a mask of serenity, or indifference. She looked into the boy's eyes.

The boy's face went slack. Slowly he raised his dagger to his throat. His eyes flashed panic.

He began to saw at his throat with the blade. Blood welled.

"There are others!" he shouted.

He kept cutting. Before long, the tendons and ligaments of his neck were visible. His face darkened as his disguise dropped away, but I could see that he was still just a boy.

"There are others!" he choked, as the blood burbled forth from his throat. "There will always be others!" Then his throat filled with blood, and he could speak no more.

It took the boy several more minutes to finish killing himself. We stood and watched until he was done. Finally, he sagged to the floor like a wine gourd, empty.

EATING MEDUSA

Aguirre whistled. "He almost cut his own head completely off before he expired. I am impressed."

Aguirre and I sheathed our weapons. We sat back down.

The blood smell from the dead boy was very strong. I heard swallowing sounds from the floor. Eager, greedy sounds. The girl was feeding.

A short time later, I smelled rain and wet wool. And blood. The girl was on the bench next to me, her hand on mine, skin warm.

Then colder. Then as cold as mine. And the skin of her hand was no longer red and rough. Instead it was smooth and white: white as marble, or chalk. Or the flesh of a corpse.

Her laughter then, and it was her own.

"Viella," I said, shaking my head. She was no longer the rawboned peasant girl who had forced the Assamite to kill himself. She was Viella, the third member, with Aguirre and myself, of our little cabal.

More laughter. "I fooled you again, Rollo. And you also, Aguirre."

Aguirre grinned at her, showing his thin, precise fangs. "I knew it was you, Viella. You didn't do the eyes right. They shifted from green to blue."

"It was the light from the hearth," she sniffed. "My disguise was perfect."

Aguirre snorted.

"Yes," I said. "Your disguise was perfect."

Her head on my shoulder. "You are so gentle, Rollo. *Si gentile*. Not like Aguirre." She snuggled closer. Her body next to mine as small as a child's.

"Then why do you love Aguirre and not me? I am a gentleman, and he is not."

"I love Aguirre because he is not a gentleman."

"I do not understand."

A giggle. "He is not a gentleman. And I am not a lady. And so we are perfect for one another."

I wondered if Viella was mocking me, decided she was. I was the only one of our party whose descent was common.

She laughed again, kissed my neck. "My precious blond beast-man. So serious."

Silence fell. Then, for a short and final time, we sat together in the taverna: Don Felix Lopez Aguirre de Garabandal, Clan Lasombra; Marchesa Viella Maria Julia di Messina, Follower of Set; and the commoner, myself, Rollo of Clan Gangrel.

Finally Aguirre said, "It is time."

We rose from the table and walked together out of the empty taverna and into the night, Viella next to me, her hand nested in mine, as tiny and fragile as a newborn bird.

But her skin was cold, the night we ate Medusa.

It was Kindermass who told us where to find Medusa. Kindermass was Nosferatu. His ugliness was stupefying, his knowledge immense, his conscience ruled by only one principle: the convenience and continued survival of Kindermass. We found him wonderfully useful.

Kindermass lived in Paris, the best place to be if you were, like him, a buyer and seller of knowledge. No, not knowledge. Information.

Most Nosferatu like to live beneath the surface of the world, like rats in a warren. Kindermass was different: he loved the night sky, passed his waking hours upon the rooftops of the Île de la Cité.

The night after I ate the Thin White Duke, we found him there, sitting against a gargoyle atop the cathedral of Notre Dame, head on the gargoyle's flank like a blue leather money pouch lumpy with coin.

We waited respectfully, as was our custom. Finally, Kindermass spoke. His voice was clipped and clear, a priest adumbrating the sins of his flock.

"You have feasted well, I see. The Duke was to your taste?"

"Yes, he was." I could still feel the Duke's blood in my veins. The feeling made me want to shout, to leap. To tear the world in two.

"I congratulate you. My assistance was of use?"

"It was. We would never have found the Duke without your help."

"My payment, please."

I knelt before him, and reached into my tunic, reluctant to part with my prize. I pulled it out and laid it upon the roof. "I hope this pleases you."

EATING MEDUSA

The payment: a small marble bust, several inches high, Roman or Greek in style. A boy's head: full lips, straight nose, tight curly hair. It could have been a bust of the young Alexander. It had once belonged to the Thin White Duke.

"Yes," Kindermass breathed. He rose to his feet, crouched before the bust. "It pleases me. You have done well, Gangrel. Payment has been made in full."

And with that, his gnarled right fist smashed down upon the head with the force of a hammer blow. The bust smashed into several large shards.

Viella was aghast. "Why did you do that, Kindermass? The head was beautiful!"

"I hate beautiful things," said Kindermass. "They are always the product of violence."

Viella, taut with disdain: "Then you must hate Aguirre and myself very much indeed."

"Not at all, little one. I see beneath your surfaces, and so am very fond of you both."

"Enough!" snapped Aguirre. "It is my turn now to do the soul-feast. Give me a target, Kindermass. Just make sure he is close to Caine, and of little power."

"A rare breed." Kindermass reached up to his left ear and pulled it, hard. I could have sworn I saw it grow. "I would be hard pressed to come up with a name."

"Well then, how about you, Kindermass? There are three of us, and only one of you. How about I eat you up, eh?"

"How horrible," said Viella, covering her mouth.

For a moment, Kindermass did nothing. Then...up from his crouch, his eyes upon Aguirre. One eye: tiny and black. The other: large as an apple, covered with white, oozing film. Rolling in its eyehole with a life of its own.

Kindermass smiled. It was not a pleasant sight.

"Would you like to try, Shadowmaster?" he said. "Test me, then. Show me your strength, the power of the Darkness you wield."

"I was only jesting, Old One," said Aguirre. This was a lie, of course, and Kindermass knew it.

"But I am not jesting." Still smiling.

Aguirre shrugged, averted his eyes from Kindermass. "Enough, Old One. You have made your point."

But Kindermass was not finished with him yet. "A word of warning to you, Lasombra. If you perform the rite of Amaranth upon one whose will is stronger than your own, you may find yourself...let me say only that you will never again suffer the pangs of loneliness. Or know the privacy of your own thoughts. And yes, Lasombra, my will is stronger than yours."

"You speak nonsense, Kindermass," said Viella. "That is a lie of the elders. I have eaten three times, and no one but myself lives within me."

Kindermass picked his nose, then looked at his finger. He seemed surprised there was nothing there. He blinked at Viella as if noticing her for the first time.

"Nonsense, you say? A lie of the elders? I have it on good authority that Tremere himself carries Saulot within his mind. And that the Salubri Ancient ofttimes takes command of the will of the Magus and has him issue decrees he later regrets."

Aguirre's lip curled. "Which explains, I suppose, why Tremere, who is really Saulot, has ordered the extermination of each and every one of Saulot's childer?"

Wheezing sounds: Kindermass laughing. "Perhaps Saulot is no longer so fond of his childer as once he was."

We joined in his laughter. Kindermass himself lived in terror of his grandsire, the Nosferatu Ancient, who wished to slay his own descendants as an offering to Caine. It amused Kindermass, perhaps, to think his clan was not alone in its predicament.

"Tell us of our next victim," said Aguirre.

"I know of a Sleeper whose blood is strong. But she rests far from here, on an island near the land of the Greeks."

"How near is she to Caine? What is she? Where precisely does she rest?"

"She is rumored to have taken the blood of an Ancient's childe, through

EATING MEDUSA

the Path of the Black Rose. As for her clan," he glanced at Viella, "she is one of yours, little one. A Follower of the Snake."

"What is her name?" said Viella, bored: not her kill. She began to fidget: one foot, the other.

"Her true name I do not know. But I have heard it said that her clan considers her to be something of a renegade. The Followers of Set call her only 'the Medusa,' or sometimes, 'Medusa.' A reference, obviously, to the snake-headed Gorgon woman from the tales of the Greeks. An unrevealing name, since it could apply to any Setite female."

Viella, very still.

Kindermass, if he was aware, gave no sign. "Medusa did a thing that was held to be insulting in some way to the priests of the Grand Temple. She was forced to flee Africa and seek sanctuary beneath the earth of a faraway land."

Aguirre was about to speak. Viella interrupted him. "What was this...Medusa's crime?" Voice tight, eagerness barely held in check.

Kindermass chuckled. "Her crime? Why, it was a very serious crime for a Setite. I believe she once performed an act of kindness."

Aguirre and I laughed. Viella said nothing.

I said, "Do you know this Medusa, Viella?"

"I have reason to believe that Medusa may be someone who offended me in the past," was all she said.

Aguirre nodded. "If Medusa once performed an act of kindness, I can see how that would offend you, Viella."

Viella seemed not to hear him. She turned away from Aguirre.

Kindermass closed his eyes, began to rock back and forth on his heels; he was about to give us a lecture.

"Listen and learn, Children of Amaranth. Here is how you will find your Sleeper."

His voice became a pedagogical drone. "South of the land of the Greeks, in the sea called the Aegean, there is an island named Santorini, an island that was once a mighty volcano. On this island is a cave, and at the entrance to this cave is an idol. It is on that island, within that cave, that you will find what you seek: the haven of the Medusa."

PATRICK HADLEY

Viella stood nearby, her face composed, distant, closed to my inspection. She did not look as if she was listening to Kindermass as he went on and on, but I could not be certain.

She was facing southeast, I saw, the direction of Greece.

❖

We walked the wind-scoured island. The rain had stopped, but the wind was still high. The rock beneath our feet was so brown it was almost black. On our right, clean-edged cliffs fell down and away to the circular bay beneath. Ahead, the island narrowed into a finger pointing southward to Crete, and to the land of Egypt beyond. Kindermass had told us that the cave and its idol would be there: at the tip of the finger.

We were alone, of course. No Greek travels the byways of the treeless heart of Santorini when he can sleep beneath a roof, warmed by the embers of his fire. Behind and below us, hugging the bay, lay Akrotiri town, its buildings squat and lifeless beneath the cloud-masked moon.

"I am still hungry," said Viella, staring back at the town. "Most of the boy's blood was wasted, spilled onto the floor before I could drink it."

Aguirre clucked his tongue. "You should have thought to feed again before we left. Now we have no time. We have not yet found Medusa. We must hurry."

"Don't be so impatient, Aguirre," I said. "Kindermass told us to watch for the idol at the cave mouth, and he has never set us wrong yet."

"An idol!" sneered Viella. "How like her to..." Her voice faded.

"Yes?" said Aguirre archly. "How like her to what?"

Viella did not answer. For a time we walked on in silence.

Finally she spoke. "I was saying only that it is just like Medusa to mark her hiding place with a religious symbol."

Aguirre winked at me. "Do religious symbols offend you, Viella? I myself think of Setites as highly religious. In their own way, of course."

To my surprise, Viella was not angered by Aguirre's mocking tone. "You are right, Aguirre. We Setites are religious. And no, I am not offended by

Medusa's use of an idol to mark her resting place. I am offended that she has chosen to mark her place of sleep at all."

"I do not understand."

"Isn't it obvious? She wishes to make her presence known to all, even as she lies alone beneath the earth. She craves attention the way we crave blood."

"I pity Medusa, then. Her sleep must be very lonely for her. Of course, that will be changing soon."

"The idol," I said. "I see it."

Ahead of us the island rose into a hillock of volcanic rock. In the hillock's center, protruding like a thumb, spired a slender white shape—the idol. Even in the cold, fingers of steam reached upward from the hillock, groping blindly into the night. The volcano that slumbered at the heart of Santorini was still alive, it seemed.

"Yes," said Viella. "That is the idol that marks Medusa's haven. I—we—have found her."

We hurried now, excited by the confirmation of our desires, up the slope of the hillock. Its surface was smooth black rock, marred by several slashlike vents. From out of the vents rose tendrils of steam, yellowish, sulphurous.

Thin, brittle grass beneath our feet crackled and crunched as we stepped gingerly about. The ground beneath the grass was hot enough that it was painful to stand too long in one place. The air around us was acrid, and as hot as a summer night.

Aguirre and I paused in our exploration of the hillock to look at the idol. It was a woman, tall and voluptuous, her face smoothed away by years of air and rain. She stood on a wide circular base, her arms held up, her breasts revealed by a robe that split open down the front of her torso. In each of the woman's hands was a snake. Something circled her smooth white neck.

"A circlet, I should think," said Aguirre. "This idol was carved by the Minoans of old, or so Kindermass said. He said also that they wore circlets such as this."

I shook my head. "It could be a circlet. The erosion makes it difficult to say. But I think instead that it is a serpent. A snake, gripping its tail in its teeth."

PATRICK HADLEY

"Or swallowing itself," said Aguirre.

"What do you make of this heat?" said Viella to me. "It reminds me of the slopes of Vesuvius when he rumbles in his sleep."

Aguirre chided her, "Did you not listen to Kindermass, Viella? This island is the remnant of a volcano that erupted long ago. It is cousin to Vesuvius."

I looked back the way we had come, toward the lights of Akrotiri on the far side of the bay. Coiled around the bay was the body of Santorini, and moving across its surface, shadows of the wind-driven clouds. And something else.

"Aguirre, Viella. Be silent."

My companions drew nearer.

"Behind us," I said. "Movement. No. It is gone."

"It is nothing," said Viella. "Only shadows."

"Perhaps not," said Aguirre. "Rollo's eyes are keen. We may have more friends of the Turk after us. Let us enter Medusa's haven and finish this quickly." He smiled. "But first..."

He let his arms drop down to his sides, stood statue-still. He closed his eyes and began to chant a monotonous, dirgelike plainsong: the Lay of Amaranth, the Black Rose.

> O Maker, Caine of Nod,
> Tonight shall bring me closer yet to Thee.
> Praised be eternal Amaranth
> Whose night-black blossom neither fades nor withers.
> Always may I feast at Her dark banquet.

He had the right to sing the song, of course. It was his turn, after all. I had eaten our last victim, the emaciated Toreador we called the Thin White Duke, and before that, it had been Viella who feasted upon the blood of the Assamite Ulic the Turk, who had tried to kill himself to stop her, but too late.

Now it was Aguirre's turn. And that was right. That was what we had agreed.

EATING MEDUSA

I thought I heard Viella speak. I turned to her, and saw her staring fixedly at the idol. Her lips moved, but she was making too little sound for me to hear exactly what she was saying.

It didn't matter. From the movement of her lips, I could divine her words easily enough.

You are mine, Medusa, she was whispering. Mine, mine, mine, mine, mine.

✥

Talk of Viella, talk of Setites: Aguirre and I in Paris, just after Kindermass told us where to find Medusa. An alleyway, inky-black, ankle-deep in slops, knee-deep in refuse.

Sprawled on the filth: two bodies, cityfolk, empty of blood. Standing over them: Aguirre and I, flushed and giddy with feeding.

"So Viella knows the Sleeper," I began. "How, I wonder."

"Perhaps Medusa is Viella's sire."

"Then why would she agree to help us eat her?"

"I think our little Setite feels abandoned." Snicker.

"That makes no sense to me, Aguirre. Amaranth is no cure for rejection."

"But it does constitute a viable revenge, no?"

I shook my head. "I do not understand Viella. Or her clan, for that matter."

Laughter from Aguirre. "They are strange indeed. Imagine, an act of kindness being a crime! How can they not know that the only real crime is weakness?"

"They wish to create more corruption, remember. That must be their reason."

Aguirre's voice, contemptuous: "More corruption? As if such a thing is possible in this world!"

I had to agree with him. "True enough. The Setites pile hillocks upon mountains—"

"—and then demand praise for the height of their creations! The gall of them!"

Silence, broken by the scrabbling of rats in the darkness.

PATRICK HADLEY

Aguirre, laughter building in his voice: "Do you know what Viella is?"

I could already guess what he was going to say.

"A saint!" he roared. "Our little Setite is a saint of corruption! So earnest! Can't you just see her, attending Snake Masses at her Snake Temple, pleading with her Snake Father to forgive her for her snaky little sins! *Mea culpa, mea culpa, mea maxima culpa.* Today I gave bread to a beggar!"

My victim's blood, together with that of the Duke, was making me feel drunk. "I sometimes think that inside every Setite there is a Christian waiting to happen."

"And I say to you, Rollo, that the carpenter's son contributed more to the corruption of the world than all the Setites who ever lived. Just think of it...him hanging there on his death-tree, oozing wound-maggots. The 'odor of sanctity,' indeed!"

I frowned. "Odin hung on a death-tree also, Aguirre."

"Ah, but at least he didn't stink to high heaven doing it, eh?"

Below: rats climbing over my feet. Sounds of gnawing.

Aguirre's voice, breathless with mock insight: "I have just thought of something, Rollo. If it is true that within every Setite is a Christian waiting to happen, then within every Christian there must be..."

I giggled. "A Follower of Set...waiting to happen."

"So the Setites are right, then! There are those who still need corrupting! There is work for them to do, after all!"

And our hilarity knew no bounds.

We journeyed to Santorini separately. Viella normally traveled with Aguirre, but she insisted this time on making her way south and east alone.

After several weeks, I finally met Aguirre in the taverna in the town of Akrotiri, not far from Medusa's haven on Santorini. Three nights before, in Thessalonika, I had first encountered the Assamite pursuing me, seeking vengeance for my part in the death of Ulic the Turk.

I had evaded his pursuit without much difficulty, I thought. A few nights later I found myself in the taverna, waiting for Aguirre and Viella to appear.

EATING MEDUSA

Aguirre entered first, looking nervous.

Even before he sat down: "She will leave me."

I had heard this all before. "No. She will never leave you. She loves you."

Aguirre was not listening. "I tell you, she has already left me. I know it in my heart. We will find Medusa, only to learn that Viella has been there before us and performed the Rite of Amaranth herself. And when I see that she has betrayed me, there will be nothing left for me to do but greet the sun."

This made me laugh. "Aguirre will never greet the sun. He is a killer, a diablerist, an eater of souls. The sun would turn away from his offering, and vanish from the sky. Then night would fall forever."

This remark struck his fancy. "Do you think so?" he asked, his eyes gleaming. "Now that would be something! Darkness forever. We would never need to sleep! Viella and I could..." His voice faded, and he grinned at me, sheepish.

"You see," I said. "I told you she would never leave you. And now you are agreeing with me."

But Aguirre only shook his head. I had convinced him of nothing. But I could see that he was thinking now, his maudlin mood broken by the cheerful prospect of driving the sun from the sky.

"Darkness forever," he said, his eyes wide at the thought of it. "Darkness unending!" He grinned again, and slapped me on the shoulder.

"Oh well," he said. "Something to look forward to, yes?"

Aguirre and I cast about for a time, looking for the opening of the cave that would lead into the earth below. Viella stood next to the idol, silent, watchful, her face a white oval beneath the ashen moon.

I felt a sudden pressure in the air, and with it a hiss that seemed to vibrate just behind my eyes. There for a moment. Gone.

Viella spoke. "The idol is not so well anchored as it appears." She pushed against the snake-woman with a single hand. To my surprise, it leaned slightly.

Aguirre and I walked over quickly. We leaned our shoulders into the snake-woman's smooth white torso and pushed. She toppled as easily as a tree whose roots have rotted away. The idol's base, I saw, had only penetrated a palm's breadth or so into the earth.

Before us, revealed by the snake-woman's fall, a black hole gaped. It was not so wide as the idol's broad base, but still wide enough for even a very large man to drop through. Steamy fingers probed upward from the depths: I had to flick one away from my eyes.

"After you," I said to Aguirre.

He knelt over the hole, turned to me and grinned. He raised a long white hand and, to my astonishment, crossed himself. "In the name of the Darkness, and of the Shadows, and of the Endless Night. Amen."

He leaned forward, and still grinning, flipped forward and down into the shadows.

"You fool," whispered Viella.

"You're right," I said. "He should be more concerned about traps."

"Yes," said Viella. "He should."

We waited for a time, then from the cavity rose Aguirre's jovial voice.

"Come," he said. "All is well. Leap down. It is a short fall."

I lifted Viella into my arms. I looked down into her face, and saw that her eyes were gleaming a deep blood red, the better to see in the darkness below. My eyes, I knew, would be the same color as hers.

Once again, I felt pressure in the air, the same odd hiss. And again, it slipped away as soon as I tried to grasp it.

"I am waiting," said Viella.

I stepped forward into the blackness and dropped. There was an impact as my feet struck a surface of flat rock.

Aguirre was right. We had not had far to fall.

I prepared to lower Viella, but she was impatient, and squirmed out of my arms like a restless child, or cat.

I looked about. We were in a chamber, its ceiling low and irregular. The walls that circled us were of reddish-black stone, broken by two lopsided, cavelike openings standing side by side. A narrow moonbeam descended through the aperture above, cutting the darkness like a blade. The air was hot and sulphurous.

The chamber was empty except for Viella, myself, and against one of the walls, a low-slung tenebrous mass, impenetrable even to the gleam of my red eyes. Aguirre, in his hunting form.

A voice from the shadows: "Welcome to Hell."

"Lead on, Master of Darkness," I said.

There. Something. A word, hanging on the edge of understanding...

"It is strange," said Aguirre. "For a moment, I could feel Medusa calling to me. Can you imagine it? She calls me to her—the fool!"

"No," said Viella, her voice trembling, avid. "You are wrong, Aguirre."

"What?"

"She does not call to you, Lasombra. She calls to me."

"What are you talking about?"

But there was no time for Viella to answer. Even if she had wanted to. No time.

The shaft of moonlight that lit the chamber disappeared, blocked by something in the opening above. From overhead rang voices, harsh and guttural. Saracen voices.

"Ulic!" they cried. "The avengers of Ulic are upon you!"

And then, true to their word, they were.

A blur before me, driving low for my gut. My fists slammed forward, and I felt something collapse. Hot wetness on my hands.

Knives flashed. Pain, burning in my stomach. In my back.

Ululations of triumph. I spun, staggered, almost fell.

Then silence. Stillness. My boots shuffling on the cave's stone floor. I reached for my dagger.

Suddenly, an Assamite in front of me, knife arcing for my throat. I sprang back.

Into silk-clad arms that whipped around my torso from behind. I was jerked up, back, my feet high off the ground. The cavern floor spun sideways, smashed into my face.

A foot pressed into my neck, pinning me to the floor.

Something flickered in the corner of my eye. Small, female. It flashed away down one of the tunnels. A hand in my hair snapped my head back and up.

Someone shouted a name—"Viella!" My voice.

And from down the tunnel, drifting back, an echoing cry, a single word, the word that had hung in the air earlier, evading my understanding.

Mine. Mine. Mine. Mine. Mine.

"Viella!" My voice again.

A low, soft Saracen voice: "Your friend has deserted you, Gangrel. We are alone now."

More silence. My head was pulled roughly to the left. I saw a body, long, dark-skinned, stretched out along the ground, its turbaned skull collapsed, oozing brains and blood.

"You slew Faisal," said the Assamite. "For that, and other crimes, you and your *munafiqun* friends shall suffer greatly."

"Viella," I whispered.

"I have already told you. The faithless one has fled into the tunnels. It will do her no good. We know that it was she who performed the Amaranth upon our master. We shall find her."

Behind the body of the dead Assamite: a shadow on the wall, unmoving.

Aguirre, help me! I cried internally.

The shadow began to slide slowly toward the same mouthlike opening down which Viella had fled. The Assamite pinning me raised my head, then smashed my face into the ground.

Once, twice. A third time. I tasted blood.

Aguirre!

The shadow on the wall merged into the blackness of the cave mouth. Was gone.

✛

They delivered me deeper into darkness. I did not struggle. The Assamite leader walked ahead of me, an elegant, silken shape. Behind me, the other assassin pushed me forward with the point of his dagger. The rapidly decomposing body of the third Assamite, the one I had managed to kill, was left in the chamber behind us.

We paused at one point. A now familiar pressure vibrated in the air. The leader stood with his head hanging low, as if listening. I saw his eyes go dead, his jaw fall slack and hanging.

He raised his head and spoke in a slurred and heavy voice. "Yes," he said.

The tension in the air eased, and we resumed walking.

I felt the beginnings of a terrible understanding grow within me. The Assamites had assaulted us openly, something their clan almost never did. Why? And why had they attacked only me and not Viella?

I glanced at the leader. He was walking slowly now, clumsily, as if unsure of his own body. He turned back to look at me. His face was as alive and aware as a stone. His black eyes were surfaces only, empty pools of night.

We stopped once more. The sensation of tension returned. The air seemed full of whispers, sibilants on the edge of meaning. Once again the leader hung his head. He seemed numbed, almost unconscious. He swayed on his feet, and spoke a single, heavy word. "Yes."

Now I understood what was happening, why the Assamites were behaving so strangely. I did not think this newfound understanding would do me any good.

We walked on, and after several minutes, we entered a chamber not dissimilar to the first.

She was there, I saw. Waiting, as I knew she would be. Medusa.

She was small, slender, naked. Her hair was so black it was almost blue, bound in braids that coiled about her head in a serpentine embrace. She sat, complacent and smiling, on a low flat slab of rock. A queen reigning in darkness, dispensing judgment from a cold hard throne.

The only light within the chamber came from her marble-white skin, which glowed as if with some inner luminescence. I could not quite make out the color of her eyes. Her lips were full and very red. Behind her throne was shadow.

She nodded at the Assamite. "Thank you Khalid, for your assistance. You answered my call with admirable haste." Her voice was low and feather-soft, strangely accented.

The Assamite said nothing. He seemed like a silk-clad statue. Something tugged at the edge of my vision. It was a patch of shadow, moving slowly across the floor at the edge of the chamber. Neither Medusa nor the Assamites seemed to notice it.

The shadow on the floor entered the greater blackness behind Medusa's throne, became indistinguishable from it.

Medusa floated to her feet and wafted toward me, her girlish hips swaying with a casual eroticism. Behind her, bereft of her light, her throne fell even more deeply into shadow.

Khalid moved to my right, the other Assamite to my left.

Medusa stood before me. She reached up a tiny hand and touched my chin. "I do believe I am going to eat you up, my precious blond beast-man."

I frowned. Her words chilled me, but not because of the threat they held. I tried to remember why. But the pressure returned, and the question became suddenly and utterly uninteresting. I abandoned it, and the pressure eased.

I looked over Medusa's head, avoiding her eyes. Behind her, her throne was now completely invisible, enveloped in a mass of impenetrable blackness. I restrained a sudden urge to laugh.

The shadows behind Medusa began to roil like a cloud of ink in water. A long thin tendril probed outward from its core, edging along the floor. Now the tendril almost touched the heels of my unsuspecting tormentor.

I felt a tug on my chin: Medusa's icy fingers. I needed to keep her distracted from the mounting threat behind her. I looked down into her face.

Into eyes of brilliant green. Then blue.

And suddenly I understood. Completely. Now I no longer wanted to laugh.

"You're not—" was all I had time to say. And then...

...Aguirre, exploding from blackness!

✣

Aguirre's attack came in fast and to my left. I felt rather than heard the whiplike snap of his shadow-clad blade as it slammed full-force into the Assamite there.

In front of me, the Setite spun, blurred, was gone—pursued by shadows.

A moment later: the impact of a heavy body hitting the ground.

I was free now. And alone with the Assamite called Khalid. I knew I did not have much time to prevent disaster from happening.

My hands spasmed, agonized. Their skin burned and split open. My fingers warped and lengthened, grew two-inch claw-tips, keen as knives.

The agony subsided. Now my hands could kill more swiftly. I circled my opponent.

"Khalid," I said. "We should not fight. I have reason to think that we are all being controlled by a sleeping Power for purposes of her own. All of us, even you. You and your companions are here only because she summoned you, made you come."

Khalid laughed coldly. He seemed himself once more, cold, self-assured. "It is of no matter," he said. "You are here. You and your friends made my sire *shahid*, a martyr. Your deaths are a matter of the vengeance that must be."

"Khalid, you must listen! The woman we saw was not—"

He sprang for me, howling, a knife in his hand. I dropped low, swung high with my claws, took him in the gut as he passed overhead.

Then he was down, rolling into the base of the far cavern wall. He flopped backward, clambered to his feet, stumbled slowly around to face me.

My claws had done their work. Khalid looked down just as his stomach opened and his heart-blood poured out, steaming, onto the ground. His face twisted into a rictus of agony. And surprise.

His eyes upon me were red with hate.

"There will be others," he said. "There will always be others."

I did not reply.

PATRICK HADLEY

Slowly, almost reverently, the Assamite knelt before me. He bowed his head, sighed like a moon-struck lover. His eyes, burning coals in his coal-black face, flickered weakly and closed.

And then, finally, he was dead.

I had no time to waste. I bolted from the chamber, racing back through the tunnels to the place where I had first fought the Assamites. It was empty.

I cursed and ran down the other tunnel. Blackness unwound before me.

I ran on. A hiss, maddening, insinuating, built behind my eyes, grew unbearably intense. I stumbled, fell, became confused.

More minutes lost. I shook my head, and the reptilian sibilance lifted from my brain. Then I heard it. Ahead, not far. I burned blood, sped forward.

I sprinted into another chamber, stumbled to a halt. My eyes made out two shapes in hideous embrace upon the ground. A female, on her back, naked, white, limbs splayed in posture of surrender. Hunched over her, a black cloud.

And from the cloud, sounds of feeding.

"Aguirre!" I shouted. But it was too late. The Rite of Amaranth was completed as I watched.

The body, bloodless now, began to wither and crack, collapsing upon itself like a punctured bladder. Within seconds, it was a mummy, then a skeleton. Then dust.

But not before I had time to see the disguise that concealed its true features drop away, revealing the face and body of Viella.

His soul-feast completed, Aguirre emerged from shadow, and leaned back from the remains.

"I have her," he said.

"It was Viella, Aguirre. Not Medusa."

Aguirre's black and depthless eyes went wide. "What? What are you saying, Rollo?"

"Back in the throne room, I looked into Medusa's eyes. They were green, and then blue."

"Viella—"

"—could never get the eyes right. Do you remember?"

Aguirre opened his mouth, closed it. I waited, until I was sure he was listening. Then I spoke.

"Viella and the Assamites were under Medusa's control. The Assamites were summoned by Medusa. That was how they found us so quickly. As for Viella, I do not know when Medusa took command of her mind. But she did. Probably above. It was strange, now that I think of it, that Viella knew about the opening beneath the idol.

"After we were inside, and the Assamites had come, Medusa made Viella abandon us. She had to get her alone, you see. Then Medusa forced her to disguise herself, pretend to be Medusa."

I paused, remembering.

"Yes," I said. "The Assamites stopped twice when they were taking me to her—to Viella, I mean. It must have been Medusa telling them to wait while Viella completed her transformation. The timing, you see, was important. I have one question for you, Aguirre. Where were you after you left me with the Assamites?"

"I pursued Viella. Then I became...confused. I wandered lost for a time. Then I heard you and the assassins, and I followed you to the chamber."

I nodded. I knew all about the confusion. "Medusa was the one who clouded your mind, Aguirre. And her stratagem worked. By the time we found Viella, she was disguised. And we thought she was Medusa. Until I looked into her eyes."

"I never saw her eyes," Aguirre whispered. "I was behind her the whole time."

I clenched my fists. Medusa's plan had been clever indeed. It occurred to me that it was not just Viella and the Assamites who had been the Sleeper's puppets. I wondered how deeply her control of us had gone, rejected the speculation as futile.

Aguirre put his head in his hands. He began to rock back and forth on his heels. "Then where is...Medusa, Rollo? Where is she...hiding?"

"Deeper in the earth, probably. Sleeping, and yet awake enough to play her little game with us. Does it matter, Aguirre? We never stood a chance. Never."

Aguirre only moaned.

"It must have pleased Medusa," I said, "to trick us into performing Amaranth on one of our own. And if Medusa really was Viella's sire, then the jest would have been all the sweeter. I guess we will never find out now just why it was that Viella hated Medusa so."

Aguirre's voice rose into a high-pitched keening wail. He began to tear at his face with his fingernails.

"Rollo!" he cried. "I can feel her! I can feel Viella within me! She is like a snake coiled inside my mind! My God, my God! Kindermass was right! I can feel her coils in my mind!"

I closed my eyes. "There is nothing more for us here. Are you coming, Aguirre?"

He only continued to moan and rock.

"Coils of the snake," he whispered. "Coils in my mind."

I turned away, left him there. I walked out of the chamber of the feast, made my way back to the opening that led to the world above.

For a moment, I stood beneath the aperture, gazing up at the empty face of the moon. Behind me, from deep within the blackness, rang echoes of Aguirre's shouts, his howls.

I pulled myself up and out of the chamber, and emerged into the cold clean air of the night. The winter storm was over, and the wind had fallen away. The sky was black and filled with stars.

I descended from the hillock, changed to wolf-form, and ran away across the island as swiftly as I could. I did not look back at the cave, or at the idol.

Eventually, some months later, I returned to Paris, where I told Kindermass everything that had happened. He only nodded.

I never saw Viella again, of course. She has left me forever, departed from my unlife utterly and irretrievably. For her and for me, there will be no reunions, no returning. She is gone. Forevermore.

As for Aguirre, I do not know if Medusa took him or let him go. I am not certain that I care.

EATING MEDUSA

Sometimes I think I am jealous of Aguirre. He was always so afraid that Viella would abandon him. But he has nothing to worry about, not any more.

She will never leave him now.

The Burden

BY EDWARD CARMIEN

JEAN

ean turned the simpleton Benedictine's correspondence over in his hands. The man slept nearby, but there was no chance of him waking.

A Letter for the eyes of Brother Eduoard, of the Bishopric of Mende:

> … I write to you, fellow clerk of the parishes, as I am preparing a new tithing list here in the Bishopric of Rodez. Let me assure you I have already posed this vexing question to our fellow Benedictines at the Aurillac Monastery. Their records have proved less than helpful…

> …It is chiefly the matter of a small village high in the mountains. It is my hope that your records at Mende can be of some assistance. For I am told with great authority by an itinerant friar, Peter, that there is an unnamed village some days west and north of the village of Aroyan. Yet this village appears not on our rolls of the Tithe, nor on any record of the Benedictines at Aurillac…

...nor are Duchy records of any use. Can you make a search of your Bishopric's records? The county in question is Rouerge, and the village itself is somewhere between the headwaters of the Tarn and Lot rivers.

Your help in this matter is of great importance, Brother Eduoard. I await your reply.

Brother Albertus
Clerk of the Parishes
Bishopric of Rodez

A Letter for Brother Albertus, of the Bishopric of Rodez:

I have made a thorough search, Brother Albertus, of records new and long past. I must say that since the county in question is Rouerge and not Gevaudan, there was little hope of my finding anything of import regarding your inquiry.

I do, however, find mention of the village Aroyan, which is indeed in county Rouerge, and of the concern of the Bishop of Rodez. I also have it on great authority that there is no pass through the mountains. It should also be said it is thought the mountains there are no fit place for agriculture of any kind, and the district is imagined to be poor if not utterly desolate.

It is my hope that this letter does not trouble you overmuch, Brother Albertus. You will find this province of France, our corner of Aquitaine, is still restless under the holy mantle of the true church.

May health and holiness be with you always, Brother Albertus.

Brother Eduoard
Clerk of the Parishes
Bishopric of Mende

Dear Brother Eduoard,

I write you in haste as my inquiries have resulted in calamity! I am ordered, by the Bishop himself, to investigate this village, in my own person! I shall be at least a month on the road, as I am

THE BURDEN

also charged with being a messenger whilst I travel. If I am fleet
of foot, I shall return before the first snows of winter.

God's ways are mysterious, Brother Eduoard, never mistake.

I needs must go now. God be with you.

> Brother Albertus
> Clerk of the Parishes
> Bishopric of Rodez

So this was Albertus? And since this collection of hovels overshadowed by mountains was named (although it hardly deserved a name) Aroyan, this mystery village was nearby, if it existed at all.

If his appointed quarry lurked in this corner of Aquitaine, Jean would find him. The clan needed him, it was said, to help rule the lovely cities mortals built and flocked to in ever greater numbers.

Jean pondered the monk's mission: tithing. Was it such an important matter? Worth the attention of one of Aquitaine's scribes, got with what difficulty from the Benedictine order? He would follow this monk, Jean decided, into the wilderness. And if he did not find his prey, he could put an isolated village to good use, he was certain.

The silly monk had given up within a short distance of what he searched for, Jean discovered a few nights later. Not two leagues from his destination, the Benedictine shivered in the cold mountain air. It wasn't much of a village. Two dozen huts, a few bolder cottages, wattle and daub. For the lucky few, fieldstone. Goats and sheep wandered aimlessly. A dog barked, and then another.

Jean had arrived: Let the dogs bark as they may, he mused. The people of the village were like ghosts before him. Someone had seen him on the rude track that led here, and they had faded indoors. Not accustomed to strangers, Jean decided, here in what was surely the rump of France in Aquitaine.

Then a door opened, and a short fat man appeared. In the dying light

Jean could see he was wiping his lips with his sleeve. The smell of mutton wafted out of the cottage, disgusting him.

The man spoke, but his Pays d'Oc was so accented Jean simply stood and stared. The man was a marvel of incomprehensibility.

Hearing no response from Jean, the man tried again, more slowly and with care.

"What brings you to our village, stranger?"

Jean doffed his cap and bowed, ever so slightly. The man was but a peasant, after all. "I am a traveler, good sir, long on the road."

The man sniffed, actually sniffed, and looked away into the night.

"You are days south of the way to Le Puy," said the man. "And if your way is to the west, to Arles, or south, to Marseilles, you will find no pass through the mountains."

Jean smiled. "And what if I mean to travel here, just here? I am Jean, good sir." There were eyes and ears aplenty upon them, Jean was sure. Dogs still barked, though many had been quieted.

"Then, good traveler, you have wasted many days. Here is only our village. And I am Marcel. It is my good fortune to have the largest house in the village, so I must ask you to stay, be my guest, until it is time for you to travel once again."

Jean tipped his head forward slightly. For all that he was a peasant, Marcel had a subtle wit about him. Placing his hat once again upon his head, Jean stepped forward. "Lead the way, good sir. Night is upon us, and I am weary from the road."

The cottage was what one would expect, a full week of travel from anything resembling a decent inn. Rough-hewn timbers stood barely above his brow. Jean met in turn Marcel's wife and grown children, but turned down a late supper.

"But know that I have eaten well on the road, Madame," Jean said, to soothe her matronly feelings. Though handsome, the fact that he looked gaunt and pale, even by the firelight, no doubt made him seem a liar.

That, too, would change, Jean thought to himself. Out of habit he asked that the dog be put out for the night, though this mutt didn't growl and snap as curs usually did in his presence. It would be a quiet night.

THE BURDEN

Pleading fatigue, Jean begged off telling current news. Village Aroyan, three days walk back down the track, had been pathetically eager to hear of Paris and how she glowed with light hours into the night.

In the darkness he waited until all the family was asleep. Marcel was silent, but his wife snored, as did the daughter. The son, too, was silent, and it was to his side Jean crept, and bit, and fed, all in equal silence. The young man would feel ill and weak for days to come, but would never know the cause.

Feeling much refreshed, Jean crept into the night, so much a shadow even the dogs did not wake. All around him the village was dark and silent. A short distance away, however, a light shone through the night.

Drawn like a moth, Jean found himself peering through the open window of a small stone chapel impossible to see from the track. In the moonlight Jean could see headstones, a graveyard. His skin prickled with fear, for it was God's ground, hallowed earth, that he trod.

An old man, reading by candlelight. It was odd, thought Jean, that a village so small warranted a chapel and a priest. Aroyan had none, that was certain.

The old man kissed the book and closed it before returning it to a box. Jean realized he read at the altar: There was no other furniture in the chapel, not even a chair. A rough, simple cross adorned the nave: no gold here! Jean watched with interest as the old man moved carefully to the rectory.

Jean followed the light from one window to the next. Although shuttered, it was not shuttered well. There the old man—a priest?—prepared for bed.

It was then that Jean was seized and thrown a dozen paces backward. He fell among the headstones, one of which gave way with a crumbling snap and thump.

Surprised and aching, Jean scrambled to his feet.

An iron grip closed around his throat and lifted him bodily from the ground. Dimly before him he saw a figure, a scarred face contorted with anger, a barely readable shadow in the starlight. Then he was borne away from the chapel at great speed.

He tried to speak and clawed at the arm that held him aloft effortlessly. The night air, previously quiet and still, sang past his ears, an eerie whistle. Rage filled him: He hadn't been so helpless since the night another had held him by the throat—

EDWARD CARMIEN

Since the night—

A door opened and shut, and as suddenly as he was gripped and spirited away, Jean was released. Within a moment a fire kindled in the darkness.

A single candle was all Jean needed to see his assailant. Disarmingly short, he smiled wickedly, making no effort to hide what such a smile showed.

Jean checked his rage. This was an old one of his kind. But how old? And was this the old one of his clan that he sought?

The short man straightened his simple linen clothing. "Be welcome," he said. He bore a scar on his face, obviously an old wound.

Jean felt for his hat, but it was long gone, torn off by the swiftness of his passage. "My regrets for disturbing you. I did not know...." He hoped his smile might mollify his host.

"Sit," gestured the man. His polite French, Pays d'Oy, if not Parisian, was balm to Jean's ears.

Jean sat. He was in a sparsely furnished room. Fitted stone, shuttered windows. Armor of a style not common for two hundred years adorned a rack. A book sat open on a small table. Jean's eye lingered on the heraldry. It sparked some memory....

"Of course you didn't know," said the man in liquid tones. Jean put himself on guard for smooth-tongued Patrician tricks. "Forgive my anger. Allow it as the mistaken get of my surprise." When Jean did not answer, the man continued.

"I am Robere. What brings you to my village?"

"My own two feet," joked Jean hollowly. He felt imperiled, but Robere showed no signs of lunging for his throat...yet.

Robere shrugged and spread his hands, open and palm up. His meaning was obvious.

"I am a traveler of the world, m'sieur. I heard word of a tiny village, almost lost in the mountains, on the way to no other place. I decided I had to see it. Little did I know such a person as yourself made it your residence." Jean tried to sound casual and urbane.

"You had to see it, indeed. Some might imagine one of our kind could have a use for such a village, no?"

THE BURDEN

Jean blanched. The message was clear. This old one was not to be trifled with.

But Robere smiled reassuringly, then shrugged. "The world grows into a smaller place," he said. Jean liked him despite Robere's rough treatment earlier.

"Indeed," agreed Jean. With the success of the Crusades, nothing seemed able to stop the march of Christendom. "Are you lord over these people?" he ventured.

Robere seemed to relax, to settle in his simple wooden chair. "These simple folk need no lord to tell them how to milk their goats, how to shear their sheep. No, I am not their lord, though they know and respect me as their better."

"What, then, keeps you here?" Jean grew bolder. With some old ones, he knew, the thirst for companionship opened mouths that otherwise stayed shut with suspicion. And the heraldry gave the man away. He was certain Robere was whom he sought.

"I'm sure it is none of your concern, sir," Robere said mildly in a tone that yet managed to convey the issue was closed.

Jean paused to collect his thoughts, then took a different path. "Do not the wild beasts trouble you, here in the mountains?" The heraldry made sense to him now, but he knew better than to mention it. Why, here was a famous soul, the bloodletter of Beziers! Jean's elders had not told him all they could of the man he hunted.

Robere grinned, and Jean was not at all sure what he meant by it. "Wild beasts do not concern me. What I wonder is how you came to hear of my little village."

Jean spread his hands in innocence. "There is a village three days from here. Aroyan. There I met a church man, some kind of clerk. He spoke of searching out this place."

Robere stroked his chin, then looked to the door. Seconds later, Jean heard footsteps approaching. "Are you expecting guests?" he said, trying to hide his nervousness.

"Just one good friend," said Robere, opening the door. The old man from the stone chapel entered. His gaze flicked to Jean.

EDWARD CARMIEN

"Ah, Father," said Robere with a smile.

Jean cringed. What was Robere doing, welcoming a man of the cloth into his lair?

"I see we have a guest. No one tells me anything anymore," said the old man. Robere directed him into his chair, then pulled up a three-legged stool.

"Father, this is…" Robere raised an eyebrow at Jean.

"Jean. I am a traveler," said Jean, turning his eyes away from the old man's silver crucifix.

"Ah, a pilgrim? This would be your hat. I found it on the path. I was roused by some commotion in the darkness—but no matter," said the old man. "You are far from the holy places, my son, although there are few places where God's greatness is so manifest as it is here, on the shoulder of the mountains."

"Jean was just telling me we're to have another visitor, Father," said Robere. "A clerk, he says. But this is Jean's tale." The old man and Robere both turned to Jean.

Jean tried not to shrink in his chair. It was crafted well: He could scarcely feel the joints beneath his fingers as he ran his hands nervously over the arms. There was something here he did not perceive. Robere spoke so kindly to the old man, and the old man…had no fear of Robere. Jean realized he had been silent too long.

"Well, yes. In the village of Aroyan, I met a holy brother who claimed he was sent by the Bishop in Rodez to investigate a mystery village. The villagers there were close-mouthed and pretended not to understand his French…."

"They profit well enough from us," said Robere.

"It must be my replacement," said the old man, who slapped his knee with sudden glee.

"Don't say such a thing!" exclaimed Robere.

"Your replacement?" asked Jean, confused. "But he claimed to be only a clerk, a Benedictine. He certainly had enough ink on his hands."

"Yes, yes, my time has come, and the village needs spiritual nourishment. Who else will lead them to God? I have tired of the task, Robere. I have prayed too long into God's ear, and it is time for me to step into his hands." The old man looked up, suddenly, and an odd glint appeared in his eye.

"Or not, as divine will might have it."

Jean cringed at the near-blasphemy, and mortal habit made his hand itch to make the sign of the cross upon his chest.

"Father, you know my mind on this...." Robere's voice held unusual concern. What haven had he made for himself here? Jean wondered. The old one did not wrap himself in the trappings of an Osiris, nor did he rule as a Fiend. Yes, there was a puzzle here.

The old priest held up his palm, and stood. "No, no, Robere. Now I must sleep. You know my mind on the question as well, but my faith will not be shaken. Besides, I've a guest to prepare for. Do you think I would leave the poor Brother to Marcel's tender mercies?"

The old man left after a few words of parting from Robere, who stood in the open door for many minutes, staring into the darkness.

Jean, deep in thought, held his peace. It was certain his elders had sent him on a fool's errand, for there was no hope in his heart that he could convince Robere to return to the intrigues of the city. Why he was certain of this, Jean did not know. Yet.

Finally, Robere spoke as he closed the door. "Well. The village is to have another guest, come the morning. We must prepare."

BROTHER ALBERTUS

At the start of the fourth day, he was certain the villagers of Aroyan had misdirected him. The mule on which his luggage rode carried practically nothing, now that he'd eaten all but a small portion of his food. The mountain springs he drank from were clear and cold but almost certainly unhealthy, and he was sure to come down with a desperate fever.

But his Bishop had commanded he find this mystery village, and so he traveled on. If only his Abbot had never made him serve as a clerk for the mother church! But by midday he was certain he'd seen smoke, and within an hour he saw the village itself. So it did exist!

Brother Albertus mentally calculated the time it would take to conduct a census and make arrangements to collect a tithe. He hoped and prayed he had not stumbled on a pagan village, for then his future would be in God's hands.

Although it would be a great boon to Brother Albertus's name in the eyes of the Bishop if he reported converting an entire village, Albertus thought to himself.

A bell tolled, then, as he rounded the last bend in the track. Not a large bell, no, but a bell nonetheless. Could there be a chapel here? There had not been so much as a plot of ground given to the church in the last village.

Villagers streamed in from the hills, and from the huts and cottages that formed the center of the village. It was barely larger than a hamlet! Could this be worth all his time and trouble? Albertus felt indignant as an old man in a worn cassock approached.

Why, the man was a priest! It could not be so! Surprise must have shown on his face.

"You seem puzzled, Brother Albertus. But welcome to our village!" Dozens of simple folk gathered around, their chattering voices all but incomprehensible to him. A ragged cheer went up upon the old man's welcome. "Come, let me show you the chapel. It is small, and the rectory, well, it's simply a small room in the back."

"Greetings, Father," Albertus finally said. His head spun with questions. How could there be a priest here, and there be no record of it? Could he be in some village known by another name? Maps were often completely wrong, he knew. Yes, that must be it.... But, then, how did the old man know his name? It was altogether unsettling.

The gabble of the villagers was no better than that of village Aroyan. He was glad the Father spoke so well.

They made their way, old priest, Albertus and his mule, and half the village around an outcropping of rock. And indeed there was a chapel, Albertus saw, complete with a small bronze bell set next to the entrance. It was still being rung energetically by a small boy.

"...so glad you've come to us," the priest was saying. Albertus was having a hard time taking it all in, and the bell didn't help. "But you must be hungry. Come with me to Marcel's. Marcel, he owns the biggest house in the village, and his wife has quite a hand with mutton."

THE BURDEN

Brother Albertus's mule was led away from him, and they dined well on mutton, bread, and cheese. There was no wine with dinner, and Albertus commented on this fact.

"Grapes will not grow this high in the mountains," said the old priest. Albertus realized he still didn't know the old man's name. "And there is little in this village that is not grown or made here."

"What little we do bring in is in exchange for what we trade with the villagers of Aroyan," said Marcel.

"What about taxes?" Albertus wanted to know. He was more collected now, and was trying to find a kind way to inform these simple peasants they would soon be tithing to the church.

"Well…" said the old priest, but Marcel began speaking. His French, too, was passable, when he spoke slowly.

"The lord of Rouerge believes we are the business of county Gevaudan."

"So you pay your tax to Gevaudan?" Albertus diligently chased gravy with the last of his bread.

"Well…" began the old priest again, but Marcel, with a grand gesture, spoke again.

"It is somewhat odd, I admit, but it seems the lord of Gevaudan believes we are the business of Rouerge."

Albertus was silent for a long moment, astonished. "And your tithe?" he blurted, all cunning plans thrown aside.

"The chapel is kept very nicely, you must admit," said the old priest. "We even have a bell. And I am kept in what clothing I require. Madame here, with the help of the village, feeds me well. You will like the arrangement, I'm sure."

Albertus would have choked in amazement, but now he was beyond surprise. "Whatever do you mean? I am here to make a report to my Bishop at Rodez. It is the year of our Lord eleven hundred and ninety-seven! You cannot evade your duty to lord and church any longer!"

Marcel, too, looked startled at the old priest's words. Perhaps, Albertus thought, the old man is a lunatic, a madman! But the old priest continued as if nothing were amiss.

"Oh, I must admit that things are quiet in the village, especially during

EDWARD CARMIEN

the winters, which can be cold and cruel. But that leaves more time for prayer, don't you think?"

Albertus shook his head with confusion. How could he correct the old man's lunacy?

The door opened, then, and two men entered. "Brother Albertus, I assume?" said one, a short, scarred man. The other was the handsome traveler Albertus recognized from Aroyan…Jean, his name was. How had he come here without passing him on the track?

"I am Robere. My companion is Jean. Please be welcome to our village." Marcel's wife puttered around the cottage, lighting candles, for the sun had just vanished behind tall peaks.

"M'sieur Robere," said Albertus. "Jean."

"Ah, it is the only man I cannot save," said the old man. He insulted Robere so cheerfully, Albertus grew certain the old priest was a doddering old fool. Even the traveler blanched at the old man's words.

"Soon he will be your burden, young man," the old priest slapped his leg and laughed. "And what a burden he is!"

Had there been wine at the meal, Albertus would have thought the old man drunk. As it was, he felt compelled to correct the old man's mistake. "I am sorry to say, Father, the Bishop did not intend me to replace you…I must say, Father, I'm not at all sure he knows you serve here!"

To that statement there was silence. The old priest nodded as if, yes, of course, Brother Albertus was right. Robere's face was unreadable, while Marcel and Jean seemed amused. "Besides, Father," Albertus continued, "I am but a holy brother, a Benedictine. I have not taken your oaths. I am no priest…."

The old man interrupted, and there was iron in his voice. "You need not put your face on the floor in front of a bishop to serve here, my son. You know the Good Book, and you have faith in your heart. Besides, would you rather count coins for the Bishop?" As if tired by his speech, the old priest sagged on his stool.

Robere bent and took the old priest's arm. "Let us go to the chapel, Father. Night is falling."

"Yes, it's night, your time," said the old man weakly as he rose.

THE BURDEN

Albertus struggled to keep from running out the door. For a moment he considered that he might have gone mad himself, and be raving and lost in the wilderness, and only imagining this strange conversation.

In a few minutes they were lighting candles in the chapel. Albertus saw sacramental tools on the altar. A silver ciborium held the host, and a simple wooden cup served as a chalice. What served as sacramental wine in this wineless country?

They stood awkwardly for a few moments, as the chapel was without seats. Albertus assumed Robere and Jean would go, having seen them safely to the chapel, but they remained.

The old priest sat himself on the flagstones, as if suddenly weak. Robere bent to help him.

"Old friend?" he said. Albertus leaned forward, to see what he could do. It was sad, the old man falling ill, but he was obviously old—very old. The village probably would never see another priest, but perhaps the itinerant friar, Peter, could be cajoled to visit once a season, to baptize and marry and sanctify graves.

"You've foregone my gift this past month, haven't you?" Robere spoke as if Albertus weren't there, and indeed, as the scarred man smoothed the old priest's brow, it seemed as if he'd been forgotten. The old man was looking worse by the moment.

"Indeed I have," croaked the old man. "Though not the sacrament. Water…did not change to wine, or blood…but it…served well enough."

Albertus came to himself and prepared to shrive the old priest as best as he was able. Robere stepped well back, as did Jean. When he was done, they stepped forward again to the dying priest's side. The old man was barely breathing now, and his skin was impossibly wrinkled. It must be the light, Albertus decided. He had looked considerably better in the late afternoon.

The old priest's eyes opened, then, and fixed upon Albertus. They were clear, and bright, and impossibly fierce. "You are to take my place. The damned is your soul to bear toward the light."

Jean hissed in dismay, then, but Albertus could not tear his eyes away from the old man. No matter what the madman's words, he wasn't and could never be a priest.

EDWARD CARMIEN

"He knows!" Jean whispered to Robere, who answered with "Silence!"

The old priest carried on, his voice barely a rough whisper. "His gift...the devil's blood...make it holy, every dawn...save the damned...each day in turn." Albertus could barely hear him now, but as he bent over further he heard the death rattle in the old man's throat, and jumped back instinctively.

Impossibly, the old man crumbled into dust around his bones, and then his bones, too, collapsed into powder.

Albertus glanced up. Robere had fallen to his knees. Jean was crouched in a corner.

Robere wept, and his tears were blood red. Only then did Albertus realize how pale Robere was, and how Jean matched him. Compared to the ruddy villagers they stood out like corpses at a harvest dance...like corpses at a harvest dance....

His heart hammered in his chest. It could not be! The devil's children, on consecrated ground! Albertus fumbled for his crucifix, held it before him, screaming, "Begone from this holy house!"

Albertus felt the power of the Lord strong in him: All his years of learning told him no creature of the devil could stand the righteous wrath of the Lord.

But Robere was unmoved, although Jean moaned with fear. A part of him noted that light was entering the windows: firelight from torches. The villagers had gathered around the chapel.

Albertus shouted "Begone!" again and again, coming closer each time, but Robere merely held to the hem of the old priest's cassock. His red tears fell to the floor, where to Albertus's amazement they hissed and boiled and disappeared in a faint vapor.

"My oldest friend," said Robere quietly, when Albertus had fallen silent.

Albertus felt an opening, then, in his soul. A peace fell upon him that he'd never known in all the long days of prayer, a silence in his mind he'd never known even when cloistered with his brothers at Aurillac.

Brother Albertus knew his purpose in life was before him. Doorways opened in his sight. It would be a lifetime's work: two, three lifetimes. He would never leave the village. It was God's will.

THE BURDEN

God showed him neither victory nor defeat in his work, yet he was content. The vision ended; the doorways shut.

Before him was Robere. Dried blood streaked his cheeks. "Rise, now, Robere. Though you be damned by…"

"Caine's blood," said Robere quietly.

Albertus nodded. All made sense to him now. "Though you be damned by Caine's blood to eternal suffering, swear you now to uphold the commandments of the Bible and the Church?"

"I so do swear," Robere said in a clear voice.

"You're mad!" shouted Jean from his corner. "You can't forswear what you are! Have the years taken your mind away from you? Come away with me, Robere. Our kind rules from the shadows in the cities of today. There are wonders you wouldn't believe! There are a dozen of us living in Paris now, sometimes more! Come away from these peasants, from this empty-headed holy brother!"

"He has sworn, Jean. If you so swore, you, too, might find peace."

"An illusion!" Jean hissed, closer now. "I have heard tales of you, Robere. Did not an Archbishop once command you, *'Tuez les tous, Dieu reconnaitra les siens?'* I remember the tale now, grown old with the centuries. I recognized your blazon! Beziers, was it not? How many thousands did you send to God that day? Women, children, the old, the weak?"

Robere nodded, his face stony, his scar an indelible line, marking him. "I know the number. And I will never forget, nor be forgiven, on this earth."

"Or in heaven?" Jean sneered. "Will not God recognize his own, along with the devil's? You pursue a dream! I should put you into His hands myself and take this village for my own!"

Albertus forced himself to face Jean. The traveler's fair face was now ruddy with rage, and hands now sported claws.

"I choose to stay, Jean," said Robere quietly.

In a flash, Jean's hands slashed forth. Equally quick, Robere raised his hands to ward off the blow to his face. Blood spurted from his palms, falling to hiss on the chapel floor.

"You can't have him!" hissed Jean, striking again, this time slicing a cut on Robere's forehead. Once again, blood ran down his face.

EDWARD CARMIEN

"Stop this!" thundered Albertus. "Begone, foul thing! Leave this damned soul in peace. He has made a sterner choice than you know."

This time his words carried more weight, and when he presented his crucifix, Jean quailed and turned to flee. In a blur he was by the door, then out and next to the bell.

Villagers in a crowd surrounded the chapel, holding staves and sticks and burning torches. Albertus watched Jean face the crowd, unafraid even in the face of such generous odds. But was that not a pallor upon his brow? Would not Jean's Satan-given weakness pull him down before the righteous?

For a moment, Albertus was afraid he had chased a fox into the henhouse, and his new flock would suffer for it. And indeed, Jean did grasp for a likely lass.

But a half-seen shape appeared before him, hands outstretched.

Jean screamed and cringed away. The villagers pounced, tearing into his body with sticks and stones. He fought like a tiger, but there were too many. Soon, a sharpened stave found his heart and he fell silent. Quickly after, his head was cut away.

Albertus turned away from the door. Robere stood, his cuts healed but blood still staining his simple linen tunic. Blood in a thick streak topped his forehead, a vivid red.

"What became of him?" Robere asked, moving to the door.

"He encountered a spirit which gave him pause." Brother Albertus marveled, briefly, at how much his life had changed in just a few hours. "And then he encountered a stake."

"This spirit…" said Robere, troubled. He turned to the dust, all the mortal remains of his old friend.

"I should not worry," said Albertus. "He tarried only to save a woman of his flock, nothing more. I am sure God has welcomed him."

"I see." Outside, the villagers streamed to a hillock topped with standing stones. There they kindled a fire and burned Jean's remains, dancing all the while.

"Still have the pagan in them, I see," said Albertus.

"My friend had two hundred years with them and couldn't change that," said Robere with a smile.

THE BURDEN

"Two hundred years?" said Albertus with disbelief, although his vision had told him this would be.

"Carrying a damned soul like mine does have strange rewards, Father."

Habit made Albertus demur. He was no priest! Merely a Brother… But he knew he was changed, and changed forever.

Robere smiled gently. "You cannot deny His will, Father Albertus. Come. We have much time before dawn. Allow me to explain…."

THE END

AFTERWORD

Letter for the Bishop of Rodez:

Your Holiness,

I have made inquiries after your Clerk of Parishes, Brother Albertus. It seems he never returned to the village of Aroyan, a small village near the border of the county. Villagers report he departed last year with a mule loaded with supplies. Careful checking reveals that the mule returned to the village during the harvest season, almost a full year later, without Brother Albertus, or his luggage.

One must sadly suppose that the good Brother was caught in an early winter storm, and that his mule, being a natural creature, survived the ordeal, while Brother Albertus, being only a man, was called to God. Village Aroyan is high in mountainous hills near the headwaters of the Tarn and Lot rivers, and the weather there, as I can attest as Aroyan's itinerant clergy, can easily take the life of a man, if he be caught without shelter.

If I can afford you further help in this matter you have but to command.

I remain
Your dutiful servant
Friar Peter

EDWARD CARMIEN

ET SANS REPROCHE

Et Sans Reproche

BY MICHAEL LEE

I am saved, Deirdre thought, watching from the trees as the knight walked his horse along the snowy forest road. Pressed against the bulk of a black, mossy oak, her long-fingered hands tightened on its ridged hide. Hunger made her delirious, made her bones ache and her veins burn. *A knight has come riding, and I am saved.*

It had been a hard winter in the woods of Lyonesse. Long, hard snows and the feudings of the local baronies meant there were few travelers on the road from Dijon to Avignon. *Pére* Renault had taken the lion's share from what little prey she had found. It was his right as her Sire, he claimed, as he gorged himself on the woodsmen and poachers she lured to the little church. Always he made her watch and wait while he fed, savoring not only the blood, but his power to hold her at bay. As though her bond would let her do anything else. Never had she been more devoted to another. Never before had she hated someone so much.

More than a fortnight had passed since they had fed. *Pére* Renault refused to share his vitae with her, even as he sent her out each night to hunt. He hoarded his strength, holding it inside his mutilated body. Soon, he said,

MICHAEL LEE

he would feed whether she returned with prey or not. Seeing the lone rider brought waves of relief and disgust trembling through her thin frame. *Pére Renault will be so pleased,* she thought, even as her jagged nails carved splinters from the treebark. The thought came unbidden, as though there were a stranger lurking inside her head. She looked forward to the day when the bond would break her mind, taking away memories and dreams that had never had the chance to be born.

She watched the knight's horse pick its way along the frozen road, burdened with rider and baggage. The knight wore his full armor, save for the kettle-like helmet that hung from a hook on the high-cantled saddle. Moonlight shone dully off rings of blackened mail, covering torso, thighs, and arms, even extending in steel mittens over his hands. His weariness showed in the way he slumped in the saddle, looking neither left nor right at the shadowed woods. Despite herself, she felt her heart go out to him, a noble warrior making his lonely way in the world. How many times had she dreamed, even after Renault had ruined her, of a knight on a shining steed that would take away her pain and shame? Now she doubted such men existed. In a world that could harbor the likes of Renault, how could chivalry survive?

Deirdre licked cracked lips and crooked teeth. Perhaps *Pére* Renault would let her have the horse. She still had a way with animals, especially horses. It could feed her for a week or more, but thinking about it gave her a pang of regret. She missed her horses. They were long gone now, dead nearly two hundred years, but she missed them still.

The rider was nearly past her hiding place. It was time to decide. Her Sire would think him too dangerous a risk; in fact, he had forbidden her to stalk the knights errant. But there was no one else. And even if *Pére* Renault's withered frame was not up to the killing, surely together they would be enough to do the deed.

Deirdre drew a rasping breath and closed her bulging eyes, hoping she had enough strength left to cloud the man's mind. If not, the sight of her would be enough to send him screaming. The blood of the Nosferatu gave power, but twisted all it touched into hideous shapes. Such was the terrible gift *Pére* Renault had given her. The true Mark of Caine.

ET SANS REPROCHE

Once I was beautiful, she thought, stirring up the power in her blood. *Once, the knights fought for my favor.* She tried to remember those lost times—a dance during Candlemas, a secret smile for a dashing paladin—memories helped make the illusion real. She straightened as much as her twisted spine would allow, and pulled her tattered shawl tightly around her shoulders. Then she stepped from the shadow of the trees and walked toward the road.

For a moment, it looked as though the exhausted rider would take no notice of her and simply ride on around the bend. She thought to call after him, but suddenly he straightened in the saddle, his head jerking around to stare at her. His eyes went wide, and for a terrifying moment she thought her power had failed her.

The knight brought his horse around, guiding the mare with his knees. Rider and mount moved as one, angling their left side to her, where the knight's lower body was protected behind a teardrop-shaped kite shield. The horse's head came up, sniffing at the air as it pawed the frozen ground. For all that it threatened her, the tableau brought back memories. She had dreamed of men such as this, after a long night listening to minstrels' poems and the gossip of her maids. Images of her father's knights came to her: fierce, bearded faces with hard eyes. She could no longer remember their names. She and her sisters had woven stories about them, going on quests and fighting the hordes of Attila for the love of maidens much like themselves. A small part of her wondered if the man before her was on a quest, or had a princess to give him tokens of love. *What if he does?* she thought. *How terrible it would be to kill him. But* Père Renault *must feed.*

She forced herself to be calm, and ventured a shy smile. The feel of her lips across jagged teeth again made her worry if the illusion had taken hold. "Forgive me if I have startled you, good sir," she said, her voice rasping wetly. The words seemed hideously comical, were the knight seeing her for what she truly was.

At first, the rider stared in silence. Then he kneed his mare into a slow walk, coming towards her. As he drew near Deirdre could make out the details of his face. He was young, perhaps twenty, with a square jaw showing a faint bristle of beard. His eyes were dark in the dim moonlight, and a tuft of sandy hair poked out from beneath the arming cap. His nose was unbroken, and no scars marked his face. When he spoke, his voice was a clear tenor.

"You're a long way from the village, lady," he said with a lopsided grin.

"I do not live in the village, sir." The words slipped easily from her tongue, well-worn and smooth. "I live in an old church not far from here."

His eyes narrowed. "A church? On the Lyonesse Road?"

Deirdre risked meeting the knight's gaze. "Not on the road, sir. The church is an old one, part of a small village. The place doesn't even have a name." She nodded her head to the east. "It's a little deeper in the wood. There is an old trail connecting it to the road."

The knight studied her a moment, then turned his gaze to the treeline. "What are you doing out here, then? The woods are dangerous for a maiden to be traveling alone."

It struck her then, like a ray of forgotten sunlight, how long it had been since *anyone* had shown any concern for her. The realization sent a shiver through her. Surprise and wonder gleamed deep inside her scarred heart, and she fought desperately to stamp it out. *It is far too late to feel such things. There is no hope left for me!*

"Father Renault sent me out to search for food," she said. *The more truth a lie has, the easier it is on the tongue.* "With the snows and all the fighting, I have to go farther and farther to find things to eat." Deirdre shrugged. "I walked farther than I thought, this time. I've been sticking to the trees, trying to be careful, but to be frank I'm more afraid of wolves than thieves. They have had little to eat themselves this winter."

The knight listened, and seemed to relax. He leaned back in his saddle and scratched his head underneath the arming cap. "You are well-spoken for a country girl."

She found herself curtsying, bending her knees and bowing her head, as she would have in her father's court. Deirdre straightened quickly. "Father Renault has taught me a great deal."

The knight frowned. "He is your father?"

"Oh, no sir." Memories threatened, reaching up from shut-away places. "My parents are dead," she managed to say. "Father Renault has...taken me under his wing. My name is Deirdre."

The young knight nodded. "I'm William. From Anjou." The young knight regarded her. "Deirdre. I've never heard of such a name before."

The question took her aback. Poachers and woodsmen were usually more interested in the body she showed them. "I'm not a Frank, Sir William, but a Celt. I was born in Britain." She stepped closer. The knight's horse tossed its head, whickering nervously and fidgeting. "May I ask the favor of your company, sir? I would feel much safer under your protection."

The young knight smiled. "The favor is mine, fair lady," William said, using knees and hands to steady his mount. "How far is this church of yours?"

Fair lady. The words tickled her heart and stung at the same time. How long since had anyone called her that? "Not more than a mile to the old path, sir. From there it is two miles more." Deirdre reached out to the horse's head, careful to catch the animal's eye. Horses, like other animals, knew her for what she was, but sometimes, if she was careful, Deirdre had learned that they could also see how much she loved them. Gently, carefully, she touched its velvet nose, and the animal quieted a bit. "Your mount is tired, sir. Surely you do not intend to ride through the night?"

William frowned. "That's exactly what I planned. I have to be in Bordeaux the day after tomorrow."

"If you come across the wolves, your mount will not be able to escape them. And without a bow, you will be hard-pressed to defend yourself. Let me offer you the hospitality of the church. It isn't much, but we have a fire and four walls, and even a stable for your horse." She considered giving him a suggestive smile, a hint of invitation, but found she couldn't do it. *He is a better man than that,* she thought, and the realization surprised her. *He is a knight, a noble man, not some coarse townsman.*

William leaned forward against the saddle's high cantle, stretching his back. "That's a kind offer, fair lady, and I would be pleased to have a little more of your company." He smiled shyly down at her.

For a moment, Deirdre found her heart aching. Again, a little gleam of hope tried to catch fire in her heart. *Too late. Oh, God, you are too late for me.* Tears welled in her eyes, and a moment of panic drowned the pangs she felt. How would her gentle knight react if she cried streaks of blood?

William nodded and swung from the saddle. Freed of its armored burden,

MICHAEL LEE

the horse showed new life. The knight took the reins in a steel-mittened hand. "Let's be walking then," he said.

Giving the horse a final pat on its neck, she fell in beside William. *Once upon a time, I would have tied a love token around your arm. Would to God that I still could.* She looked over at him, studying his features in profile. They would have written legends about him, she and her maids, once upon a time. *When the time comes, I will try to be quick, and give you no pain. It's all I have left to give.*

The winter snows brought a hush to the great forest, broken only by the mournful cries of the owls and the whisper of their feet along the road. They walked for a while in silence, and Deirdre's mind began to wander.

The last time she had traveled with a knight was on her way to her wedding, at the court of Charlemagne. A Saxon princess given to cement an alliance with the Sun King's family. Her husband had sent a score of knights and a half-dozen gilt carriages to bring her from Normandy. That had been in the summertime, when the woods of Lyonesse were green and smelling of flowers. She had been seventeen, and she never wanted the trip to end.

She remembered the paladin who had caught her eye. *Etienne, with the green eyes, and a voice like honey.* As the days passed she caught his occasional stares, revelling in his bold smiles. She fashioned wild schemes to win his heart, dreaming of how he would challenge the fat old baron that waited to wed her. He would set her free, she had dreamed, and she would give herself to him when they returned to the wild hills of Eire.

"What waits for you in Bordeaux?" Deirdre said, studying the young knight's face.

She seemed to startle him from a reverie of his own. "Oh—there is to be a tournament outside the city. Over a hundred knights will be there—some even say William Marshall will attend, though I pray to God he stays in Britain this season."

Deirdre smiled, remembering the minstrel's songs, and the pride of the ladies at hearing how their knights had fared in the melee. "Is this William Marshall a great knight?"

ET SANS REPROCHE

William shook his head. "There is no better in all Christendom. I saw him in the tournament at Tours last season, and he bested a dozen knights before the day was done." The young knight shook his head in wonderment. "He started from nothing, a peasant, but has made for himself a fortune in ransoms and prizes."

"Do you fight in many tournaments?"

William grinned ruefully. "I ride the circuit every season. My older brother has the family's fortune, so I'm left with either making my own way or joining the clergy." An edge of frustration sharpened his voice. "So far I've had to give up most of my winnings in ransom money. It seems like there's always someone who is a little faster, a little stronger..." He shrugged. "But I can't give up. There is a prize of land and title for the knight who fights best at Bordeaux. If I could win that..."

She listened, and something moved within her, stirring up the dust of ages. Without thinking, she laid a hand on his arm. "You are a brave man, Sir William. My father often said that courage counted for more than muscle on the field of war."

Deirdre could feel the warmth of his flesh rising up through the icy rings of mail, and her hunger threatened to consume her, twisting her heart and singing in her bones. She jerked her hand away as though stung, screwing her eyes shut against the growing frenzy. *Please oh please don't let him see my face, please oh please—*

She might have stood there for moments, or hours. When she opened her eyes William was staring at her. "I'm sorry, Sir William," she said shakily. "Forgive my forwardness."

"It's all right," William said. "You weren't forward—"

"It's been a long time since I've had someone besides Father Renault to talk to." *To love,* came the thought, unbidden, and she nearly screamed from the ache that welled up inside her. "I forgot—"

William raised his hand. "Deirdre!"

She stopped. "What?"

William opened his mouth, then caught himself. He studied her a long moment, his expression guarded, then abruptly he said, "Why don't you come with me to Bordeaux?"

MICHAEL LEE

All she could do was stare at him. "I—I can't." But she saw in her mind the tents of the knights, the brightly-colored pennons and the ladies in their finery. There would be a festival before and after the war games, dances and minstrels—*oh God, why did I meet this man? I would have rather starved!*

"But why?" he said gently, and reached out for her cheek. "It's not right that someone so beautiful as you should be trapped here, in this desolate place."

"I can't!" she cried, backing away from him. "Would that I could—you have no idea! You're too late, William!" The words came pouring out of her, as though alive, desperate for freedom. "I should never have asked to travel with you. This is a terrible mistake." Part of her yearned to run, but another part of her yearned to be with him. *Because I hunger. Because I'm trapped.* Her insides felt as though she were being torn apart. *Pére Renault must feed. Pére Renault must die!* Yet he was her Sire, and she loved him. She had to.

Just as she turned to run William grabbed her arms. His hands held her like a vise. "What kind of madness is this?" he said. "What kind of hold can this Renault have over you?"

She twisted in his grasp, but could not break free. She was too weak from hunger, and the frenzy was building again. "Let me go! You have no idea— Renault is a monster, and so am I! For the love of God, let me go!"

"You're no monster, Deirdre! This man has twisted your mind. Take me to him. Tonight you will be free."

His words cut through her. With all her will, she forced the frenzy away. *I cannot hurt him! I will not hurt him! Sweet God, I love him!* "You are too late, William. Far too late," she said, choking back crimson tears. "Please let me go! Renault is...he is a terrible man. He has great power. Magical power. His strength is greater than any two men."

William stopped. His eyes grew thoughtful. "He is some kind of sorcerer?"

"Yes. Something like that. Now please..." For all that she hated Renault, there was still the bond, and she could not bring herself to betray him.

And then the determined look was back in William's eye. "What is the secret that gives him his strength?"

At that moment, she felt her heart tear apart. Here at last was the noble paladin of her dreams, determined to face all manner of peril for the sake of a lonely princess. Slowly she shook her head, and the tears began to flow, heavy and bitter. "You cannot do this, William. With all my heart I wish you could, but there is nothing you can do. If you go into Renault's den, this is what awaits you."

And she let go her illusion.

William screamed, recoiling from her. He fell to his knees and became sick.

Deirdre threw back her misshapen head and howled her anguish to the skies, then leapt for the shelter of the trees. She ran and ran, back to the church, back to *Père* Renault. He would feed on her tonight, she was sure, and it would be a blessing.

Père Renault's village had once thrived under the Sun King, providing furs and timber to the Holy Roman Empire. Renault had been a pious shepherd of a simple, untroubled flock. Until the night he came upon a leper begging along the Lyonesse Road. A hideous figure with long teeth and a hatred of priests.

The forest had all but reclaimed the thatch-and-sod huts where the villagers once lived, reducing them to little better than sagging, mossy mounds. Presiding over their remains, lost in the shadows of the trees, the twisted hulk of the church lingered on. Its thick, oaken doors hung half-askew from rusted hinges, and the gray walls around the windows were still blotched with smokestains, nearly two hundred years after the burning. When the timbers were consumed, the roof had mostly collapsed, but the walls still stood.

Deirdre moved through the funereal mounds of the village. A small part of her was afraid; worse, a part of her was also ashamed at having failed her Sire. It sickened her. *God damn you Renault. You took everything from me. Everything but the waking moments of this world. Hell has no place for devils like you.*

The darkness beyond the church door was cold, and smelled of smoke. Slanting rays of dim moonlight etched the ruins into stark relief. She could sense his presence, watching her from the deep shadows. She could feel his hunger.

MICHAEL LEE

"*Pére* Renault," she said dumbly, stepping into the blackened nave. "I've returned."

"Empty handed, my Childe." The voice was a thin, sharp whistle, like wind over stone. Then she saw the figure of her Sire, rising up from the rubble of stone and timber in the center of the church.

He still wore the rags of his cassock, stained with blood and filth and soot. The blood of the Nosferatu had twisted his bones, giving him a hunchbacked posture and pale, translucent skin. His hair had gone, and his ears were long and pointed. But what the blood had turned into a blasphemy, the church fire had made into an abomination. When the villagers had spiked the oaken doors and set God's house alight, the flames ate away half his face and shriveled his left arm and leg. Only the collapsing roof had saved him, covering his body from the fire and the sunlight of the next day.

His movements were a halting shamble, painful to watch. But his one good arm was still deathlessly strong, and he had the power to cloak his shape faultlessly.

Enough to resemble a dark-eyed knight with a voice like honey. Enough to lure a princess from her bed and into the deep forest with words of passion and undying love. Oh, sweet Etienne, he would never tell me what became of you.

"There is nothing left to eat, Father," Deirdre said grimly. "Nothing."

"You haven't looked!" Renault's one good eye blazed. "The night is not even half over." The maimed Nosferatu drew closer, flexing his one good hand. "Is this rebellion? Are you defying me at last, little princess?"

"Don't call me that! Not ever. You have no right!"

Renault's hand crashed against her face, his claws tearing parallel lines across her cheek. His strength sent her sprawling, but there was no pain.

"You dare speak to me this way?" Renault's tortured voice screeched with outrage, but a look of pleasure glazed his one eye. "Have I not looked out for you for these many, many years? Have I not provided for you—"

"You took everything from me!"

"—did I not give you your freedom? And this is the thanks that you give?"

The smell of her own blood, the taste of it on her lips, drove all thought from her mind, and with it the shackles of Renault's bond. The frenzy came, and this time, she sheltered in its madness.

When the black tide faded, the world was burning.

The church was on fire. The old, blackened timbers blazed, and the remnants of the oak benches. The heat beat against her skin, and she could feel her clothes beginning to smolder.

Her throat was torn. She had flung herself at Renault, but he still had his hoarded vitae, where she did not. He had handled her like a child, driving her to the floor, then his fangs found her throat. Her last memory was the mad gleam in her Sire's bulging eye.

Yet she still lived, and hell was loose again in the little church. Renault was nowhere to be seen. Deirdre felt utterly weak; she had little strength left, but the thought that the fire might do with her as it had with Renault drove her crawling to the doorway.

As she emerged into the night air a powerful hand closed on her arm and she found herself dragged over the snowy ground. The hand turned her over, and she prepared again to face her Sire. But the bloody visage that looked down on her was a man in armor, carrying a sword red-tinged from the firelight.

"William?"

The young knight's face was torn and bloody, and his eyes were wild. The front of his mail hauberk had been torn like paper, and the tunic beneath was in tatters. His shoulders heaved from exertion, and his breath came in great, ragged sobs.

He had ridden after her, Deirdre realized. She had shown him what she truly was, and yet he still had come for her. Somehow, he had set fire to the church, and when Renault had fled outside, William was waiting. And he had won, else he would not be standing over her now. *My knight has come riding, and I am saved.* The knowledge took away her pain, like a salve on her soul. "My paladin," she said, choked with wonder and long-denied love.

"Your master is dead," William said. The words came out in a growl. "I threw his head back into the fire. He was everything you told me, and more. Now tell me his secrets!" The sword drew back. "With strength like his, I can be the greatest knight in the kingdom! Tell me the secret, or so help me you'll join him."

Her smile faded. "What do you mean? He was a Nosferatu—"

"I don't know what that means, and I don't care. I just want his strength. With that I can have anything else I want. No knight in the world could best me. Now tell me—or should I get a torch and see how you like a taste of fire, you damnable fiend?"

She understood then. She understood it all too well, and her dead heart went cold. She had been so wrong, so terribly wrong...

With all her will, she turned on her dreams, crushing them, driving their pieces back down into blackness. She wove the pain around her like a cloak, shielding herself from what she once had been.

Deirdre found that when she gave herself over to the pain, it did not hurt anymore. Her memories vanished, sinking into a black void that swallowed all feeling, all thought and reason.

She reached out to the man standing over her. "Give me your hand," she said quietly, without emotion.

Still holding the sword over her, he gave her his hand. She drew away the armored mitten, exposing his wrist, and then sank her fangs deep into the vein.

William screamed. The sword flashed down, burying itself in her shoulder, but that was all right. It would heal. And the pain became her strength as she drank deep of the mortal wine.

The knight fell to his knees, taken with the ecstasy of the Embrace. His eyes turned up to heaven, and he moaned softly, then sank to the cold earth.

Deirdre awoke to a shrill screaming, a few hours before the dawn. But her knight still lay sleeping, a blush of crimson coloring his pale lips.

It was a horse, tied to a nearby tree. The church still burned, and embers had carried on the breeze and set the tree to smoldering. It pulled at the reins and shrieked, unable to escape.

With a growl she rushed at the beast, savaging its long neck with her claws. It screamed and screamed, rolling its huge brown eyes, until finally her hunger drove her to gorge on its bitter blood. At last, it collapsed and died, and the forest was silent once more.

She returned to her paladin, kneeling down to study his sleeping face. Already the blood was working upon him, thinning his skin.

He would be strong, and far swifter than any man. A knight *sans peer et sans reproche*.

MICHAEL LEE

THREE DAYS OR SIX

Three Days
or Six

BY DON BASSINGTHWAITE

ome time during the day, the mistral had emerged from its hiding place in the mountains. Now it ravaged the valleys like an invading army. Plants, birds, animals, and men all gave way before it, plants immovable but bending, animals and men fleeing to whatever shelter they could find. Most birds also took shelter, but some few played in the mistral, challenging the cold, roaring wind. It carried them far higher than they might normally have flown. Once, as a child, Veran had watched as a raven ascended into the dusk, carried in the arms of the mistral, until it vanished above the sinking sun. At dawn the next morning he had found a raven, perhaps the same bird, dashed against the wall of his parents' house. There had been crystals of ice caught in its feathers.

Tonight there were no birds in the sky. The mistral flung itself howling against the mountains and the old tower that grew out of them. Veran stood concealed in the darkest shadows of the tower doors and watched as the travelers dismounted in the little courtyard before the tower. The wind caught his hair, rich red-brown and worn long in the manner of scholars, and sent it lashing across his face. It was a poor night for traveling—if any travel at night could be counted as good—and the travelers were bundled against the wind. Veran didn't feel the cold of the mistral now, though he did sometimes miss the warmth of the sun on his skin, even after fifty years. And in fifty years, plus twenty before in which he'd lived in the villages below, he had never known anyone from outside the mountains to come to the tower.

Two of the travelers were armed with swords, and one of those two wore a crested surcoat, suggesting that he was a knight and the other perhaps a mercenary. Additionally, there were a neatly dressed man Veran guessed to be a personal servant, a servant woman swathed in a heavy traveling cloak, and three roughly dressed men. The knight, the mercenary, and the servants all rode horses Two of the three rough-looking men led laden pack horses and carried lanterns that bounced and swayed in the wind. The third was dressed even more coarsely than the others—a guide, perhaps. The knight looked around, then said something to his companions in a language that Veran didn't understand but that might have been some dialect of German. He could guess what the knight was saying, though; there were lights in the narrow tower windows, but no one was visible. All within had been ordered to stay out of sight. The lights of the travelers' lanterns had been visible as they climbed the path to the tower, and it was always wise to be wary of any who traveled by night.

One of the knight's companions offered comments in that same foreign tongue, then the knight turned back to the tower. "Hello!" he bellowed in French. His voice echoed off the tower walls and was lost in the mistral. "Hello! We seek the master of this tower, the man who is called the Patron!"

Veran stepped out of the shadows. "I speak for the Patron." He replied in French, but pronounced his master's name in proper Provençal fashion. "What is your business with him?"

Much to his surprise, it was not the knight who answered. Instead, the servant woman stepped forward. "Please—is this the Patron's school? I have come a long way to meet him." She spoke in flawless Provençal and, as she began to loosen the enveloping folds of her traveling cloak, Veran realized he had been hasty in his assumption of who led the party. The woman wore a fine dress and mantle. A gold signet ring flashed on her finger. Long blond hair framed a delicate ivory face and clear blue eyes. Red lips parted slightly. Thin eyebrows arched. She moved to one of the packhorses. "I have brought gifts for him."

Veran blinked. "The Patron has no need of gold, silver, or other riches." The words should have flowed smoothly, but in this woman's presence he felt as if he were learning to speak all over again. *Idiot*, he cursed himself, *so she's beautiful. You have no more need of beauty than the Patron has need of gold.*

The woman simply smiled. "No," she said, "I didn't think he would. But precious metals are not the only form of riches." She opened a pack and produced a square parcel tightly wrapped in waxed cloth. "Lost knowledge, copied in Baghdad from scrolls rescued from the Alexandrian library." She gestured. "Other works. Fine paper. Inks. The riches of a scholar."

Veran's mouth dried. Riches, indeed. Abruptly, the Patron appeared beside him, a lean man with iron gray hair and a few of time's lines in his face, no older in appearance than many men with wives and children and fields to tend. The Patron, though, was infinitely older. All of the glories of Rome lay within his memory, and Rome marked his face more than time. "What is your name?"

A touch of color came to the woman's cheeks, and she sank down, the wrapped book in her hands. "*Patroun?*" she asked humbly.

"Answer my question."

"I am Elsbet von Steyr, from the city of Linz. These are my companions, Tibault," she indicated the knight, "and Angelin." The mercenary. She didn't introduce the servants.

"I see." Calm and self-possessed always, was the Patron: the embodiment of Rome. "Pray tell me, Elsbet von Steyr, what do you want? No one travels this far into the mountains of Provence simply to deliver gifts. And how did you bypass the villages along the valley? They should have stopped you."

Elsbet's blush grew deeper. "We rode past the villages in the dark. Our guide told me your school was close and I was eager to reach it. As it please you, *Patroun*, I wish to study with you for a time."

The Patron froze. After a moment, he said slowly, "I must consider your petition," and stepped back inside the tower without another word. Veran stared after him, then hastily nodded to Elsbet and her party and turned to follow his master.

He found him just inside the entrance, staring pensively into the bright light that spilled out of the great hall. Noise spilled out of the great hall as well, the excited talk of the Patron's young students. Once Veran had been one of those boys. No more, though he still considered himself a student when compared to the Patron. He still had a student's respect for his master. Perhaps that was what made the thing he saw so surprising: The Patron was chewing on his thumbnail. The action was so shockingly human that Veran could only stare. The Patron glanced at him, then realized what he was doing. He lowered his hand, becoming once more the stoic Roman.

"Three days or six, Veran?"

"What?" This was an old game between him and his master, though it hardly seemed relevant to the moment. The tales told in his village—and in virtually all of the villages of Provence—said that the mistral could always be depended upon to blow for a number of days divisible by three. Three days or six were most common, but nine was not unusual. Whether the villagers of Provence truly believed the tales was another question. The Patron certainly didn't. The first time Veran had quoted the tales to him, he had asked Veran if he thought the mistral would blow for three days, then, or six. Confident, Veran had said six. The Patron had given him a stick and told him to notch it once for each day. The mistral had blown out in less than two days. Now the Patron asked the same question each time the mistral blew.

"Three days or six?" The Patron asked again.

"Six," guessed Veran. "But why?"

"Perhaps," the Patron replied distantly, "I think it may last longer, though." His hands twitched. "I want her gifts, Veran, but I don't want her. If I let her stay, there is too much she could discover. The refuge I've built here is delicate." He looked at Veran. "What do you think?"

A second shock for the night—a third if Elsbet's unexpected arrival at the tower was considered. The Patron had never asked his opinion before. "Me?"

"You're at risk as well should she discover anything, Veran."

THREE DAYS OR SIX

The younger man considered. "*Patroun*, do we really have that much cause to worry? We are what we are."

"Are you already so sure of yourself, Veran?" The Patron looked at him again. A great sadness enveloped him, an aura of loneliness so strong that it made Veran's head feel numb and hollow. The bond between sire and childe could be very strong. "I was Embraced two hundred years before your Christ was born, and exiled from Rome to these mountains while Christianity was still a persecuted cult. I have been almost a thousand years in this place. I am afraid of the strength of humans. I have seen what it can do. What do you know? What have you seen of the world?" He turned away.

The excruciating loneliness of his master vanished from Veran's body, replaced with frustration. Veran's own frustration at the Patron's exile. His master had never told Veran why he had been exiled from Rome, only that he had and usually with the observation that exile from the civilization of Rome was sometimes considered the equivalent of death in his day—for humans and Damned alike. Veran could well imagine the provincial exile as a hardship for the Patron, sent away not only from the society that fed his intellect, but from the nourishment that fed his body. Like all members of ancient and aristocratic Clan Ventrue, the Patron could feed only on a specific type of blood. In the case of the Patron, that was the blood of students. And there would have been very, very few students in the mountains of Provence a thousand years ago.

So the Patron had created a school. A secret, hidden school where the students belonged to him alone and studied at night—and where he could feed freely. The villages down the valley provided him with students, young boys who stayed at the tower for seven years and returned home with the finest in Roman educations—not much, perhaps, but a wonder in the mountains. In return, the villagers protected the Patron, hiding him from the eyes of the world. Veran had asked him once why they hid. Why the Patron was still in exile. Why they had no contact with the world beyond the valley. The Patron answered him in the same way he answered questions about the circumstances of his exile. With silence. And that silence only served to fuel Veran's frustration at his confinement to this isolation.

But now, at least, he had chance to end at least one silence in the tower.

"Yes, *Patroun*," he agreed. "But what if we did grant her petition and let her stay?" He held up a hand, forestalling the Patron's response. His master wanted the woman's gifts. From the moment the travelers' lanterns had been spotted in the darkness, Veran had wanted something else. "For a short time. A month? And we allow only her into the tower. Her companions can stay in one of the outbuildings. And we provide an escort for her every waking moment."

"I could simply entrance her."

"No!" Veran bit back the vehemence of his outburst. The Patron was more than capable of controlling Elsbet's mind so thoroughly that she would obey his slightest whim. If he told her to remain seated in the great hall for a month, she would. That wasn't what Veran wanted. "Her companions would surely suspect something. If she's alert, she may talk with her escort. We may be able to learn as much from her as she wishes to learn from you. If we befriend her."

"If we befriend her?" The Patron smiled slightly. "Dare I guess that you have someone particular in mind to play the role of the fair lady's escort?"

"I believe," Veran answered, "that such a responsibility would naturally fall upon me."

"And what would you want with such a responsibility?"

Veran hesitated, trying to think of the best way to respond. The Patron didn't give him a chance. Instead, he patted Veran on the shoulders. "Don't worry. I know. You want her news of the outside world. My tower is no fit place for your mind, Veran. It should be allowed to wander. Sometimes I regret keeping you here, but I have no other choice." He nodded. "It will be as you suggest. Rolant!" His eldest student—or rather, his eldest mortal student, seventeen and almost ready to leave the school and return to the valley—came running from the great hall. Rolant and Veran shared the same red-brown hair, the same round face, the same sloping nose. There was good reason for their similarity. They came from the same village down in the valley, although a generation apart. Rolant's father had been the youngest child of Veran's youngest sister. "Convey my regards to the lady in the yard. She is welcome to study here for a month, but only she may enter the tower. Veran will accompany her by night. She must remain in

THREE DAYS OR SIX

her chamber by day. Her companions may lodge in the outbuildings." Rolant nodded and ran to the doors, slipping out into the night. The Patron watched after him. "Take care that you watch her, Veran."

Veran smiled. "Yes, *Patroun*." The tower doors swung open and the roar of the mistral echoed in the great hall as Elsbet entered, walking into the light with an expression of rapture on her face and the precious book still clutched in her hands.

Two months later, Elsbet was still at the tower. A candle beside her, she sat at a table in the great hall, studying a volume of Sophocles intently. Veran studied Elsbet. She had become like any of the other students. She was quiet. She was modest. When the villagers had come with supplies, she charmed them as she had charmed him. As she had charmed even the Patron. The ancient vampire spent most of his nights closeted with the books she had brought, occasionally shouting in the excitement of discovery. Even her companions, the knight and the mercenary and the grooms, made themselves useful, catching game in the forests and gathering wood against the coming winter. When Elsbet's first month had ended, the Patron had very simply and quietly asked her to stay on. It seemed certain that he would do the same at the end of the coming month. He had even relented a little and allowed Elsbet's personal servant, the neatly dressed man from her party, to accompany her into the tower. Veran had spent many hours watching the man brush Elsbet's shining hair before she retired in the gray hours of morning. Elsbet had adapted easily to the dusk-to-dawn lifestyle of the tower, never questioning it in the slightest. She almost worshipped the Patron, and Veran didn't doubt that she would happily have stayed the rest of her life in the tower.

And Elsbet was more than simply beautiful, quiet, and modest. She was brilliant. She was educated. German was her native tongue, but she spoke and read in Latin, Greek, and French. She could converse in Provençal, Italian, and other languages Veran had never heard before—musical Venetian, tongue-defying Hungarian, and flowing Moorish. He persuaded her to teach him some German and a little Venetian in exchange for a pretty Roman ring that the Patron had neglected in a cupboard for centuries. She gave him news of the world beyond the mountains freely, though. As her servant brushed her hair, she told Veran of cities and merchants and crusades. And while she talked, he could simply sit and...

Elsbet's hand paused as she turned a page of her book. "Veran," she asked without looking up, "are you watching me?" He started, embarrassed, and tried to fumble out an apology. She turned and smiled at him. "Please. Don't. You don't have to explain yourself." She flushed a little and her smile turned bashful. "The Patron's tower *is* isolated, isn't it?"

"No," Veran said quickly. "I mean, yes...I mean, not all that..."

Fortunately, he was saved from any further embarrassment by a sudden yell and a commotion on the far side of the great hall. Veran turned. The Patron's students had been gathered on the other side of the room, waiting for their nightly lessons in Latin and Greek. Two of them were fighting, rolling together on the ground. That was unusual. More unusual, though, were the identities of the combatants: Dalmas, a quiet, withdrawn boy; and Rolant, old enough to know better. Rolant was red-faced and shouting, hammering away at Dalmas with a rage that Veran had never seen before. As Veran watched, he rolled up on top of Dalmas, got a grip on his head, and began slamming the other boy's head against the floor. Veran lunged across the hall to wrench Rolant away from the other student. Rolant spun around, hands up to strike. Veran seized him by the front of his tunic and lifted him up onto his toes. "Rolant!" he snapped. "Stop this!" Snarling, lost in his anger, Rolant just lashed out again. Veran grabbed Rolant's jaw. He met Rolant's eyes and glared into them, the force of his will slamming into the boy's mind. "Stop now!"

Rolant's eyes went wide. For a moment his body was tense and rigid, then he slumped in Veran's grasp. The great hall was silent except for Elsbet's concerned murmurs as she comforted Dalmas and helped him sit up. The injured boy gasped loudly in pain. As if that noise were a key, all of the students began talking at once.

"What happened here?"

The Patron stood at the base of the stairs that led out of the great hall and up into the tower. His face was impassive, but his stance was angry. Once again the students fell silent, though this time they also looked away, leaving only Veran and Elsbet to face the Patron. "Rolant attacked Dalmas," Veran said simply.

"Why?"

Veran could only shake his head. Elsbet didn't answer. One of the students, however, coughed and mumbled, "Marot's mouse bit him, *Patroun*. Then he got sick."

Veran touched Rolant's face. "His skin is very hot."

"I see." The Patron regarded his students. "I have never seen a mouse in my tower. Where did it come from?"

"Outside," confessed Marot. "From the fields. I was watching Elsbet's horses." The boy, no more than eleven, was pale. "*Patroun*, the mouse died two days ago. That's not going to happen to Rolant, is it?"

The Patron's face grew stony. "I hope not." He looked at Veran. "Come to the door and talk with me for a moment." He turned and crossed the floor. Veran set Rolant down gently and went after his master nervously. The Patron paused just before the tower doors, out of sight of the students in the great hall. His eyes were sad. "I was afraid something would happen because of Elsbet's presence," he said heavily. "I wasn't expecting this. Rolant is a good student."

Veran looked away. "I feel responsible, Patroun. I was the one who urged you to bring her into the tower. He may still recover."

"That's what I'm hoping." The Patron sighed. "It's not your fault. Take Rolant upstairs. Find an empty room and tie him down. Make him comfortable. If he has taken sick from the bite of a mouse, I don't want him to injure any more students in his madness. Do what you can to help him recover." The Patron patted Veran's shoulder. "But I think it may be time for Elsbet to leave us. Before anything else happens."

Veran blinked in surprise and shook his head. "*Patroun*, she hasn't done anything. It's not her fault that Rolant is sick."

"Not directly, no. But he wouldn't be sick if she hadn't come—Marot wouldn't have gone out to look at her horses and he wouldn't have found that mouse." The old vampire turned back toward the great hall. "I know you want the news that she can give you, Veran. It's your nature. Remember your other nature, though. You're not human anymore. You have all the time in the world to indulge your curiosity."

"All the time, but only a corner of the world," Veran replied bitterly. The Patron paused. Veran flushed. "I'm sorry, *Patroun*. But your exile…"

"Look after Rolant, Veran," his master said coldly. The Patron swept back out into the great hall. Shamed, Veran followed silently. Rolant still stood where Veran had left him. Dalmas was gone, as was Elsbet. She had probably taken him away to look after his wounds. The other students had taken their places for the day's lesson, as silent and still as the crosses in a churchyard. The Patron seated himself in the big chair that was his alone and began to lecture in Greek. Veran picked up Rolant's unresisting body and carried him upstairs.

There was an unused room on the third floor of the tower. Veran took Rolant there, then fetched a pallet and warm sheepskins to make him comfortable—and ropes to keep him restrained. He tied Rolant's ankles together and lashed his hands to a post. It wasn't the best position for a sick person, but it would keep him from hurting himself or others. Veran kept a sharp little knife in his belt. A swift slash opened the veins of one arm, allowing blood to drip down along his hand and fingers and into Rolant's mouth. The blood would help Rolant's body to heal itself. When he judged that enough had fallen, Veran willed his wounded arm to close. And then he woke Rolant.

The human shouted in his first moment of consciousness and lunged at Veran. The ropes held him, though he snarled and spat bloody saliva, showering Veran with red gobbets. Veran simply wiped them away and waited. Waited and thought about Elsbet and the world beyond the tower. Waited and thought about the ancient exile that kept him here. About his curiosity. About the inhuman nature that kept him from Elsbet.

Eventually, Rolant stopped fighting his bonds. He lay on the floor, shivering uncontrollably. Veran squatted down next to him. "Rolant?" The boy looked at him with wild, fevered eyes. "I'm sorry."

"For what?" Rolant's voice was strained.

Veran smiled. "For asking Elsbet to stay at the tower. If she weren't here,

THREE DAYS OR SIX

there would be no horses. If there were no horses, Marot wouldn't have gone into the fields and brought home that mouse. If there was no mouse, you wouldn't be sick."

Rolant laughed, but it was like no sound Veran had heard him make since he had come to the tower six years ago. Normally Rolant's laugh was short and full, falling quickly back into an easy grin. This laugh was short as well, but hard and bitter, and when it fell, it collapsed into a thin twist of Rolant's lips. "You and the Patron have no idea what happens during the day, do you? Marot's had that mouse for a couple of months. Well before Elsbet came. Marot was lying."

"Hush, you're sick." Veran touched Rolant's face again. His skin was fiery and wet with sweat. "Do you want some water?"

Rolant turned his face away. The vampire reached down and turned it back. Rolant was crying. Veran frowned. "Rolant?"

The boy squeezed his eyes shut. "In God's name, Veran, if you would only rise once during the day instead of remaining in that damned cellar, you'd see what kind of perversion the Patron has invited into the tower! I'm not sick—I'm cursed!"

Veran rocked back, almost stunned by the force of Rolant's angry snarl. Rolant pulled away from his hand. "What are you talking about?" Veran asked, bewildered.

"Elsbet," Rolant choked, "and her servants, and her men Tibault and Angelin. You and the Patron have been so busy fawning over her and her books, that you haven't seen through her. They're evil, Veran. Elsbet's not here to study with the Patron. She's here to destroy him."

"You're delirious." Veran stood. "Elsbet?"

"Elsbet!" Rolant jerked against his bonds. "I can prove it. Have you seen the guide who came with them lately? You won't. He's dead. They murdered him and buried his body in the woods above the tower. They're cunning. Everything happens during the day. Elsbet is some kind of witch. I'm not here because a mouse bit me. I'm here because I refused to..." He grimaced.

"To cooperate with her?"

"To service her." Rolant spat the words. "She cursed me. She must have. Elsbet likes her men young. Tibault likes them even younger, but he uses them in a different way." His face contorted in disgust. "Little Aliot bled for hours. They're drawing the students in, Veran. We're frightened of her. That's why Marot lied. We're all afraid. And you and the Patron can't help us. During the day we can't reach you. And at night, we're afraid to." Rolant was breathing hard. "But now I've got nothing to lose. Look at what Elsbet has done to me! I can't control myself. I didn't want to attack Dalmas. It was as if some spirit was riding my body like a horse."

Veran stepped away from the raving student. "Elsbet?" he asked again in disbelief.

Rolant's struggles ceased abruptly. "You don't believe me." His voice was flat, hopeless.

"Rolant, you're sick."

"Am I?" A mad smile split Rolant's face and he laughed again. "Rise during the day, Veran—if you can. See what happens while the Patron sleeps. Elsbet holds court in the great hall, reading from a book that drips blood from the pages!"

"Perhaps," said Veran slowly, "I should ask another one of the students about this. I could ask Marot or Aliot."

"They'll lie. They're afraid." Rolant's voice rose to a shout. "Throw her out of the tower, Veran!" He began to struggle again, thrashing in his bonds. "Throw her out! Drive her away! Elsbet von Steyr is a monster, a witch, a child of the Devil—"

Veran seized Rolant's head, holding it still and forcing him to look into his gaze. "Sleep, Rolant!" he ordered. "Sleep!"

The student fell silent. Veran sighed and released him, then drew a sheepskin up over his sweat-soaked body. He looked down sorrowfully at the sleeping boy. He well remembered the delirium that came with fever. He had seen it in the village and experienced it himself before the Patron had saved him. Rolant had no control over his tongue. If he was lucky, he would regain his wits before he died. And it seemed very likely that he would die. Veran sighed and stood up, turning to go back and tell the Patron the news.

Elsbet was standing in the doorway, her face pale. Veran paused. "You heard him?"

THREE DAYS OR SIX

"It's not true, Veran." There were tears in her eyes.

"Of course not." Veran wiped a tear from her face with his thumb. "He's delirious."

"But it's so…" Elsbet swallowed. "It's such a horrible thing to hear." Impulsively, she threw her arms around Veran. "Please. Don't tell the others."

He smiled at her. "Don't worry. I won't. It's all in Rolant's mind."

Or was it?

Veran had never known the violence and delirium of a fever to come on so quickly without at least some warning signs. Rolant had been fine one moment and raving the next. And there had been a night not so long ago when Aliot had remained in his bed—ill, the students had said. Veran had visited him and he had looked so pale and drawn that the vampire could only imagine illness as the cause. But perhaps… And Elsbet's guide. Veran had always assumed he had simply left one day, his job done. Could Rolant be telling the truth? Could something be happening in the tower?

Veran turned on his bed in the darkness of the tower's cellar. The lethargy that he felt told him the sun had risen, though he had no idea what time of day it was. His body was sluggish, but his mind worked furiously, churning in circles. Rolant had unknowingly been at least partially correct. Veran and the Patron knew nothing of what happened in the tower during the day. They normally slept from dawn to dusk, as unconscious and insensate as the dead. They could rise if they had to, though sunlight was always a danger. Veran lay in bed, staring blindly into the shadows. Could Elsbet…?

He had to know.

Veran rose, went to the door of his chamber and opened it a crack. He and the Patron slept in separate chambers in the cellar, heavy stone walls protecting them from daylight that might somehow filter in or unexpected attacks of a more physical nature. Veran half expected an ambush now. There was no one in the gloom of the cellar, though. The door to the Patron's chamber was closed. Veran crept up the stairs and down the corridor

DON BASSINGTHWAITE

that led to the great hall. There were no windows in this part of the tower, another precaution taken by the Patron against sunlight.

With the day sealed outside, the tower should have been dark. It wasn't. Like the darkness of the night he had first seen Elsbet's party from the tower top, the shadows of the tower were spoiled by light spilling out of the great hall. Veran froze, stunned.

Like the lord and lady of a castle, Elsbet and Tibault sat in the great hall, a blazing fire throwing light and heat into the huge room. Tibault sat in the Patron's big chair and bounced little Aliot on his knee. The knight's face was alight with unholy rapture; Aliot's face was white with terror. Elsbet sat quietly, a large book in her hands. A great black book that bled when she turned the pages.

"Oh, Rolant!" Veran breathed, "You were right." As if an apology whispered here made any difference to the student locked away in an upper room. As if Rolant was still alive. Veran had only to look at Elsbet's red-stained hands to guess that he was dead. She had heard everything he had said.

But the other students were another matter. She couldn't have killed them all. Veran stepped back into the shadows of the corridor. He would rouse the Patron. The vampires might be slow, but they would still be more than a match for Elsbet. She and her foul companions would be gone by nightfall and Rolant would be avenged. He began to turn, to flee back down into the cellar....

The sharp point of a crossbow bolt poked into his ribs. The bolt was still in the crossbow, but the crossbow was cocked, and holding it was Angelin the mercenary. "Don't move," he said softly. "Or this will be in your heart. Not lethal for one of your kind, but not comfortable." He smiled crookedly, or perhaps it only seemed that way because his eyes were fixed on the floor. Veran could only gape at him. A crossbow bolt in his heart to paralyze him. Eyes averted to avoid the power of his gaze. *Angelin knew what he was.* Veran's stomach twisted. If Angelin knew...

"Bring him here." Elsbet's voice was different—brisker, crisper. Angelin pressed the crossbow into Veran's chest, forcing him back out into the great hall. Elsbet was standing and setting her book aside. Tibault was slower to

THREE DAYS OR SIX

react, caressing Aliot before releasing him. The child dashed away into the shadows. Elsbet circled around Veran, inspecting him as if inspecting a horse. Angelin took the opportunity to step around behind Veran, out of range of his gaze, but still able to keep the crossbow trained on his heart. Elsbet nodded. "Well done."

"Traitor," hissed Veran. "Witch."

"Vampire," replied Elsbet. "Demon." Giggling, swiftly silenced, emerged out of the shadows. Elsbet smiled and gestured. The Patron's students appeared, eagerly clutching crude crucifixes and sharp stakes. Veran gasped. "Oh yes," said Elsbet. "They know. I told them the truth about you."

A snarl grew in Veran's chest and lashed out of his mouth. Some of the students stepped back. Others just pressed forward. "Who are you?" Veran demanded. "Why are you here?"

"To study with the Patron, of course." Elsbet flashed him a dazzling smile. "To learn what he knew and what he was hiding, and then to destroy him utterly. His students, the source of his sustenance, turned against him. You, his only ally, turned to ashes in the sunlight." The Patron's students murmured eagerly and Elsbet laughed. "You see?"

"You've enchanted them, witch! Or mage, or sorcerer, or whatever you choose to call yourself!" He was shouting. Angelin jabbed him sharply with the crossbow. Elsbet merely shook her head.

"Did you really believe so deeply, Veran? Let me tell you that I'm not a mage. The bleeding book, a charlatan's trick. Not that I am utterly without power." Suddenly, Elsbet seemed to undergo a change. She looked exactly as she had a moment before, but abruptly she was radiantly beautiful in the way she had been when she arrived, in the way she had seemed from time to time over the last month. "Wouldn't you agree?"

"Yes," he breathed helplessly. It was a trick. He knew it. He recognized the power. The Patron had the same ability, and had told him that he might learn it as well, that it was common to many vampires. But Elsbet was no vampire. The Patron would have seen that immediately. Veran would have seen it! He had to look away, had to break the power of her…beautiful…intoxicating…. He couldn't. He stared at Elsbet as the sheer weight of her sorcerous beauty overwhelmed him. As it overwhelmed the students. She stepped up to him, sliding her fingers across his face, and along his jaw. She looked into his eyes.

Her mistake. Now he had a chance. Desperately, he focused his will, driving it into hers with the force of a knight's lance.

His will skipped across hers like water across a hot pan, leaving him gasping in defeat. Elsbet laughed and stepped back, her beauty only human once more. "What do you think of that enchantment, Veran?"

"How...?" Veran blinked and shook his head. "What are you?"

"What I am is a being born to resist and deceive your kind. What has your master told you of the clans, Veran? Has he told you of the Tzimisce? Has he told you of their servants, families of ghouls bred like prize swine? The Grimaldi, the Zantosa, the Obertus, the Bratovitch—the Ducheski? That's my real name. The other families tend the Tzimisce hounds or spy for them in courts. The Tzimisce created us to spy on the other clans. We've left them, though. They crafted too well. We serve new masters now, masters who value our talents." Her face was haughty. She turned and sat down in the great chair that Tibault had vacated. "Don't feel bad, Veran. Wiser vampires than you have fallen into my trap. After all, I have deceived your great *Patroun* as well."

"Don't be certain," Veran snarled.

"Why not? I don't see him here. He would seem to have fallen into the trap as well."

"A trap baited with the life of one of his students."

"Rolant? Is that what you think?" Elsbet looked pleased. "You should look beyond the obvious, Veran."

She gestured. Rolant stepped out of the shadows in the darkest part of the room and walked up to the great chair. Elsbet rose to meet him. They kissed. Rolant spared Veran a brief glance. "It was simple, my lady," he told Elsbet. "He always underestimates others. He believed it all. He's too smart for his own good."

"You..." spat Veran. "How could you? Don't you see that she's enchanted you, Rolant?"

"No." Rolant smiled savagely. "She hasn't. Take Elsbet's advice. Look beyond the obvious. I've always wanted more. The Patron's *education* taught me that. I'm leaving the mountains, Veran. I've always planned on it. Except now I'll be doing it with Elsbet."

"So it was all a lie?" Veran clenched his teeth. "What you said about refusing to service Elsbet? What you said about Tibault and Aliot?"

Rolant grinned. Tibault laughed. Elsbet shrugged. "Not all of it."

"Fiends. Why? *Why?*"

Angelin poked Veran again, reminding him of the crossbow. Elsbet merely returned to her seat and regard her captive with a steady, cool gaze. "The world beyond the Patron's mountain exile is complicated, Veran. Far more complicated than you know, far more complicated than the world your master knew. There are certain ancient Ventrue of Rome, old enemies of his, who remember that he was exiled to these mountains long ago. They wanted to know if he still existed, and if he did, they wanted that fact corrected. I work for them. And there is another clan now, the Tremere, the new masters of the Ducheski. There are those among that clan who have learned that when he fled Rome, the Patron took books and scrolls with him, and they want to know what secrets he might be hoarding. I serve them as well, on behalf of my family." She clenched her left hand into a fist. "But no one—not the Ventrue, not the Tremere, not the Ducheski—appreciates failure. I have spent almost two months sifting through the library of this tower. I have looked through the tower from roof to cellar, even your chamber. I have found nothing that my masters do not already know. Before I destroy you and move on to your master, let me ask you this directly, Veran: Does the Patron keep any books or scrolls in his cellar chamber?"

Veran glared at her. "No," he snarled.

"Really? Are you sure? Perhaps you'd like to reconsider." Elsbet opened her fist.

It must have been a signal. From behind him, Veran heard a familiar creaking groan. The tower doors, but only opening a little way. Golden sunlight etched a narrow, burning line across the floor barely a foot to Veran's right. Involuntarily, Veran twitched, horrible, irrational terror striking through him. Every vampire feared sunlight, feared it more than anything else. "*Patroun!*" he screamed desperately. Then Angelin's arm was around his throat and the crossbow jammed hard into his back.

DON BASSINGTHWAITE

Elsbet stood. "Call if you want to," she said mockingly, "but you won't rouse him. Don't you think there have been louder screams in this hall over the past month? Did the cries of his students arouse the Patron? No. Now, tell me what I want to know or you will die slowly, inch by inch of your body disintegrated in warm, innocent sunlight." She stepped into the light, letting its radiance wash over her harmlessly. "What secrets does the Patron keep in his chamber?"

"None, betrayer." The voice that echoed through the hall was cold. "None at all."

All eyes—Veran's, Elsbet's, Tibault's, Angelin's, the students'—snapped to the end of the hall. The Patron stood at the edge of shadows, magnificent rage darkening his face, an ancient and dangerous power in all of his glory. He glared angrily at Elsbet. "You underestimate the power of a childe's frightened call for his sire."

Elsbet didn't hesitate for a moment. "Open the doors!" she ordered. "Now!" She grabbed the nearest students. The radiance of her magic poured out of her. "Attack! Attack the creature that imprisons you!"

With a yell, the students charged forward even as the doors resumed their creaking groan and sunlight filled the hall. Veran didn't see what happened when they reached the Patron. Elsbet and Tibault were racing for the doors, fleeing the tower for the protection of daylight. "Finish him!" Elsbet snapped to Angelin. Half-blind in the brilliance, Veran felt Angelin whirl him around so that he faced full into the streaming light. He howled at the pain, but he knew what would be coming next and he forced himself to keep turning, throwing Angelin off balance. Angelin snarled, a small sound in the cacophony of shouts and screams that echoed in the hall. Veran dropped even as the mercenary released the crossbow bolt. His struggle had been just enough, though. The bolt pierced his shoulder—but missed his heart. Veran stumbled forward. Through the haze that clouded his vision, he saw Angelin run to join Tibault and Elsbet. He ignored him, fighting instead to make his legs carry him out of the light and into the blessed shadows. The smell of blood filled his nostrils and he could feel it slickly underfoot. He fell. One flailing arm caught something and clung on for support. Another hand seized his and helped him stand.

THREE DAYS OR SIX

"*Patroun?*" Veran asked. Then he blinked and saw who was holding him.

Rolant. Beyond, young bodies lay on the floor. A final few clung to the Patron like choking vines to a tree. One by one, he was picking them off and draining the blood from them. Only Rolant stood apart. "You," Veran whispered.

"Me," Rolant rasped harshly. His face twisted. He hurled Veran away, back into the sunlight. Veran screamed. Over the scream he heard Rolant shouting Elsbet's name as he fled the tower as well. Then he knew nothing but pain until strong hands picked him up once again. This time, however, they carried him out of the light and down into the embrace of darkness.

Veran stood beside the Patron in the courtyard of the tower and looked out into the night. The stars shone down. The air was still. The path down to the valley was pockmarked by the hooves of galloping horses. Elsbet was gone, Tibault and Angelin with her. Rolant was gone as well. Elsbet's strength had been in secrecy. Her plans revealed, she would have been no match for the power of the Patron. She couldn't have hoped to destroy him now. And yet she had. In the great hall of the tower, eleven corpses lay where they had fallen. Veran could name them all. Renier. Enric. Aliot. Perona. Luquet. Dalmas. Marot. Perin and Perot, twins. Carlemaine. Nadal. The Patron's students, so twisted and maddened by Elsbet that he had had no choice but to slay them.

The moon was a waning crescent low over the mountains. In the distance Veran thought he could see the villages. "Elsbet will have stopped and told the villagers the truth about us."

"Perhaps." The Patron was studying the stars. "Let her. The villagers may riot. They may storm the tower. It will do them no good. I will deal with them. I will send them back to the villages. Their sons are dead." He sighed and brought his gaze back down to earth. "Elsbet has already destroyed me. My hold on the villages is broken. My school is closed."

Veran blinked in shock. "How will you feed, *Patroun?*"

"Perhaps I won't," replied the Patron. He sounded tired. "Perhaps I will

descend into torpor and sleep the sleep of ages. My exile will be complete."
He patted Veran on the shoulder. "Then you could leave this isolation. You
could travel."

"I could travel." Veran thought of Elsbet, riding in triumph through the
night. "She said that she had been sent by those who remembered your
exile, *Patroun*. Will you tell me about it now? Will you tell me why you're
here and why I cannot leave?" He realized that his voice was hoarse and
desperate.

The Patron merely looked at him—and then away. "I had powerful enemies
long ago, Veran. It appears I still do. As for the secrets she sought—" He
spread his hands. "She was wrong. I took no great secrets from Rome."

"Except for the secret of your exile." Veran stared out into the night.
Beyond the villages was the world. Elsbet's world.

"You have time, Veran. Forget Elsbet. Forget Rolant."

"They betrayed us. Elsbet destroyed you, and the school, and the students."
Veran's gaze remained fixed in the distance. "And all because of a secret
you will not share."

"A secret I cannot share."

"*Why not?*" Veran turned on the Patron, howling at him. "You said it
yourself. Elsbet has destroyed you. If I am to be alone in the world, can you
not at least tell me why? Why would someone destroy a peaceful school?"

The Patron was silent before his anger. And then he said, "Because once
I refused a student. His name was Commodus, the son of Emperor Marcus
Aurelius. Certain others of the Damned desired that he be made emperor
after his father died. They wanted him taught, but only what they wished.
They wanted me to teach him. I would not. I knew that he was a fool, a
vicious, incompetent fool. I refused to teach him. And because I dared to
resist their wishes, the others exiled me. The eldest among them forced me
to look into her eyes and told me to leave Rome for the edges of civilization
and never to return. The strength of that command is still with me, Veran.
And Commodus went on to be made emperor in spite of my refusal—a
disaster for the empire."

"That's all? That's the reason you were exiled?" Shock washed over Veran.
"Your school destroyed because you refused to teach a tyrant?"

THREE DAYS OR SIX

"Exile was the lightest of the punishments that were proposed. I suppose that some of my old enemies still bear a grudge against me. Maybe they think that if I had taught Commodus, he would have been a better emperor and their plots would have succeeded. Elsbet was right, Veran." The Patron's voice was tired. "The world beyond these mountains is complicated. Infinitely complicated. Our kind play games that would confound the most brilliant philosopher with their intricacy and amaze the most bloody tyrant with their cruelty. My school—your home—was destroyed, the students killed, and Rolant turned against us all because of that game."

Because of a game. Because of a game, and because of a lust for imagined secrets, and because of a grudge carried for a thousand years. Veran turned away.

Into the silence of the night there came a roaring like the wrath of God. Invisible strength bent the blades of grass and the limbs of trees. Good men already indoors fastened shutters tight. Ungodly men and beasts and birds sought sanctuary. The mistral was back.

"Three days or six?" asked the Patron.

The scream of the wind, cold, ancient, and uncaring, beat at Veran, freezing brittle anger in his heart. "Forever," he said.

DON BASSINGTHWAITE

MY BROTHER'S KEEPER

My Brother's Keeper

BY JOHN STEELE

ANNO DOMINI 1093

The creature paused on the moonlit hillside, clawed fingers and toes kneading at the exposed rockface. Wolfish nose twitched, revealing canines too long for the once-human form. There was a scent on the winter breeze, a new scent, not far away. Distracted by an itch, the beast scratched behind an ear with its foot, then picked a louse from the toenail with its teeth. More sniffing the night air. Definitely a new scent. Not sheep or boar or the blood-rich stench of peasant. Something else.

Owain stepped from behind a boulder and with the momentum of three powerful strides thrust his spear into the back of the crouching Gangrel, raising the creature to its feet by the force of the blow. For a brief moment the skewered beast grasped at the spear protruding from its chest, then the last strength fled from its body. With a snarl of pain and rage, it dropped to its knees and then collapsed to its side.

"Forty years since I've hunted these hills, and still I'm able to track you three nights running before you notice my presence." Owain fairly spat the words as he stood above the impaled, convulsing figure. "And you *Gangrel!* What elder would choose you as progeny?" He noticed blood splattered on his dark cloak; the stain would not show, but still he raised the cloth to his lips and licked the damp patch. "Was your sire's mind fouled with tainted blood, or maybe the years have caught up with him? More animal than man by now?"

The Gangrel struggled to speak, but could only gasp as blood gurgled in its throat.

"Where is your sire?" Owain asked leaning down close to the Gangrel's face. "The deep cave a league to the west by the birch stand?" The surprise and the fear—the elder Gangrel was not an understanding master, then—in the Gangrel's eyes told Owain that he was right. "Yes, you led me there last night." Owain smiled and patted his prey roughly on the cheek. "I'll mention you to him."

Finally the Gangrel forced out stuttered words: "B-Bl-aidd…will t-tear…"

Owain stood and placed a booted foot firmly against the Gangrel's face, pinning its head to the ground. "Blaidd. Wolf. How quaint. What the peasants call him, no doubt. And he's going to tear me apart? Limb from limb? Perhaps." Owain drew his sword and with one fierce blow rent the Gangrel's head from its body.

"And so it begins," Owain said solemnly to the night. *I've been away from Wales for far too long,* he thought as clouds obscured the moon and a mist of rain began to fall. *Far too long.*

Morgan ap Rhys strode briskly into the great hall, all but deserted at this late hour of the morning, and found red-haired Iorwerth. Morgan called to his older brother, the lone occupant of the hall, who hardly looked up from where he sat oiling his boots. "He's dead, Iorwerth! Robert of Rhuddlan is dead!"

At this, Iorwerth did stop his oiling. "According to whom?" he asked, eyes narrowed.

Morgan ignored his brother's skepticism. "Riders from the north. It was Gruffudd that killed him—raiding at Degannwy and Robert tried to stop three shiploads of Welshmen with only one man, and Gruffudd took his head!"

MY BROTHER'S KEEPER

"Answer my question," Iorwerth pressed impatiently. "What riders?"

Morgan scoffed. "He's *dead*, I tell you."

Iorwerth threw his boot and oiled rag to the floor. *"What riders?"*

Morgan stared back into the hard eyes of the man who would be lord of Dinas Mynyddig, king of Rhufoniog, when their father died—*if* their father ever died. Morgan took a deep breath and replied more calmly. "Cynwrig. And others."

"Did they see it?"

"They heard."

"Hearing doesn't make it so."

Morgan bristled, slammed his fist down on a table. "Do you have to be so damnably thick-skulled?"

Iorwerth stood. He clenched his fists by his sides and looked down at Morgan. "Until I talk to someone who was there, someone who has touched his swollen tongue, he's not dead."

It was more than Morgan could take. House Rhufoniog had supported Robert and his overlord cousin Hugh the Fat, earl of Chester, because it had been the practical move. Morgan had never liked it. He hadn't liked losing the northern lands near Rhos, and moreover he hadn't liked his family swearing fealty to a Norman. And now that the situation was changing, his brother was too damned slow-witted to see it! Morgan grabbed Iorwerth by powerful shoulders. "Robert is dead, and Gruffudd is on the move! They can't hold Degannwy; they can't hold Rhuddlan. The Normans will be running back to Chester."

"Gruffudd has *been* on the move," Rhys ap Ieuan, their father, corrected Morgan. The old man had shuffled into the room unnoticed among the shouting.

Morgan released Iorwerth. The two brothers stood only a foot apart, the tension between them palpable. They watched in silence as their father came closer. He was older than a man had a right to be, especially a Welsh lord whose sons waited for their inheritances.

Rhys placed a hand on either son's shoulder. He spoke through one side of his mouth, a concession to the rotting teeth that pained him. "Didn't I tell you when news arrived of Gruffudd's escape that either he or Robert would soon be dead? I knew it." Rhys patted Iorwerth on the cheek. "Gruffudd ap Cynan is not a patient man, not a man to let twelve years of imprisonment go unavenged."

Morgan had always felt that both sons were reduced somehow in the presence of their father, much as Morgan sometimes felt lessened in comparison to his brother, who had once killed three cattle thieves single-handedly. Did greatness recede so much with each birth?

Rhys patted Morgan's cheek also; Morgan pulled away from the gesture meant for a child. "No," Rhys continued, "Gruffudd is not a patient man. Neither is he a man on whose behalf one should act rashly. Robert *may* be dead." Iorwerth, vindicated, smiled. "But there is no cause, just yet, to act."

Morgan could feel his color rising. Their father was taking Iorwerth's side. "But this is our chance to push the Normans out of Wales!"

Rhys grunted contemptuously, as if disgusted that a son of his could be so dense. "And then what? Fight the Normans? So that instead of paying a reasonable tribute to Robert, or to the earl of Chester, we are under Gruffudd's yoke? Think, my boy."

Morgan had no response to this. *At least Gruffudd is a Welshman,* he thought, but that would carry no weight with his father. Besides, it would be Iorwerth who would someday rule House Rhufoniog. Morgan was resigned to his fate of holding a *cantref* or two to the south, guarding against incursions from Powys. He would own land, but the real decisions would be made by his father, and by Iorwerth.

"Even if Robert is dead, the Normans aren't turning tail for Chester just yet, I'd wager," Rhys crooned through the stench of decay. "Hugh will come, or he'll send someone else. Before Hugh, William the Bastard sent Gherbod the Fleming. There will always be someone. The trick is to be ready for him. Not to throw in our lot before we know which way the wind blows." He jabbed a gnarled finger at Morgan's chest. "You're not the risen Rhodri Mawr here to unite all of Wales."

Neither are you, thought Morgan. *Neither are you.*

"When the time comes," said Rhys, "we will act."

❖

Owain stood in the rain and the darkness just beyond the earthworks that had been maintained and expanded over the years. Would the young noble—young compared to Owain's true age, at least—respond to the message delivered by his ghoul Gwilym? Owain thought so. He had watched the noble, as well as all the other members of House Rhufoniog, for many nights. Owain could pick out the sounds of their differing heartbeats—calm and regular, angry and pounding, fluttering with the flush of sex—and he fancied he could fairly read their thoughts.

And Gwilym was dependable. He had led the loaded mules to the empty summer hunting lodge that was exactly where Owain had said it would be. Surely the ghoul could deliver a simple message.

Owain's prediction was borne out as Morgan ap Rhys, wrapped in hides and furs against the cold and wet of the night, cautiously picked his way through the muddy defensive works of Dinas Mynyddig. Owain did not feel the cold.

At length the vampire moved, allowing himself to be seen by the mortal, who had been peering ineffectually into the dark. Morgan seemed faintly surprised to see someone where a moment before he'd seen no one, but if he found this disconcerting, he hid it well as he sauntered over to Owain.

"Your man said you'd be here."

"He did, and I am." Owain kept his wide-brimmed hat pulled low. No need to reveal too much too soon. Morgan eyed him suspiciously. *As well he should*, Owain thought.

"And that you had news of Robert of Rhuddlan," Morgan continued.

"I can only confirm what you have already heard," said Owain. "He has died the death from which none may return." Even through the gloom, Owain could see Morgan's eyes narrow as he weighed the value of information from an unknown source. "No. You have no reason to trust me," Owain answered the unvoiced question, "but I would earn your trust if you will allow me. I bring a token of my good intent."

Morgan's hand instinctively shifted to the hilt of his sword. "Yes?"

Owain smiled at the haughty attempt at intimidation. *Time enough for that later, my boy*. The vampire, with exaggerated caution, handed over a small bundle. Morgan gingerly unfolded the rag to find a fang half the size of his middle finger and coated in still-moist blood.

JOHN STEELE

As Morgan held the rag, the rain began to wash away the blood from the tooth. "Who are you and what do you want?" Morgan asked sharply. "Your man called you *arglwydd*. Are you a lord? What's the meaning of..." he vacantly waved the bloody rag and tooth, "all this?"

"All this," Owain imitated Morgan's gesture, "is my way of proving how I can aid your people, this land, you." All hint of facetiousness left Owain's voice. "There is a beast that prowls your land. Blaidd, the villagers call it—wolf. This tooth is from its spawn which is dead, but if you do not kill this Blaidd, there will be more, and your people will die."

Morgan considered this for a moment. "But there have always been tales of the wolf."

"And you have believed them while others have not. 'Tales of dodderers, and of mothers to frighten their unruly babes,' your father calls them."

Morgan tried unsuccessfully to hide his surprise at hearing his father's words parrotted now. Owain had eavesdropped on Morgan teasing a serving girl he bedded about her fears of the wolf. Later the vampire had also listened as the young noble had mentioned the peasants' fears to his father and had been admonished. Owain wondered for a moment if he had given away too much, set the younger man too keenly on guard, but then realized that it didn't matter. The moment Morgan had ventured out into the cold night, into the rain-soaked unknown to meet with a complete stranger, at that moment the hook had taken hold, and now was the time to pull it true.

"Listen carefully," Owain said with great urgency. After giving terse instructions, he slipped away before a protesting Morgan, merely feet away, knew the vampire was gone.

The clouds gave way to stars and moon during the night, and the morning dawned bright and chill. As Morgan gnawed a cold biscuit and waited, as he had been instructed, at the edge of the forest for Gwilym, the second son of Rhys ap Ieuan couldn't help but wonder what manner of man was the stranger, who had vanished so quickly and completely into the night. The man's audacity had angered Morgan, especially since, as far as Morgan could tell in the deep shadows and with that hat, the stranger had looked so young. But his words had not been those of a young man; they were spoken with an inherent authority, with the expectation that they would be obeyed, much like…Morgan's father.

Morgan had been prepared to disregard the arrogant words, to ignore the stranger's instructions, but had changed his mind for two reasons. The stranger had quoted, word for word, Rhys's rebuke of Morgan for his concerns about the wolf. How was that possible? The stranger didn't seem the sort of man with whom Morgan's father would consort.

And there was the tooth.

"Dry it off and expose it to the sunlight," the stranger had said, and when Morgan had done so early this morning, the tooth had crumbled to dust in his hand. Mere trickery? Perhaps. But worth investigating, and if Morgan could rid his family lands of the beast…

So he waited with spear and torch as instructed. "It fears fire," the stranger had said. "Also, the beast will be sluggish during the day, even in its cave. Attack it at noon and you will have a chance. Drive your spear through its heart—it must be the heart—and then wait for me to join you at nightfall."

What manner of man, indeed? Morgan wondered.

Eventually Gwilym arrived. He was a short, stolid man, probably from southern Wales, Morgan guessed from the accent of the few words the servant uttered. He led Morgan to the east, away from Dinas Mynyddig, out of the forest, up into the unforgiving mountains. For several hours they kept up a brutal pace without speaking, sweating even in the cold, steam rising off their bodies. Just before noon, they stopped.

"My *arglwydd* commanded me to go no farther," said Gwilym. His breath hung in the air before him. "There is the cave." He pointed up the hill to a small opening near a stand of weather-beaten birch trees.

Morgan doubted he would ever have noticed the entrance on his own. He proceeded alone, stopping before he reached the mouth of the cave to light the sap-soaked head of the torch. Flame sputtering, spear lowered, he entered the cave.

Morgan was a born hunter. He had brought down all types of game and, on necessary occasions, had tracked human prey. But this was different—

JOHN STEELE

he sought a beast he'd heard stories of since his childhood. Morgan adjusted his grip on the spear. The torch cast dancing shadows on the cave walls. Once beyond the entry and the whistling breeze, he could feel that the air in the cave was slightly warmer than that outside. The cave's damp, musty smell was familiar to Morgan, but there was something else as well—an odor similar to the kennels at Dinas Mynyddig, except with a fouler edge, less aired-out, and the farther Morgan advanced into the tunnel, the stronger the smell.

A stillness descended around Morgan. The only sounds were those of his measured footsteps, the distant dripping of water, and the pounding of his heart. It wasn't fear that caused sweat to trickle down his back, but rather the intense alertness that he'd only ever experienced when death was at hand. Morgan was thinking that he must be close, as overwhelming as the odor had become, when he heard it—growling from around the next turn.

His mouth went dry.

There was no way to surprise the beast; the torch had certainly given him away already, but there was no getting around that. Spear levelled before him, Morgan stepped around the corner and came face to face with the beast—Blaidd, wolf, the monster of his childhood, the bane of the peasants of Rhufoniog.

For a moment they regarded one another. The beast looked much like a wolf—pointed snout, bared fangs, ears laid back, hackles raised—yet it stood on two legs against the back wall of the cave. Its glaring eyes were thick with sleep, but it looked anything but sluggish.

One heartbeat passed, and the creature pounced.

Morgan thrust the torch at the wolf and it veered away from him with an angry snarl.

He attacked immediately, but the beast countered with inhuman speed and strength, almost tearing the weapon from Morgan's hold.

Again the wolf charged and Morgan warded it off with the flame, and again his counterattack was easily turned aside. Each time the creature struck the spear, the force of the blow sent jolts of pain up Morgan's arm. His hand tingled.

Morgan thrust with his spear and the beast's downward slash almost ripped the shaft from his hand, this time wrenching his smallest finger to the side with a loud pop. He howled with pain and dodged to the side as the wolf's jaws snapped shut inches from his face.

Morgan lurched off balance. The ancient beast swiped sideways at the torch and connected, burning its own hand but knocking the firebrand from Morgan's grasp.

Morgan lunged for the torch—more potent than any shield—but the wolf had expected that. Its claws dug into Morgan's flesh just below the neck and tore down across his chest and belly.

He felt shock more than pain as he stumbled backward and fell.

Now it was Morgan's turn to anticipate his opponent's next move, and his ability to do so saved his life.

As the beast surged forward with a roar of triumph, Morgan hastily braced his spear under his arm against the stone floor, jerking the point upward in line with the charging creature's chest instead of its stomach. With the terrible, bone-shattering force of its killing lunge, the beast crashed onto the spear, imbedding itself well down onto the oaken shaft.

As the dead weight of the wolf yanked the spear from Morgan's quivering hands and blood welled up in his wounds, the torch on the floor sputtered and there was darkness.

Owain arrived shortly after sunset to find Gwilym caring for the half-dead Morgan just inside the cave entrance. "The Gangrel?" Owain asked.

"Staked." Gwilym nodded toward the inner cave. "In its lair."

"And young Morgan?"

Gwilym's expression remained neutral. "Got himself cut pretty badly. Lost a lot of blood. If the claws had gone much deeper, he wouldn't have made it this long." Owain saw that it was true; the heap of blood-soaked hides and rags with which Gwilym had been able to stop most of the bleeding attested to the fact. Gwilym looked up with an unusually intent expression. "Was it this way with me, *arglwydd?*"

It was the only time Owain could remember Gwilym asking about his transformation into a ghoul. "You were worse, I think." Gwilym nodded, apparently satisfied.

Owain knelt down beside Morgan. The vampire forced himself to ignore the enticing scent of so much blood. He drew his dagger and with a forceful jab pierced his own right palm. Blood flowed freely. "From the stigmata the fallen are given eternal life. Eh, Gwilym?" Gwilym frowned. Owain smiled, still amused that his ghoul had not yet shed the ingrained piety of his former life. "I shouldn't blaspheme, should I? Who knows what torments the powers of heaven might devise for us?"

He lowered his bleeding palm and after a moment of blood dripping into Morgan's slack mouth, the unconscious noble began sucking at the wound, weakly at first, then more forcefully, greedily. Gwilym pulled back the bloody rags and watched with Owain as the torn flesh of Morgan's chest and abdomen miraculously knitted itself back together, closing over the exposed bone and muscle below.

Satisfied that Morgan would survive, Owain pulled his hand away. It, too, was already healing. Owain chuckled, "Physician, heal thyself," again to Gwilym's obvious discomfort.

Owain headed deeper into the cave. As he advanced, the smell of wet, dirty beast that dominated the cave became atrocious. *How far from humanity some Cainites have fallen*, Owain thought. This was no occasion for compassion. Having been defeated by a mortal, the beast had earned its fate.

When Owain emerged from the depths of the cave, he was ruddy-cheeked with the blood and power of a vampire of elder generation. Morgan was awake now, sitting up against the cave wall. Owain dropped the head of Blaidd at the noble's feet. "You did well."

Morgan blinked, dumbfounded. "I should be dead."

"You're a quick healer," said Owain dryly.

Morgan was in no mood for trifling. "Who are you? *What* are you?"

"All in good time, dear Morgan. All in good time." Owain raised a finger for silence as Morgan began to protest. "For now, the night is young and you are a hero. You must return to Dinas Mynyddig and present your father with this trophy." He indicated the severed head and waved away Morgan's question. "You're too weak still to journey alone, so Gwilym will aid you. Do not mention me. I want none of the glory. We will speak again." And for the second time, Owain stepped away from Morgan and disappeared into the night.

Owain, too, would return to Dinas Mynyddig, but not yet. Instead, he turned east and passed over mountain and through forest with the speed and grace of a stag, the strength of a bear. None saw his passage as leagues fell away behind him. He travelled until he reached a hilltop above the abbey of Holywell. From above, he could see within the outer walls—the spring, the shrine—and he knew that she was there, but he went no closer that night.

After covering the distance back from Holywell, it was no great task to slip past mortals into the manor house at Dinas Mynyddig. Owain was but a shadow in the night to them. He could hear the celebration in the great hall. Morgan had staggered in and pulled from a sack the head of the beast. He was met first with confused silence, then with whispers of awe, and finally with cheers of triumph at his heroic deed. This night would be remembered for many years to come. *Oh, yes. It will be remembered*, thought Owain.

The revelry continued without sign of abatement, but not all would drink and cheer and sing until dawn. Owain entered a particular bedroom and waited.

When Rhys ap Ieuan returned to his room, Owain was on him before the door had completely closed. With preternatural speed and iron grip, the vampire clutched the old man from behind, wrenching his head to the side so his ear was within inches of Owain's lips. "Do you remember my voice, Rhys?" Owain hissed. "Has it haunted your dreams for these forty years, or have you slept peacefully at night?"

Owain could see Rhys's eyes bulging.

JOHN STEELE

"Do you still have a tongue, old man?" Owain twisted Rhys's head a bit farther, so that the king of Rhufoniog cried out, then threw the old man to the floor.

Rhys, confused and in pain, held his strained neck and licked his dry, cracked lips. "Owain?" He stared unbelieving at the impossible sight. "But…you're alive? Young?"

Owain laughed. He had looked forward to this moment for decades. "Greetings, brother."

Rhys struggled to speak. "How…?"

Owain lifted Rhys to his feet by the shoulders. "Don't worry. Your assassin didn't botch the job. I'm dead." Rhys's mouth hung open; his eyes blinked rapidly, vacantly. "It was Angharad, wasn't it?" Owain's knuckles were white with rage. "You married her, but I loved her."

"No, no, no…" Rhys stared ahead, mouth agape; reason was quickly fleeing him.

"What size *galanas*, do you think? How large an honor-price do you owe me for forty years of unending death? Hundred head of cattle? Five hundred?" Owain snarled and bared his fangs. Rhys moaned; his eyes fluttered, began to roll back in his head. "I think there aren't enough cattle in all of Wales, dear brother." Owain held the king's face in his cold hands. "You've lived too many years, old man. Your body stinks of rot." The vampire moved his face closer to Rhys's. "And your son Morgan, he has become a great man tonight," Owain whispered, "and he is *mine.*"

Rhys began to let out a doleful wail; pus and frothy drool ran down his chin. Owain snapped the old man's head violently to the left—*crack!*— then let the body crumple to the floor.

With singing from the great hall echoing in Owain's ears, he waited in vain for the relief he had always dreamed would come at this moment.

✣

Morgan was in bed, taken with sudden illness, when he received his brother's summons. Three days ago Morgan had felt the chill grip of death. As he had lain on the cave floor next to the impaled beast, he had prayed to the risen Christ to intercede on behalf of his soul.

Someone else had interceded.

Morgan had awakened to find what should have been an open, mortal wound healed as if it had happened weeks before—the stranger's doing, somehow.

Just as peculiar, as Gwilym the Tight-Lipped had helped Morgan back to Dinas Mynyddig, instead of collapsing from fatigue and physical strain, Morgan had grown stronger and increasingly energetic. Throughout the impromptu feast honoring the death of the beast, he had felt flushed with vigor and praise. Even Iorwerth had embraced Morgan while their father looked on admiringly—enviously in all probability, considering the old king had no such heroic deed to his own credit.

Don't think ill of the dead, Morgan chided himself. Early that next morning, a servant had found Rhys ap Ieuan's body at the bottom of a staircase, his neck broken by a fall.

The next evening, last night, there had been a mass and then a feast in honor of the late king of Rhufoniog—and in honor of the new king, Iorwerth ap Rhys. By the end of the mass, however, Morgan had been beset by spells of dizziness and had almost fainted. The feast barely begun, he had been forced to excuse himself and had retreated to his bed, where he had remained throughout the past day, wracked by vertigo if he so much as sat up to relieve himself in the chamber pot.

Presently, his head was clearing somewhat, and, with the aid of an attendant, he was able to make his way to the study that doubled as an audience chamber on informal occasions.

"Uncle Morgan!" Iorwerth's six-year-old daughter Branwen hugged Morgan; so enthusiastically, in fact, that she nearly upset his fragile balance.

"Hello, Branwen. Easy, child." The room began to swim slightly before Morgan.

Iorwerth sat in a padded armchair by the fire, his glittering hair seemingly an extension of the blaze. Beside him sat delicate Blodwen, cradling their infant son Iago in her arms. Morgan's other two nieces, Elen and Siaun, red-haired like their father, sat at a table nearby practicing their letters on a piece of slate with chalk.

"Morgan," Iorwerth greeted him.

Morgan, trailing behind Branwen, her tiny hand gripping his finger, approached the royal couple. He felt surrounded by the comforting warmth of family, but distinctly separate from it, an outsider glimpsing that which was denied him.

Against the wall to the king's right stood Brochwel, *penteulu*, captain of the household guard, listening, watching with his fierce eyes.

"Morgan, you've not been well," said Blodwen, the beautiful new queen of Rhufoniog. Her eyes sparkled blue in the light of the fire; her small nose and strong chin framed the smile that induced forbidden stirrings in Morgan. She still radiated strength and vitality, even after giving birth to four children. "You should settle down. Stop your carousing and find a woman to care for you."

"How can I, when my brother has already taken the most lovely woman in Wales for himself?" The words were offered as flattering jest, but struck closer to truth than Morgan would have cared to admit.

"I must speak with Morgan," Iorwerth said gently to his wife.

Blodwen nodded, then gracefully stood. "Come, children." As she ushered them from the room, she turned one last time to Morgan. "Guard your health well, Morgan," she said, and then closed the door behind her.

Morgan saw the way that Iorwerth's eyes followed Blodwen's progress across the room. Whatever differences lay between the brothers, Morgan freely acknowledged that Iorwerth was easily ten times the husband and father that their father had been, and, though Morgan was not a man of great sentimentality, Blodwen and the children held a place close to his heart.

"You have been ill, brother." The eyes which had shown such affection toward Blodwen were more guarded with Morgan.

"I have, but I will survive."

"I will not keep you long," said Iorwerth. "As was Father's wish, you are granted Penllyn and Dyffryn Clwyd. I imagine you will want to take up residence at your new holdings as soon as possible."

The news itself was not a surprise to Morgan. He had expected to receive one or two of the southern *cantrefi* while Iorwerth retained the more central lands of Rhufoniog, but the abruptness with which the grant was presented and the haste in which he was apparently expected to leave Dinas Mynyddig caught Morgan up short. He scrutinized the closed expression of his brother, and then looked over to the more openly challenging gaze of the man-at-arms Brochwel. There was a new facet in how they regarded him, Morgan realized. Now that Iorwerth was king, now that Morgan was a hero, the slayer of the beast, they no longer saw him merely as a younger brother, but as a rival, a possible claimant to the kingship of Rhufoniog; the sooner he was safely tucked away in the isolated lands south of the Hiraethog Range, the better.

Morgan's blood rose at the thought of no longer being welcome in the ancestral lands where he had spent all the days since his birth, at the thought of being hustled off beyond the mountains. "I am loyal to you, brother," he said more tersely than he'd intended.

"I do not doubt that you are."

The two brothers regarded one another for several moments, neither's gaze wavering. Morgan saw in Iorwerth's eyes no hope of reconciliation, no possibility of cooperation. Their father had torn the two brothers apart more completely in death even than in life. Morgan turned and, fighting the vertigo that once again assailed him, made his way to the door.

"There is news from the north," Iorwerth said finally. Morgan stopped but did not turn. "Robert of Rhuddlan *is* dead, and Gruffudd ap Cynan has driven away Hervé, the Norman bishop of Bangor."

"Then we must throw in with Gruffudd," said Morgan quietly, still facing the door.

"We must do whatever I decide we must do," Iorwerth responded.

Morgan left without further comment. *So, there it is,* he thought as he closed the door behind him.

Climbing up the outer wall and easing through the shutter that a moment before had been latched, Owain found Morgan sick in bed, feverish and furious. "So, you've been ordered to the south." The mortal started at the sound of the icy voice. "This is your moment of destiny, Morgan."

Morgan raised himself on his elbows. "Who in damnation *are* you, and why don't you leave me in peace?" he snapped.

"Your question nearly answers itself," said Owain with a wry smile. The vampire, now by the bed, looked down intently at his pale nephew. Though Owain was more than thirty years older, he appeared to be at least ten years Morgan's junior. "But all things in their time. Do you plan to tuck tail and slink off to the southlands like an obedient little brother?"

Morgan opened his mouth to issue a sharp retort, but Owain's glare snatched the words from the young noble's mind. "I...I am loyal to my brother," Morgan forced out.

"As he is loyal to you?" Owain asked with raised eyebrow. "Tell me, Morgan. Does he treat you like a brother? Does he seek your counsel, confer with you as a trusted advisor?" A harsh strain crept into Owain's voice. "Or does he treat you more like a leper, ordering you far away from your home?"

Owain held Morgan's gaze; the mortal's eyes blinked and began to water, but he could not look away. "I...am loyal...." he repeated weakly.

"Do you know why he treats you so, Morgan?" Owain leaned very close now. "Because he fears you—you who destroyed the beast. Your name is whispered in awe throughout Rhufoniog. People will follow you, and he knows it. He harbors ill feelings against you. He sees that he is slighted by your leaving the feast in his honor. He jealously parades his wife and children before you. He fears you."

Morgan opened his mouth but was unable to speak.

"You have proved yourself worthy. Unlike your brother, unlike your father, you are a man approaching greatness." Owain towered over the mortal, knowing that Morgan was incapable of looking away from the mesmerizing vampire eyes, black as death. "You asked who I am, Morgan. I am Owain ap Ieuan, your father's brother."

Morgan lay on his bed, breathing shallowly, hearing the words but robbed, in his stuporous state, of the profound shock that would otherwise have accompanied them.

"Three nights ago you asked what I am. I am accursed by God," said Owain, "but that is just as well, for God has failed me. I am the devil's spawn." Owain turned away, began pacing methodically around the sparsely furnished room. "Forty years ago," he continued, "my brother was to be anointed *subregnum*, king of Rhufoniog, by Edward the Confessor, but Rhys was taken ill and sent me in his stead to Westminster. Looking back over the years, I have no doubt it was an illness of convenience, for Rhys hired an assassin to kill me in Westminster. It was to appear a common robbery, a visiting Welshman caught unawares in the city."

The rage of decades washed over Owain; he flexed his fingers, all lengthy claws now. "What my dear brother could not know was that the assassin he chose was no mortal. He was a vampire of royal blood, and he did more than kill me; he took me beyond death, into the world of the Cainites."

Morgan stirred as the haze began to clear from his mind.

"You see, your father and I had argued about…" Owain paused. "About many things. But it was his fear of me, his fear and jealousy, that condemned me to be what I am."

Owain raised a clawed finger and with one slow motion slashed his own forearm. For the first time—too late—Morgan looked with fear upon the creature leaning over him. A second time, Owain's deep, black eyes took control of the mortal, holding both muscle and will immobile as Owain presented his bleeding arm. Morgan drank. Owain smiled as his cursed blood flowed into his nephew. Shortly, the vampire pulled his arm away and stood. Morgan, seized by a spasm of coughing, fell back onto his pillows.

"Do you feel it?" Owain asked. "Do you feel the power of the blood?"

Morgan struggled to prop himself against the headboard, took a deep breath. "The power of the blood or the curse of God?"

"They go hand in hand."

"Then I, too, am cursed?"

Owain laughed derisively at the question. "Idealism is the luxury of the young and the foolish, Morgan. Loyalty to your brother, loyalty to God— they do not exist, not in this world or the next." Two powerful strides and Owain was again by the bed, lifting Morgan into the air by his collar. "I have given you what you want, what you all but asked for." Owain bared his fangs; he had no stomach for self-pity, not from a mortal whose suffering could never match his own. "Or would you rather pad away quietly to

Penllyn or Dyffryn Clwyd? Is that what you want? To give up all you've ever known? To never again walk the paths or hunt the forests that have always been yours? To bow before your brother?"

Morgan stared deep into the animal eyes. "No," he finally answered in a subdued voice. "That is not what I want."

Owain lowered his freshly fed ghoul back to the bed. "Somehow, I thought not." The vampire smoothed the wrinkles from his cloak as the rest of the trap fell into place. "You have no great love for the Normans?"

"No."

"Good. I am of the vampire clan Ventrue, but with the Conqueror from Normandy have come a new breed of Ventrue wishing to drive before them or rule over those of us already here." Owain gnawed at a speck of blood beneath his now-receded fingernail. "Needless to say, London is no longer so hospitable as it once was. I have returned home, and I never again wish to see a Norman on my soil."

All the old wrongs will be redressed, thought Owain.

Morgan, overwhelmed by all that he had been subjected to, sat quietly.

"By morning," the vampire continued, "your strength will return, more strength than you've ever felt. This is my next gift to you, Morgan. You need not submit to your brother's designs for your fate. Challenge him. Challenge him, and after you defeat him, declare the allegiance of House Rhufoniog to Gruffudd ap Cynan. *You* will be lord of Dinas Mynyddig. *You* will rule Rhufoniog. All of Wales could be at your feet."

Morgan did not protest.

Good, thought Owain. *He will do it. So easy when you give them what they want.* "One matter remains to decide—your brother's family. You must take his wife and children as your own."

At this, Morgan balked. "I will not."

Owain could see the struggle within Morgan, could remember what it felt like, the struggle to separate family from politics, power from blood. "Blodwen is not an unattractive woman," the vampire pointed out, "and wouldn't you like young Iago to grow with love and respect for his uncle rather than with vengeance in his heart?"

A bit of Morgan's fire had returned now. "I will *not* take my brother's wife as my own."

MY BROTHER'S KEEPER

The vampire sighed. "So, you'll kill your brother but not bed his wife, eh? How noble of you, Morgan." Owain smiled, only partially amused. "Very well, then. That is your decision to make." He returned to the open window. "I have taken shelter in the hunting lodge on the ridge three days to the south. You know which one?" Morgan nodded. "Good. Come to me there as soon as you can. Eventually you will not need to feed so often, but for now we must keep up your strength."

And then the window was again latched, as if Morgan had been without a visitor that night.

All singing and merriment died away as Morgan entered the great hall with a naked blade. The crowd parted before him, all except Brochwel and his second in command, Cynwrig, who stepped forward to block Morgan's way. "What is the meaning of this?" barked Brochwel.

Behind the *penteulu* sat Iorwerth, king of Rhufoniog, at the high table, Blodwen's seat empty beside him. "Yes, brother," said Iorwerth, "what is the meaning of this? Treason?" He did not look surprised, nor particularly worried.

The ties of blood weighed heavily on Morgan—on one side, the undeniable bond with a brother, regardless of any rivalries that persisted over the years; on the other side, the strength and ambition that, magnified by vampiric power, flowed through his veins. Such thoughts had plagued Morgan all night and all day. He had neither slept nor eaten. When he spoke amidst the confusion of the great hall, he heard the words as if from a distance, as if they were spoken by someone else. "I challenge you, Iorwerth. I claim the kingship of Rhufoniog."

Brochwel drew his sword; Cynwrig stood ready with hand on hilt. A worried murmur rippled through the hall.

"Hold, Brochwel," called Iorwerth.

"Such traitorous dogs should be put down," responded the *penteulu*.

Iorwerth ignored his retainer's ire. "Morgan," said the king calmly. "Put down your sword, ride south tonight, and this is forgotten."

JOHN STEELE

"Do you fear me, brother?"

"I fear *for* you."

Morgan bristled at such condescension. "I challenge you, Iorwerth, I claim the kingship of Rhufoniog."

Iorwerth sighed deeply. "Very well, then." He reached out his hand and an attendant brought him his sword. Iorwerth drew blade from sheath with the grace and power of one well versed in the arts of war. He stepped forward around the table. "Brochwel, go make sure that Blodwen and the children remain in their chambers."

"But, *arglwydd*…"

"Do as you're told," said Iorwerth evenly. "And let all know that Iorwerth ap Rhys accepts the challenge of his brother. House Rhufoniog will be led by who survives here."

Morgan had been sure that Iorwerth would accept the challenge. Whether it was arrogance or nobility that forced the king's hand, Morgan could not decide. Either way, the result would be the same. Brochwel stormed out of the room, and Cynwrig, also, stepped aside.

Challenged and challenger circled each other for only a moment, as tables were pulled back and goblets overturned, before Morgan attacked. Iorwerth parried and swiped at his brother's knee, but Morgan easily sidestepped the stroke.

Neither man gave ground as they traded blows. The sound of steel on steel echoed from the rafters of the great hall. They offered no witty banter, only grunts and gasps of exertion as they swung and parried and dodged.

Twice Iorwerth's blade struck glancing blows and bit into Morgan's flesh— once on the calf, once the forearm—but Morgan felt nary a prick. He pressed his brother relentlessly, attacking at every turn, and as Iorwerth's breathing became labored, Morgan still moved strong and fresh. Iorwerth was clearly the more adept swordsman, but Morgan was skilled enough to hold his own, and his ceaseless aggression was taking its toll. It was soon apparent that fatigue would tell the tale.

As Morgan pressed his increasing advantage, he saw, for the first time he could remember, fear—*real* fear—creep into his brother's eyes. *Is he thinking of his lost kingdom?* Morgan wondered. *Or of the wife and children he will never again hold?*

MY BROTHER'S KEEPER

It was time now for Morgan's blade to strike true. He caught Iorwerth's left side, and then his wrist, and then his bicep. None of the blows were crippling, but they added to Iorwerth's mounting exhaustion, and Morgan was not yet winded.

The king fought on, his jerkin stained with spreading blood. His attacks came less and less frequently, and Morgan brushed them aside with ease. Iorwerth backed away, but Morgan gave him no quarter.

When the final blow fell, a thrust that dug deeply into Iorwerth's belly and left him with blood on his lips, the king seemed surprised. He staggered, then slumped to the floor.

Morgan, standing above his brother as the last of his life fled, felt none of the exultation he had expected. All he had wanted, all he had dreamed of, was in his grasp now. Dinas Mynyddig was his. House Rhufoniog would stand by Gruffudd ap Cynan, the Welshman, and drive the Normans from Wales.

Blood pooled around Morgan's feet.

He heard his own voice, again from far away, "Cynwrig, fetch Brochwel."

Morgan was only vaguely aware of the murmurings around him of the household and of the few guests remaining after the feast in honor of Rhys ap Ieuan. The victor, the new king of Rhufoniog, could not turn away from his brother's lifeless body, from the eyes that someone should close. He must have stood there for some time, because now Cynwrig was back, speaking quietly in Morgan's ear: "Morgan, come with me."

Morgan, the lord of Dinas Mynyddig, allowed himself to be led from the great hall, away from the shocked silence, to the family chambers of Iorwerth ap Rhys. The king stepped from the corridor into a room of madness.

Littered among Blodwen's modest decor were the sprawled bodies of Iorwerth's loved ones. Elen and Siaun, tangled young limbs, on the floor. Little Branwen crumpled on the bed. Blodwen was propped in a chair, her head tilted back, while Iago, barely a year old, lay limp across her lap. Blodwen's gown was torn, and two red punctures stood out at the top of her left breast.

Off to the side lay Brochwel, his head at an impossible angle to his body. Of all the carnage, there was no blood—not on the floor, not on the clothes, and not, Morgan was sure, in the bodies.

JOHN STEELE

Very well, then. That is your decision to make.

Morgan had not wanted this. But hadn't he known? Hadn't his ambitions set this in motion? Had he actually thought that he would be able to shield Blodwen and innocent Branwen from the fury set loose by his unsheathed sword? Morgan wanted to throw down his bloodied blade, to run far away from the evidence of his crime.

"Is this your doing?" Cynwrig stood behind Morgan, horrified at the thought, wanting to be told otherwise.

Morgan did not turn, did not weep. "Yes," he said. "This is my doing." *As surely as if I slit their throats myself.* "I am king."

Owain had been vaguely unsettled for the past four nights since his brother's death. Not since the first weeks after his embrace had he felt so. *Forty years thirsting for revenge, and now I have drunk of it fully.* Yet still he thirsted.

He had tried to kindle his rage in dispatching Blodwen and the children— *It had to be done. Morgan will see that in time. Send a message of ruthlessness to the other petty nobles that they'll not soon forget, and no rival claimants to the kingship*—but of all the lives taken, only Brochwel's had been at all satisfying, an amusement.

As rain fell again from the dark skies of Wales, Owain, flushed with the family blood that ran in his veins, passed across the countryside more swiftly than an eagle, more silently than a shadow. He sought the one loose thread that still tied him to the past.

Stolen warmth radiated from his body as he stood atop the hill above the abbey of Holywell. He paused not long, what might have been a heartbeat for the living. The outer wall was low, not meant particularly for defense. Within, the power of faith hummed about the spring, so Owain took a wide route around. He had no use for faith.

He found her by scent. She was kneeling in prayer by the bed in her cell. Even as quietly as Owain entered, she heard. She looked in his direction.

"Angharad," he whispered, the ability to speak almost escaping him.

She cocked her head slightly; a bemused smile played across her features. "They said you were dead these many years." Angharad's voice was still musical, though huskier, richer. Like Owain's brother had been, she was old now, nearly sixty, and the years had not passed her by as they had Owain. Her skin was leathery where once it had been supple, though it did not droop overly much. The once-bright eyes were obscured by cataracts. She was blind. "I must finish my prayers," she said.

Owain waited silently while she prayed.

Finally she stood, then sat on the bed.

"You look well," Owain said quietly.

"I may look well," she smiled as she spoke to him, "but I no longer see well. It is good to hear your voice, Owain." She did not see his smooth, young skin, his still-dark hair.

They remained in silence for many minutes. For perhaps the first time in his long life and unlife, words deserted Owain. He had thought to snuff this last smoldering ember of his past, but he no longer knew if he could. After some while, he again found his tongue. "I never wanted Rhys to send you away."

"I know," she nodded quietly. "He needed children."

Again there was silence.

"I always..." Owain faltered. "I always cared for you, Angharad." He realized as he spoke the words that, though the memories lived, the passions were long dead. "But I was loyal to my brother. How the years have changed me." Loyalty dead, love dead; Owain was an empty husk, consumed by insatiable hate.

"Owain?"

For a brief moment, he had deluded himself that redemption might lie with this woman and her infinite capacity for tenderness. *Redemption*, he thought as he looked at the crucified Christ on the wall. *Humanity*.

Owain left her on the bed and slipped from the candlelit cell back into the infinite night.

JOHN STEELE

TOUJOURS

Toujours

BY JACKIE CASSADA

"The meddlesome troubadour must be silenced!"

Guerard de Vitreaux delivered his pronouncement in a voice as casual as if he were remarking on the weather.

Etiénne carefully lowered his head in apparent submission to the desire of his lord. In reality, he wished to hide his dismay at the seigneur's request.

"How can one mortal so discommode you, sire?" Etiénne couched his question in cautious tones, hoping to avoid arousing the ire of the lord of the chateau.

Guerard smiled coldly.

"Already his songs have caused trouble for me in the court of Alphonse de Courcy. If you doubt me, then perhaps you will not doubt these." Guerard thrust a piece of parchment toward Etiénne. "This was delivered to me yesterday evening. You do read, do you not?"

Etiénne nodded. "If the hand is clear, I read well enough," he said. It took most of his control to keep his voice diffident. Although Guerard's blood was stronger, Etiénne was older by several centuries than the Cainite who claimed the lands near Toulouse. Not only did he read and write the *langue d'oc*, but he was fluent in both Latin and Greek, a product of having witnessed the last struggles of the Roman Empire. Still, here in southern France, where he had but recently come, he preferred not to make known his true age to those in power.

He examined the writing on the parchment by the light of the single candle which provided illumination for the small tower room that served as Guerard's private reception chamber.

"They are transcriptions of the troubadour's latest compositions," Guerard offered as Etiénne picked his way through the shaky script.

"Obviously written in haste," he murmured. "And from memory, no doubt?"

Guerard nodded. "My agent's memory is quite accurate," he replied. "I trust his rendition of the troubadour's lyrics."

> And if love's blossom is sucked dry
> By bloodless lips, who hears the cry,
> Who bears the blame? Who bears the blame?
> Cold the hand, the still heart cold and dead,
> Speak not of love where hunger dwells instead
> Nor speak his name, nor speak his name.

There were several more verses, each one expanding on the same morbid theme. Etiénne read through the words several times until he had committed them to memory before he handed the parchment back to Guerard.

"How do you know he sings of you?" he asked. "This could apply to any number of callous lovers in de Courcy's court, or so I have heard."

"This was written at the request of a certain lady who entertained me when last I visited Alphonse to reaffirm his loyalty to me," the elder Cainite said. "I had thought she would retain no memories of our dalliance, but it appears I was mistaken."

"Do you think this was meant to reach your ears?" Etiénne asked.

"Most certainly," Guerard responded almost immediately. "Furthermore, I believe that it was meant as a warning." His fist came down with a crash upon the delicate wooden table that stood by the window. The table shattered from the blow.

"No one threatens me!" Guerard thundered. Etiénne stood silently until his host's fury dissipated. "Least of all some mortal troublemaker who, by my reports, is even now traveling toward Toulouse. I will not have songs such as these corrupt the thoughts and passions of those who live beneath my rule." He whirled around to face Etiénne. "Will you do as I command?"

Etiénne heard the danger clothed in silken tones and nodded. "As you will, my lord," he said. "I will seek out and remove the cause of embarrassment to your good name."

Solange found that if she bound her breasts beneath her loose tunic and roughened her face with a small chafing stone, if she did not mince her stride or allow her voice to assert its natural timbre, no one suspected that she was anything other than a wandering troubadour. Adopting the small differences that distinguished the actions of men from the actions of women had become second nature to her, so that her heart no longer pounded in her chest whenever she arrived in a new town or made her way to the estate of the local lord to proffer her services as a maker of lays and a composer of tunes. She called herself Séverin de Ville and practiced thinking of herself as the man she would have been had God so designed.

Some days earlier, Solange had marked her eighteenth birthday and the third anniversary of her decision to defy her family's wishes and make her own way in the world. Since childhood, Solange had wanted nothing more than to pursue her natural gift for music. Her family, though they indulged her desire to master the lute and praised her first girlish performances, expected her to put aside her frivolous interest when she approached marriageable age. When her father announced his intent to marry Solange to his nearest neighbor, a prosperous baron with an avowed distaste for vain pleasures such as music and dancing, Solange could not accept the prospect of so dreary a future. Clad in her older brother's second-best tunic and hose, she sought refuge in flight.

At first, when she feared that her father and brothers would follow her and force her into a loveless union that would unite two sizeable estates in

Anjou, her disguise served as her only protection against discovery. Now "Séverin's" reputation as a troubadour made a return to her true gender impossible.

The wayside inn was crowded with travelers, many of them headed ultimately for the three-day festival at Toulouse, another two days' journey beyond. The inn provided shelter against the darkness, protection from the bandits—and, some said, worse—that infested the forests of southern France. Solange hoped that, in Toulouse, she would find a patron to replace her last one. Hélène de Courcy, wife of Baron Alphonse de Courcy, had requested from Solange a particularly bitter reproval of her latest lover, who had abandoned her, she said. Her tales of the individual, whom she refused to mention by name, had troubled Solange. While she dutifully composed a lay to express the unnatural passion her patron ascribed to this lover, her performance of it had only increased her feeling that she was treading on dangerous ground.

Shortly after she had satisfied Lady Hélène's request, Solange had made her excuses and departed the de Courcy household. That was nearly a fortnight ago, and now she hoped in Toulouse to find another lovesick lord or lady who would compensate her for composing songs about love unrequited or unfulfilled, preferably one who did not maintain that the beloved was a demon. That such creatures existed, she did not doubt. Nor did she question the wisdom of avoiding their displeasure.

Solange sat by herself in a corner of the room, watching the crowd that packed the long trestle tables that occupied the central portion of the inn. It was from a chair place....d atop her own small table that she had performed and now, her evening's entertainment over, she found herself somewhat separated from her audience. *This is how I knew it would be when I chose the life of a troubadour.* Idly, she brushed an errant strand of sweat-dampened hair from her face. Her shoulder-length ebony curls, though acceptable for a troubadour, would soon need cutting to preserve her disguise.

The room was close, filled with the odors of bodies too long on the road, of slightly rancid stew and watery beer. The smoke from the candles and torches that lit the room created a thick haze that searched for some escape and found none. The heavy wooden door stood barred, the windows shuttered.

Solange had more than earned her night's lodging. It was not every day that a troubadour deigned to perform to a crowd of unsolicited listeners, but she had agreed, upon her arrival, to play a selection of her compositions for the entertainment of the lodgers in return for a meal, all the beer she could drink, and a place upstairs in the common sleeping room. As the evening wore on, she became less and less comfortable with the idea of sharing a bed with strangers. It was simple enough to preserve her secret when there were only one or two other bedmates. All she needed was a corner of the bed. She had learned to sleep without moving about, to minimize the likelihood that she would accidentally brush against another body. Tonight, the common room would be crowded—too crowded for comfort. Solange toyed with the idea of requesting a place in the stable instead.

A flagon of ale appeared before her, along with a small pouch—filled with coins, from the sound it made as it clattered upon the table. She looked up at the figure now blocking her view of the rest of the room.

"I enjoyed the music." The stranger spoke with a slight accent that marked him as a foreigner, although Solange could not immediately place the region of his birth. "I hope you will allow me to demonstrate my pleasure by these small offerings."

He was small and slender, with pale blond hair and fine features, as if carved from marble by a master sculptor.

"I am afraid that I do not know you, m'sieur," Solange said.

"And I do not know you, except for your talent," the stranger replied, a slight smile warming the cold mask of his face. "May I?" He gestured toward a second chair, one which now held her traveling pack and her lute.

Despite her usual reticence with casual acquaintances, Solange found herself unable to refuse him. She reached across the table to retrieve her possessions, placing the lute carefully upright against the wall behind her and laying her pack on the floor beneath her feet. The leather satchel contained her only other clothes, ones more suitable for the presence of nobility, and she could not afford to replace them until she was once more ensconced in the home of a patron.

The stranger seated himself across from her. "My name is Etiénne Le Chaisseur," he said, bringing his head up to meet Solange's dark eyes.

JACKIE CASSADA

"Séverin de Ville," Solange replied, suddenly becoming lost in contemplation of the contours of her companion's face and the precise shade of blue that represented the color of his eyes.

Etiénne smiled as he noticed the troubadour's rapt concentration. He leaned forward, deliberately taking a deep breath that brought to him the aroma of his quarry's pulsating vitae, a delicate vintage decidedly lacking the spice of violence so necessary to his refined Ventrue palate. His smile faded with the realization that he could not dispose of this mortal so easily as he had anticipated. He had hoped the troubadour would possess both the rashness of temper and the lack of conscience his tastes required. His discovery had proved him wrong.

Etiénne looked deeper, behind the deliberately roughened skin of Séverin's face, behind the bulky clothing that almost concealed a decidedly unmasculine softness of form. In an instant, the troubadour's face became transformed from the pretty mask of a callow youth into the graceful countenance of a resourceful maiden. The revelation aroused in him an unexpected tenderness. *I cannot do this, knowing what I know.* Etiénne made a sudden revision of his plans. *I will find another way to silence her.*

"The company this evening does not bode well for a good night's sleep," he observed, directing the troubadour's attention to the still-crowded room where, in fact, a few heated discussions threatened to erupt into more than verbal battle.

Solange shrugged, affecting a calm she suddenly did not feel. Something about this well-dressed, obviously noble-blooded gentleman both aroused and repulsed her, yet she was loath to have him leave. "It happens, sometimes," she remarked. "One cannot always choose one's bedmates. I shall manage."

"I can offer you another choice," Etiénne said. "My own villa lies but a short distance from this place. One of your obvious talent would be a more than welcome guest in my household." He hesitated, wondering if he should simply employ a more direct method of eliciting her compliance. The ability to command the obedience of mortals was something Etiénne was skilled at.

"I would not wish to impose upon your hospitality, m'sieur," Solange replied, but Etiénne heard the reluctance in her voice.

"Except for a few servants, I live alone," he said. "There is a spare bed kept for guests—" he allowed the temptation to hang in the air between them.

Solange thought about the last time she had luxuriated in a bed all to herself and, before she could reason herself out of it, she made up her mind.

"Then, if it would be no trouble," she said, "I accept your kindness."

The innkeeper looked relieved when Solange informed him that she had found other lodgings for the evening. Although he mouthed a few stale warnings about the dangers of traveling so late at night, it was obvious to both of them that he saw her departure as an opportunity to charge another customer for whatever available sleeping accommodations her absence would provide.

Together, Etiénne and Solange set out along the road that led away from the inn and toward the city of Toulouse. Only after they had proceeded for several paces did Solange notice that her companion's gait was noticeably slower than hers and that he seemed to favor one leg. She bit her lip before voicing a query as to the cause of his injury, realizing that such a short acquaintance did not make her privy to his frailties. Nevertheless, she shortened her stride to accommodate him. They walked for some time in silence, Solange listening to the sounds of the night, Etiénne seemingly lost in some contemplation he did not care to share with her. After perhaps a mile, he touched her elbow and steered her gently away from the main road to a smaller path that led into the forest.

"This is the way to my home," he said. "It does not lie directly along the road."

Solange glanced upward at Etiénne's face just before they left the road. The moonlight illuminated her companion's face, casting it in tones of alabaster, giving it the pallor of death. *To what place do I go so trustingly? And in what company?* She stopped abruptly, covering her action with an attempt to adjust the strap of the lute that hung from her back.

Beside her, Etiénne stopped as well.

"It is only a little farther," he said, pointing through the trees. His sleeve brushed Solange's face and she caught the aroma of cloves and other spices from the fabric. Of the man himself, there was hardly any scent. "Once there, you can rest and take some refreshment that I hope will suit you far better than the inn's dismal board."

The sound of his voice, soft and mellow with the tones that she had heard used to calm a frightened horse, allayed her fears. She found it only natural that she should finish her adjustments and step into the forest along the path that wound before them through the trees. Once they were away from the main road, the darkness engulfed them. Beside her, Etiénne put a hand on her shoulder, guiding her steps with a light pressure from his gloved palm. As they walked, he spoke of the history of his villa, which had once belonged to a knight lost on crusade and which had now fallen into his keeping.

"There is a small garden within the courtyard," he said, "planted with flowers that bloom only at night. Some have called it a witches' garden, but I have yet to see any proof of that." He described the profusion of evening primroses, baby's breath, alyssum, aquilegia, cleome and satinflowers. Solange lost her fear as she listened to his speech.

The trees ended in a clearing, but the path, now broader, continued up a small hill that rose from the center of the forest. Instead of the dark woods, the night itself was all around them, and as they climbed toward the small stone fortress—Etiénne's "villa"—that sat atop the rise, Solange lifted her head toward the starry sky, drawing in a deep gulp of air as if she had just learned how to breathe.

"It is like this, most nights," Etiénne said, throwing his head back as well to gaze upward at the pinpoints of light outlined against the sky's impenetrable blackness. "There sits the Crab and next to it the Lion," he continued, pointing upward, his hand sketching imaginary shapes as he named other groups of stars. Solange tried to see the stars as he described them, but instead her attention focused more on the form of the sketcher, and she marveled at his angular profile and the pale waves of blond hair that framed his face. *His pallor is only the natural consequence of his coloration.* The thought seemed to rise of its own accord in her mind. *Perhaps he comes from some northern land, where the sun gives less color to the flesh.*

"I was born when the sun was in the house of the Water Bearer, so I'm told," Solange said. Etiénne regarded her, his eyes narrowing in intense concentration. Finally he nodded. "Yes, that much is evident," he said. "My own celestial ruler is the Scorpion. We will see neither of those until winter." Still talking about the stars, he motioned for them to close the distance from the forest to the villa.

Solange awoke in a strange bed, the late afternoon sunlight streaming in through the narrow slitted window to pool in one corner of the small room. She had not meant to sleep away most of the day, but no one had come to waken her, and the rigors of her recent travels had finally presented their toll upon her body. Her head felt groggy, and she lay awhile luxuriating in the sensation of having a bed—no, a room—all to herself. Even in her most favorable appointments, she usually had to share sleeping quarters with her patron's other retainers, those artists and other musicians and poets who were not fortunate enough to win a place beside one of the ladies of the household. The rumors, started by Solange herself, that "Séverin de Ville" labored under the curse of a great tragedy *d'amour* which had turned him away from the pleasures of the flesh had allowed her the liberty of refraining from the amorous pursuits that might otherwise have been expected of one of her station and calling. It was said, by some, that the young troubadour's voluntary abstinence informed his compositions with an acute poignancy known only to one who had savored and abandoned love's delights.

One of these days, someone will challenge that reputation and unmask me. The thought had occurred to her before, and served as a constant goad. So far, she had been fortunate, managing to conceal her true sex by affecting a modesty that many found strange, but none had dared to question. She glanced from the bed to the wooden door, barred from the inside.

Last night, Etiénne had delivered her into the care of one of his servants, a dour-faced woman who seemed oddly unperturbed at having been roused in the early hours before dawn to attend to a strange guest. Without her asking, a bath had been drawn for her in a small room behind the kitchen, apparently reserved for the washing of clothes and, occasionally, bodies. She had requested privacy in order to clean herself, and the serving woman had voiced no protestation, leaving Solange alone to wash several days' worth of travel from her skin. When she emerged, clad in her good clothes for lack of anything else to wear, she found that a meal had been set for her in the kitchen, where she dined on stewed capon and potatoes flavored with rosemary and onions, and drank copiously from a bottle of fruity amber wine.

Etiénne made no appearance until after she had eaten, when the servant informed her that her host was prepared to receive her.

Solange experienced a brief sensation of curiosity, wondering for a moment whether this lavish treatment was the preface to the discovery that her host belonged to the ranks of nobles whose carnal desires led them toward their own sex. Instead, Etiénne wanted only to conduct her through the rooms of the villa, pointing out his private library—a collection of more than a dozen bound tomes and more scrolls, some of which bore signs of great age— and his great hall before conducting her to the corner room which was to be hers for the night. She noticed that, under the light of the torches that burned from their sconces on the walls, Etiénne's complexion seemed almost flushed, a detail which she found somehow reassuring.

He left her at the door to her room. "I would show you the garden of which I spoke, but I fear that it is nearly morning and its beauty is best appreciated in the darkest part of the night. Perhaps tomorrow—"

"You speak as if I will be staying beyond tonight," Solange said. "I am headed for Toulouse, as you must have determined."

"Ah, yes," Etiénne said, as if suddenly coming to himself and remembering that he had but offered her the gift of a night's lodging. "Well, we shall let tomorrow happen as it inevitably will. There is an inner bar on the door, should you wish to ensure that you are not disturbed until you are ready to awaken." He wished her good night, with an ironic glance through the narrow window at a sky just beginning to grow light, then took his leave of her. A sudden weariness overtook her and she made haste to seek the comfort of the narrow bed, only at the last remembering to bar the door so that she could, for once, sleep without fear of discovery.

✤

Feeling profligate for wasting so much of the day, Solange roused herself to full wakefulness. She dressed quickly, and unhooked the bar from the door, nearly stumbling over a neat pile of clothing—the soiled garments she had discarded in the bathing room—now clean and smelling of the sun's drying warmth. Some sprigs of mint and savory were tucked into the folds, freshening the cloth with their spicy aromas.

The villa bustled with servants, all of whom greeted her with a polite deference. A chambermaid informed her that M'sieur Etiénne had gone out on business and that he would not return until evening. She found her own way to the kitchen, where there was more food for her. The thought of leaving so late in the day seemed ludicrous, so she sought out her host's library and spent the remainder of the afternoon poring over the pages of an illuminated manuscript on herbs. She hardly noticed when a servant entered quietly and lit candles to replace the natural light that had faded with the passing of the day.

"I see that you have reconsidered the urgency of your journey."

Solange jumped at the sound of Etiénne's voice and looked up from the book, now open to a page describing the properties of St. John's wort.

"You startled me," she said, hoping that her surprise had seemed less girlish than it felt. She quickly closed the book and stood to greet her host.

"I know," he said, coming across the room to stand beside her, his slender fingers tracing the worked leather covering of the book. "Forgive me for not being available earlier. I hope you have not been bored with solitude."

Solange shook her head. "It seems I was more tired than I realized," she confessed. "I awakened late."

Etiénne nodded. "I suspected as much," he replied. "And I admit that I so seldom have visitors, I have been looking forward to your company this evening. I am glad that circumstances have arranged themselves so as not to disappoint me. Have you supped? I have already dined at the home of an acquaintance, but Genevre assures me that there is food aplenty for you, if you are hungry."

Solange realized that her last meal had been some hours before, and made a wry face. She followed Etiénne to the dining room, where he sat with her, sipping occasionally from a silvered goblet, as she ate her fill of roast mutton and small, whole onions mixed with baked apples. Afterward, he took her into the garden. He had not exaggerated the beauty of the pale pink, yellow and white flowers that blossomed beneath the waxing moon. She looked up from her contemplation of the garden to find Etiénne staring at her, a look of profound sadness—or, perhaps, lingering pain—on his face.

"Does it pain you?" she asked. "Your leg, I mean," she added as his expression grew puzzled in response to her question.

"Oh, not overly much," he replied. "It is an old wound, from a particularly nasty war I was fortunate enough to emerge from intact. Perhaps one day I will tell you about it."

Solange recognized the unspoken request to speak of something else and so she obliged him by asking about the names of the flowers in the garden. The look that had prompted her inquiry disappeared from Etiénne's face as he moved slowly from blossom to blossom, giving them both their Latin and common names and demonstrating a copious knowledge of their properties and requirements for growth. Some of the words sounded familiar, and Solange realized that she had read them only a short time before, in the pages of the book in her host's library. *It is as if he wrote them himself, though the book seems far older than he.* Finally, he paused, having made the rounds of the garden.

"It seems that I have been practicing my skills at oratory," he said, a small smile making his face seem suddenly very young and very vulnerable. "You are the troubadour. It would please me greatly to hear more of your efforts."

"Of course, M'sieur," Solange replied. They parted company briefly while she returned to her room to fetch her lute, rejoining her host in the great hall where he had gathered his entire household, some half-a-dozen servants. She sang, accompanying herself on her instrument, for close to an hour before she stopped, her fingers sore and her voice beginning to tire. Her small audience rewarded her performance with claps and smiles of appreciation, and though she acknowledged the accolades of the servants— who she came to realize enjoyed a status halfway between servants and retainers in this household—her attention focused on her host. It was he whom she so fervently hoped to please. The look on his face told her she had succeeded. *Why does his approval mean so much to me?* she wondered.

The servants left, and she and Etiénne sat together in the hall, watching the fire in the great hearth burn to ashes. It was nearly dawn before she rose to seek the comforts of her bed, leaving her host to his own contemplations.

After a handful of days marked by late awakenings and nights of long conversations and visits to the witches' garden, Solange realized that she was falling into a routine from which she had no desire to escape. Etiénne made no attempt to discourage her from remaining as his guest; in fact, he seemed relieved each evening to find her still there when he arrived from whatever business occupied his daylight hours. The festival at Toulouse had come and gone and, with it, her prospects for finding a suitable patron in the area. She would have to seek further abroad, perhaps even as far as Poitiers or Tours or even Paris itself, but somehow, the thought of taking to the road once more only aroused in her strong feelings of dismay.

More and more, she found herself wondering about her host, who seemed full of knowledge about plants and herbs, the stars and their courses, and the history and thoughts of ancient warriors and philosophers, but oddly reluctant to elucidate for her his personal history. She gathered from one or two passing comments that he originally hailed from somewhere in the territory of the Holy Roman Empire, though the exact place of his birth remained a mystery. For her part, she responded with bits and pieces of gossip and rumor that she had picked up during her stays with various noble patrons throughout southern France, remaining equally as reticent as he about the particulars of her past. It was as if both of them had agreed to a conspiracy of privacy about themselves while speaking with absolute openness about everything else. She suspected, after one night spent discussing theology, that Etiénne might not even be a Christian but might, in fact, hold to one of the false religions of the pagans. She decided that prudence required that she keep her suspicions to herself, lest she anger one whose regard was coming to mean more to her with every evening spent in his company.

"I am not becoming enamored of him," she told herself sternly when she found her thoughts straying to him, as they did with increasing frequency. To counteract her growing emotions, she began to gather together a mental list of oddities about Etiénne and his household—beginning with his nocturnal habits and including the equanimity with which his servants seemed to accept their own unnatural schedules of wakefulness and slumber. Her list ended with the fact that not once since her arrival had he actually taken a meal with her. Some nagging thoughts began to stir within her, intimations for which she had no name but which rang in her head with an uncanny familiarity.

Still, she remained and, still, she found herself inescapably drawn to Etiénne's presence. She thought of confessing to him her deepest secret, but found that she was afraid that he might find "Solange" less interesting than "Séverin." She kept her silence.

One evening, nearly a month after her arrival, Etiénne informed her that he would be absent from the villa for at least two days. "I have my own obligations to my superiors," he had said by way of excuse. "I look forward to seeing you upon my return."

In his absence, Solange moved like a ghost through the villa, finding no consolation in the beauties of the garden or even in the pages of the manuscripts in Etiénne's library. She retired to her room early and sat up for most of the night composing and rejecting song after song.

Finally, she arrived at a verse that seemed to suit her feelings.

> *The midnight garden blooms with palest light,*
> *But far more fair the flower that rules the night,*
> *In darkness sweet, in darkness sweet.*
> *My heart lies still and silent, left alone,*
> *The garden flowers surround an empty throne*
> *Till next we meet, till next we meet.*

She practiced it until she had fitted melody to words, but knew that it would be a song she would keep to herself. As the sun rose, she sought her bed and felt, for the first time, that it was too large.

The next afternoon, she woke with a name thundering in her head.

Hélène de Courcy.

Sick dread coursed through her body, followed by an instinctive denial. *It cannot be possible. Etiénne is no monster.* Reluctantly, Solange remembered the tales the wife of Alphonse de Courcy had told her of her own affair with a demon. The nocturnal ways and odd mannerisms of Lady Hélène's lover sounded far too much like Etiénne's. Although she knew that he and that unholy creature that had so entranced Mme. de Courcy could not be one and the same, still, where there was one, there could easily be others.

Solange opened the heavy wooden shutters and stared out through the tiny window of her room, watching the pale afternoon sun sink lower in the heavens. Her warring thoughts marched to one inexorable conclusion. *I have stayed here far too long. Whether or not he is a demon, I have fallen prey to Etiénne's charms.* Hastily, she donned her traveling clothes and packed her gear. Although it would be night again in a few hours, she could not risk remaining in his villa any longer, lest the sight of him sway her resolve.

Even so, she took the time to pen a farewell to her host. Then, careful not to attract the attentions of the servants, she slipped from the villa and made her way down the hill into the forest.

Guerard de Vitreaux was not pleased. From across the room, Etiénne could feel his lord's displeasure.

"You have had the creature in your household for a month and still he lives!" The Ventrue elder's voice rang with barely suppressed anger. "I thought my orders to you were clear."

Etiénne steeled himself. He had never before gone against the commands of Toulouse's reigning Cainite, but he knew that this time he must defend his actions.

"Sire, I did as you asked. The troubadour has not performed in public since you ordered me to silence—him." It had taken an effort to refer to his guest as masculine. Etiénne hoped de Vitreaux did not notice his near slip. "I have done that."

JACKIE CASSADA

"It is not enough," de Vitreaux said. "I will have this scoundrel removed from the face of the earth."

"I cannot harm someone with so little malice in his heart as Séverin de Ville," Etiénne said, his voice insistent and bordering on defiance. This was the closest he had come to confessing his exclusive feeding habits to another Cainite.

De Vitreaux nodded curtly. "That has become obvious to me," he said. His face, which had grown almost feral with fury, became preternaturally calm as he regarded Etiénne coldly. "I have, therefore, taken matters into my own hands. When you return to your villa, as I expect you will do as soon as we have finished speaking, you will send your guest away by whatever means you have at your disposal. All I require of you is that you make certain he heads into the forest that surrounds your lands. Do that, and those lands may still be yours. Now, *begone!*" His final statement held the force of a command backed by all the power of his blood. Etiénne felt himself physically compelled to leave the presence of his lord.

Perhaps her panic had disoriented her senses, or perhaps she had simply missed the place where the forest path joined with the main road between Toulouse and Narbonne. Solange had wandered through the woods until nightfall and had come no nearer to its end. Still she pressed onward, hardly allowing herself to stop for more than a few minutes to rest before her fears drove her onward again.

Exhausted, she stopped to catch her breath and look around her, trying to find some familiar landmark and finding only an endless darkness full of eerie sounds and looming trees. The single torch she had thought to bring with her was beginning to gutter and she feared that soon she would be left without any light at all. She had finally decided to gather some fallen branches in the hope of fashioning a makeshift torch, lighting it from the dying flames of the old one, when the bandits attacked.

A cracking branch and a muttered oath were the only warnings she had, but they were enough, in her agitated state, to give her time to drop her torch and draw the twin daggers she wore—though seldom had occasion to use—at her belt.

"This be the one!" she heard a rough voice call out just before something struck her, cutting into the pack on her back and propelling her forward, where she collided with a second body. The sound of splintering wood as the lute she wore slung behind her shattered alerted her to the presence of yet a third assailant.

Vaguely, she became aware of still others standing a few paces away, holding torches aloft, forming a circle of light that provided just enough illumination for the battle. *How could I have missed them?* She thrust blindly in front of her and felt the momentary satisfaction of feeling the points of her daggers connect with soft flesh. She prayed the bandit would go down from the wound, and he did, though only to his knees, clutching his belly with both hands. She was still trapped between his kneeling form and the two opponents behind her. A sharp pain in her upper thigh, followed by the sticky heat of flowing blood, forced from her an angry cry that was only partly in response to her agony. She had lost one of her daggers, buried too deep in the belly of the man she had wounded—mortally, she hoped—but she managed to whirl around and slash at the face of one of the two men at her back. *I will die here tonight, but I will not give them the satisfaction of coming through unscathed.*

"That were a woman's scream!" a deep voice from one of the torchbearers cried out, and one of her attackers stepped back for just a second. Solange took advantage of her unmasking and attempted to flee, heading for the darkness between the torches' range. Her foot came down on part of her broken lute and she fell, moaning with despair, commending her soul to the mercies of God and the saints; then she felt the stale, hot breath of her attackers as they grasped her and plunged their swords into her back. Even as she began to lose consciousness, she heard a commotion. The voices of her attackers changed from crudities and grunts of encouragement to gasps of surprise and then screams of agony.

"'Tis a demon from hell! God save us!"

She turned her head, a motion which cost her more effort than she could have believed possible, to see what was happening, but all she could make out through eyes that were already dimming was a whirlwind of movement that left pieces of what had been men in its wake.

✥

Even before the battle was over, Etiénne knew that it was too late for the young troubadour maiden. He had left de Vitreaux's manor and traveled as fast as he could, riding his horse to ground in an attempt to reach his villa in time to warn his guest. He had thought to spirit her away, rather than deliver her into the arms of the men he knew Guerard had hired. That was the only explanation he could find for the Cainite's comment about taking matters into his own hands.

It did not take long for him to dispatch the bandits. Years of practice on such as they had honed his fighting skills to a sharp pitch, while anger had driven him to excesses of speed and strength that few of his bloodline possessed. His roused passion allowed him to ignore the weakness in his leg, the result of a wound gotten during the sacking of Rome. Mere mortals, even hired killers, could not stand against a Cainite in the throes of bloodlust.

Wiping the blood from his hands, he sought the troubadour's body, and was amazed to find faint signs of life, though those signs were quickly and irretrievably fading. He sat cross-legged on the ground, bloody tears streaking his face, and lifted her head to rest upon his knees. She moaned once, and then he heard the harsh rattle of death as she struggled for one final breath from lungs that were bubbling over with the last of her life's blood. He felt something tear at his heart, the seat of his remaining passions, and knew what he must do.

I have grown too fond of her to let her God have her. She and I will have to leave this place, but even if I did not take her into our society, I would not be able to stay any longer in the presence of he who brought her to such an early death.

He watched her until he was certain that the spark of life no longer held her to her mortal existence, and then, with the tenderness of a lover, he Embraced her. *She will need much blood to heal her wounds and give her strength.*

He looked around at the fresh corpses strewn among the trees. *Fortunately, there is plenty to hand for both of us.*

Solange did not seem surprised at what she had become. When Etiénne explained to her what had happened and who had sent the villeins after her, she only nodded sadly. Her wounds took several evenings to heal completely, and since she could not yet hunt for herself, Etiénne fed her from his own veins. On the second night, she told him her true name, and thereafter he referred to her as Solange. He sent a message to Guerard, informing him that Séverin de Ville had met his death at the hands of bandits, whom Etiénne was then obliged by his own principles to dispatch.

"We will have to leave here," he said to her. "It will not be safe in these parts for either of us for many years to come. Perhaps we will go to Paris, or even better, to England. I find myself longing for a colder clime than this."

Solange nodded, still overwhelmed by the strange sensations coursing through her once-living, still animate body. Once again, Etiénne became a font of information, this time about her new existence as one of the descendants of Caine.

On the third night, he warned Solange of the consequences of drinking his blood for the third time.

"An oath of blood that will bind me, heart and soul, to you?" She seemed bemused by the concept.

He nodded. "I would not force it upon you, but you have yet to learn the art of seeking your own prey—or of considering children of Adam and Eve as mere sources of nourishment."

Solange looked up at Etiénne with a heart suddenly untroubled by all the doubts and fears that had once seemed so important. She reached out for his wrist and brought it to her lips.

"A bond of love," she murmured. "Is that not at the heart of all troubadours' songs?"

Seeker

TIM WAGGONER

The dense canopy of trees allowed only a trickle of light from the full moon to penetrate to the forest floor. But it was enough illumination to allow a grizzled old warrior like William to make his way through the thick wood—and far more than enough, he was certain, for the creatures who paced him.

They moved among the trees and through the underbrush silently, like liquid shadows; the only indications of their presence a fleeting glimpse of darkness seen out of the corner of an eye, or an almost inaudible rustle of one leaf against another, as if stirred by the faintest of breezes. Another man would most likely not have noticed them at all. But William had been a warrior and knight for the better part of the last forty years. He needed only the tingle on the back of his neck, a cold tightness in his innards, to tell him he was not alone in the wood.

He laid a hand on the pommel of his sword—a blade which had delivered more Saracens than William could remember into the arms of Allah—and smiled. This was what he had come here for.

TIM WAGGONER

"Show yourself," he whispered as he continued deeper into the wood. But he wasn't talking to the shadows that flitted through the forest around him. Not at all.

⟊

"Come here, William."

William hesitated. At twelve, he was still enough of a child to be afraid of Father Abernathy, but at the same time enough of a man to be reluctant to demonstrate that fear. So instead of running across the courtyard and into the castle—where he knew he could easily lose the priest among the numerous corridors and alcoves—he did as Father Abernathy bade and walked over to him.

The priest was a lean man with pale, unhealthy skin. His eyes were always half-lidded, as if he were perpetually sleepy, or perhaps some manner of lizard masquerading in human form. When William stopped before him, the priest laid a cool bony hand on the boy's shoulder and smiled thinly.

"You haven't been to confession in some time now, have you, lad?"

Something about the Father's manner of speech always bothered William. It was as if he didn't mean the words he spoke, as if they served only to cloak his true intentions.

Ideally, the identity of the confessor was supposed to be a secret from the priest, in order to encourage people to admit their sins. William knew that in practice, however, this was rarely the case.

"No, Father."

Father Abernathy's lips tightened in disapproval. "Don't you have any sins to confess?"

"No, Father. I mean, yes, Father. We all sin." William lowered his eyes as he said the latter, lest the priest take the comment the way William meant it.

"Then you must be unconcerned about the state of your soul. I can think of no other reason for someone to avoid the confessional."

William had a very good reason; he didn't like Father Abernathy. But he knew better than to say so. With William's father and older brothers off crusading, Father Abernathy, as the family priest, was the closest thing to a lord the castle had at present. And besides, as a cleric, he was God's voice on earth, wasn't he?

"I think you'd best come with me, William." And without waiting for a reply, the priest gripped William firmly—and a bit painfully—by the shoulder and steered him toward the castle. He didn't relax his grip until they had reached the family chapel. Father Abernathy lit no candles, didn't even open the shutters; the only illumination came from the thin space between the oaken panels.

The priest didn't go to the confessional as William anticipated. Instead he sat on one of the simple wooden benches before the altar and gestured for William to do the same.

Father Abernathy nodded. "Go ahead."

William knew better than to question the Father. If this was the way he wanted William to confess, then this was the way he would do so. He crossed himself and said, "Bless me, Father, for I have sinned." He had no clear idea how long it had been since his last confession, so he left that part out.

He related a list of minor sins—disobeying his mother, envying his father and brothers who were off fighting to reclaim the Holy Land, putting a dead mouse in the stew to frighten the cooks—and when he was finished, he waited for Father Abernathy to pronounce his penance.

But instead the priest said, "Are you sure that is all, William?"

William fought to keep his face from reddening, sure that Father Abernathy would see even in the chapel's gloom. "Yes, Father."

"Come now, William. You're a young man. And young men commit...special sins. Sins of the flesh."

He felt a cold stab of fear at the base of his spine. God saw everything, and if priests were God's servants, then perhaps they knew what God did. Still, William couldn't bring himself to admit to his most terrible sin.

"I don't know what you mean, Father."

"Do you touch yourself, lad?" The priest's voice was low and throaty, and for some reason it frightened William. "Touch yourself...down there?"

William looked at the floor and nodded. He could feel tears threatening.

"Such an act is a great affront to the Lord, and can only be undone in a special way. Unless of course you wish to continue with this stain upon your soul."

William shook his head.

Father Abernathy reached out and gently stroked William's shoulder. "Good lad. Let us then begin your penance. And remember: as serious as your sin is, it is a far worse transgression to speak of what occurs in confession. Do you understand?"

"Yes, Father." Nearly a sob.

"Good lad," he repeated, and began to remove his robe.

When it was over, Father Abernathy left William huddled on the stone floor of the chapel, crying and hurting. He wanted to run to his mother, wanted her to hold him in her arms, wanted to tell her what the priest had done, wanted her to order him killed. But even if he were willing to commit the sin of speaking of what had happened to him, he knew his mother would not believe him and would do nothing about it if she did. To her, the Church's word was law in all things. William's father would have seen it differently, but he was far away, perhaps never to return.

And so William was left alone to cry, to ache, and to contemplate the ways of Father Abernathy's God.

The shadows were closer now. Sweat broke out on William's brow, night-air cold. His pulse grew more rapid, and he felt a tightness in his chest that edged toward pain. He concentrated on keeping his breathing regular, measured, and the sensation subsided. Without willing it or even being completely aware he was doing so, William assessed his physical condition, a warrior preparing for battle. His right shoulder was stiff, thanks to a Saracen dagger wound he'd taken nine years ago, his knees ached from all the walking he had done to penetrate this deep into the wood, and his fingers felt thick and clumsy from the night's chill.

His was an old body, well-used, perhaps ill-used, but it was all he had and thus would have to serve.

This section of the forest was too thick for swordplay, so William knelt and drew a dagger from his boot sheath—a silver dagger. If he still prayed, he would have prayed now that the legends were true, that silver would prove effective against the shadows in the wood. Assuming, of course, that they were indeed what he hoped.

The first one came at him from the left. A snarling black shadow that detached itself from the surrounding darkness, eyes a baleful hungry yellow in the moonlight. The beast bounded forward and leaped for William's throat, slavering jaws stretched wide. But the old warrior was still nimble enough to sidestep in time, and as the wolf flew past, William sliced his dagger along the animal's side.

The creature fell to the ground, howling in pain. William fell into a battle stance, weight evenly distributed on his feet, dagger held at the ready. The creature thrashed about on the forest floor, its howls falling away to whines. In the patchy moonlight the animal was revealed to be a wolf. A rather large wolf, perhaps, but there was nothing in its features to mark it otherwise, at least not that William could discern. He experienced a surge of disappointment; he hadn't come all this way merely to strike down a mangy wolf.

The whining ceased, along with the wolf's exertions. The animal lay still for a moment, then rose stiffly to its feet. William squinted, trying to determine how badly he had wounded the creature. But while the wolf's pelt was bloodstained, there was no sign of the deep gash William was certain he had caused. He risked a quick glance at his blade; it was well blooded, dripping wet-black.

The animal began to circle him then, growling low and deep in its throat, soft and weak at first, but louder and stronger with each pad of its paws.

TIM WAGGONER

The wolf moved easily now, all sign of its earlier stiffness gone. William wasn't sure, but it seemed that there was even less blood on the creature's fur, as if the wolf were actually drawing the precious fluid back into its body.

William cautioned himself. Perhaps he had only thought he had struck such a deep blow; perhaps there had never been that much blood, and he had been merely deceived by the forest gloom. Still, he couldn't keep from hoping otherwise.

He matched the wolf's actions, turning as it circled, never taking his eyes off its blazing yellow orbs. Together, they made three complete circles before the wolf stopped and stared at him with eyes that seemed more intelligent than a wolf's had a right to be. More human.

William pondered his next move. His choices seemed simple enough: attack or retreat. And really, wasn't that what all war boiled down to in the end—perhaps all of life? Well, if it was a choice between fight or run, William knew which he preferred. He gripped his silver dagger tight and prepared to rush the wolf, but before he could move, a dozen sleek shadows slipped out from between the trees to join their packmate.

Perhaps, William thought, *it is time to rethink my strategy.*

When William turned sixteen, he informed his mother that he intended to join his father and brothers in liberating the Holy Land. The baroness pleaded with him to stay, but he was firm in his resolve. She asked him at least to consent to accompany her on a pilgrimage before he left, not only so that she would have the memory of the trip to keep her company while he was away, but also so that he could go off to battle without her worrying about the state of his soul.

William didn't want to go. He had been six during the family's last pilgrimage and once the novelty of travel had worn off—which had taken all of three days—he had found the journey deadly dull. But the baroness insisted, and cried, and in the end it was not her words but her tears which swayed William to say yes.

The baroness chose as their destination the abbey at Roxbury, where the abbot, who had been a most holy man, had supposedly lain in state for three months after his death without the slightest sign of decay.

William didn't know what they were supposed to see at Roxbury Abbey; from what Father Abernathy said, the purported miracle had occurred seven years ago, and the abbot had long since been buried. Still, Roxbury was where his mother wanted to go, so Roxbury it would be.

The trip itself was only slightly more eventful than William's previous pilgrimage. One afternoon, they stopped at a village in order to attend mass at a small stone and wood church. But Father Abernathy got into a shouting match with the vicar over the image of what the former called a "pagan idol" carved above the entrance to the church. William examined the figure as the two clerics argued. The being resembled the renderings of Christ he had been familiar with as a child, but instead of a crown of thorns, there was a garland of leaves which encircled the figure's head, neck and shoulders.

The local priest attempted to explain that the Green Man, as he called it, had been added to the church long ago, when it had been originally constructed, in order to connect to the locals' pagan beliefs and make Christianity seem more familiar, more acceptable.

But Father Abernathy would have none of it, and so the baroness's retinue departed the village without so much as setting foot within the tiny church. As they rode, Father Abernathy lectured long and loud for anyone who would listen on the evils of paganism, but William paid no attention. He couldn't get the unearthly image of the Green Man out of his mind.

A quarter of the way to Roxbury, they encountered another band of pilgrims, a duchess and her servants, also bound for the abbey. They fell in together, the duchess and William's mother getting on like two long-lost sisters, despite their differences in station. They rode together in the duchess's coach and William, who insisted on riding horseback rather than in their wagon with Father Abernathy and the baroness's servants, would sometimes ride alongside the coach and eavesdrop out of sheer boredom.

"You jest!" His mother.

"Not at all. My lord the duke truly did once take me nine times in a single night. Of course, he was a much younger man, then. The best he can manage now is three or four."

They giggled like two girls, and then grew quiet.

"I miss my husband terribly," said his mother.

"As I do mine," echoed the duchess. "Though, in truth, I have found other ways to…occupy myself."

"What do you—" The soft rustle of clothing being removed. "Oh, I see."

Silence again, but this was a silence punctuated with sharp intakes of breath and long sighs. William decided he had heard more than enough, and fell back.

The baroness and duchess were inseparable for the remainder of the journey to Roxbury Abbey—which turned out to be a small, squat stone building hardly any different from any of a dozen village churches they had seen during their journey. They stayed for all of the day, praying several times at the abbot's graveside before heading back.

William's soul did not feel any different, but then he hadn't expected it to. At least now he could join his father and brothers without having to worry about his mother. If she got lonely, she would have the memory of this most holy pilgrimage shared with her youngest son to keep her company, wouldn't she?

That, and a certain duchess who had agreed to come visiting as soon as William departed for the Holy Land.

William reached into his leather vest with his free hand and removed a small bottle. Keeping his eyes on the wolves, he brought the bottle to his mouth, bit into the cork and pulled the stopper free. He spit the cork out and then began sprinkling the contents of the bottle around him in a tight circle, all the while whispering the Lord's Prayer to himself in Latin.

He had no idea if the holy water would prove effective against these creatures—assuming, of course, that they weren't just ordinary wolves. But that was one of the things he had come here to find out, wasn't it?

When he was finished, he dropped the empty bottle at his feet, transferred his silver dagger to his left hand, then drew his sword. There still wasn't enough room to wield a sword properly, but he doubted the dagger alone would serve against so many foes.

And then he waited.

The wolves lifted their muzzles and sniffed the air, then, one by one, they began making a soft, snuffling sound. It almost sounded as if…as if they were laughing.

The lead wolf, the one who had attacked William, grew darker, seemingly drawing the forest shadows closer and wrapping itself in their cool, black embrace. And then its lupine form began to soften around the edges, to flow inward, as if the creature were no longer made of flesh at all, but rather night-shadow. The blackness pooled on the forest floor for a moment before fountaining upward and coagulating into a bipedal shape. The darkness fell away, rolling off the night-creature like water to reveal its new form—a naked man, so pale as to be nearly bone white, lean taut muscles like sculpted marble; shaggy black hair spilling past the shoulders, nearly down to the waist; glittering yellow eyes, still more wolf than human. The being laughed softly, displaying long, sharp incisors.

William felt a thrill run through him. It was possible that the manlike thing before him was a hallucination brought on by age and fatigue, but in his heart, William knew this was not so. The creature was real; the tales about this place were true! And if beings of darkness existed, then that meant…

The other wolves followed their leader, becoming first shadow and then men. Or rather men and women, for both sexes were represented in the pack. They all stood laughing as they regarded him.

William felt anger begin to rise. "May I ask what you find so amusing?" His voice sounded flat and muffled by the surrounding trees, but still strong and unafraid.

The lead wolf—or rather lead creature, since he no longer wore a lupine shape—nodded at William's feet. "You are, man. You and your superstitions."

The being had a strange accent, one William couldn't place, but he was nevertheless able to make out the thing's words.

TIM WAGGONER

"An odd statement coming from a superstition made flesh," William countered.

The creature gestured, and the grass at William's feet began to writhe as if caught in a wild wind. But the night air was still. He watched the blades wrap around the discarded bottle and then pass it forward to other blades, which in turn grasped it and passed it farther along. Within seconds, the bottle had made its way to the pack leader's feet. He reached down and plucked the bottle free from the blades which encircled it. He then held it to his mouth, extended a tongue slightly too long to be human, and upended the bottle.

William watched as several drops fell onto the creature's tongue—with no effect.

The leader tossed the bottle over his shoulder and grinned. "There are superstitions, and then there are superstitions." He gestured again, more forcefully this time.

The grass around William's feet came to life once more, wrapping tightly around his legs, growing and lengthening as it did so. William raised his dagger, intending to slice himself free, but a tree root burst forth from the ground and encircled his wrist, tightening, tightening, until his hand was forced open and the blade fell to the forest floor. He raised his sword, but a second root pushed free of the earth and caught his sword arm, likewise tightening until he dropped his last remaining weapon.

He fought to pull his way free, but the roots proved too strong. He felt a sudden stabbing pain shoot through his left arm, felt a heaviness settle in his chest. He stopped struggling and took several deep breaths. The pain subsided, but it did not entirely cease.

The creature—what it was precisely, William didn't know; a shapeshifter, a drinker of blood, perhaps both—came toward him. Not walking so much as appearing to glide across the grass, as if it were somehow bearing him forward. As it neared, its form altered once more. Its hair became as strands of vine, its skin rough and craggy like bark, its fingers lengthening and twisting like tree twigs. But its eyes remained feral yellow, its sharp teeth stark white.

It passed across the line of holy water William had surrounded himself with, and stopped a mere inch from his face. Its body smelled of forest loam and decaying vegetation, of leaves freshly wetted by a spring dousing, of rich dark topsoil, of oak, ash and pine.

William found himself staring into the face of the Green Man he had once seen carved above the entrance to a small village church.

"I'm curious, man, as to what brings you to my forest." Without waiting for a reply, the creature reached its twig fingers toward William's head. He felt their sharp tips puncture his flesh, burrow through his skull and sink into the soft matter of his brain.

His scream echoed throughout the forest.

The Green Man smiled.

William had fought in Outremer, the land beyond the sea, for nearly five years—without ever seeing his father and brothers—before realizing the Crusades were more about glory, personal enrichment and bloodlust than they were about liberating the Holy Land from the Saracens. But he had gone on fighting for decades after that, for he knew nothing else; after all the killing he had done, was fit for nothing else. But eventually he started to grow old, started to slow down. More, his mind and heart were weary of battle and blood. And so like many who had come crusading, he decided to settle in Outremer. He had saved some money. Not much, but a sufficient amount to purchase a small house in the village of Kalila, not twenty miles from the Mediterranean.

He lived alone in his humble abode, not having taken a wife (or several) from among the local women as so many former crusaders had done. He had seen and done much during his days as a warrior, and these memories haunted him, often causing him to brood for weeks on end, and wake screaming in the night. No, he wasn't fit to be a husband. Besides, he liked living alone. At least, that's what he told himself.

TIM WAGGONER

William made it a habit to take a walk around the village just before dusk every evening, often stopping at the fruitseller's to purchase a handful of dates, walk, eat, and, as usual, be alone with his dark thoughts.

After fighting over this land for so long, William felt more at home here than he would have in England. He had come to understand and respect these people. What did it matter if he did not share their particular set of religious beliefs? True, he had slain many Saracens in his time as a warrior, but unlike some others, he could at least say he had killed no children, raped no women.

At least not many.

He was admiring the subdued red and orange of the sunset as he passed a chapel in what had previously been a mosque. But despite it now being a place for Christian worship, Moslems were allowed to use it for prayer as well, provided, of course, that they behaved themselves. As William walked by this evening, he saw a young Frankish knight escorting an old Moslem man out of the chapel. Well, escorting was too genteel a word: The knight was forcibly removing the man.

"Out, heathen!" proclaimed the young knight as he threw the man into the dirt. "This is a house of the Christian God now, and not for the likes of you!"

The Moslem, whom William recognized as Ousama, a rug merchant, rose indignantly to his feet. "Both our peoples have shared the mosque since you were suckling at your mother's teat, boy! Now let me pass!"

Ousama attempted to force his way into the chapel, but the knight shoved him back down to the ground and drew his sword.

William dropped his dates and started running toward the chapel, but he was too late. The knight's sword rose and fell and Ousama's blood stained the earth. The youth grinned in satisfaction as he knelt to wipe his sword on Ousama's robe.

William intended to shout at the young knight, demand to know why he had slain a man who had only wanted to pray to his god. Wanted to demand of God—either God, any god—why He would let one of his worshipers die like this.

SEEKER

Instead, he found himself drawing a dagger from his belt.

The knight was young and strong, but William was far more experienced in the ways of killing. It wasn't long before the youth's body lay in the dirt alongside Ousama's.

The next morning William packed up his meager belongings and said farewell to his few acquaintances. He left his home to Ousama's widow, for whatever money it might bring her. And then he bought one last handful of dates from the fruitseller, and set out on the long journey back to England.

And so you came looking for us, following legend and rumor until you found our Wood. Soundless whispers echoing from the cold, cold places where the Green Man's finger-roots penetrated. *But still I do not understand why.*

William couldn't speak, couldn't move at all, save to breathe. But he sensed the Green Man delving deeper into his mind until he found what he was looking for.

Ah, I see. Once you were a devout man, an unquestioning believer in your God. But you have lived too long, seen and done too much to believe so easily now. So you came here seeking proof. For if shadows such as ourselves exist, then must not there be a Light to cast them?

I am sorry to disappoint you, man. We cannot answer the question you have brought before us. Does your God exist? We do not know. All we know is the Wood, and all it knows is Us.

The connection between William and the Green Man evidently worked in two ways, for the old warrior caught jumbled impressions and images, few of which made sense. There was one word, one concept he was sure of, however: Gangrel. The being before him had once been that, been Gangrel, a night-creature, one of what his kind called the Damned. But he had found the Wood, or perhaps the Wood had found him; it made no difference. And the two had become One. Others of the Damned had been drawn to the Wood—Brujah, Ravnos, Nosferatu, Ventrue—leaving behind their clans to become vassals of the Green Man, to partake of the ancient power and knowledge of the Wood. And in the process, they had been transformed into creatures such as the Green Man; in a sense, they were his progeny. His and the Wood's.

The dark ones before William were incredibly old, had forgotten far more than he could ever hope to learn. Still he sensed the Green Man was telling him the truth: Neither he nor his pack knew the answer to William's question.

If William had had control of his voice, he would have moaned in despair; if his body had obeyed him, would have slumped in defeat. To have come all this way, fought so hard, endured so much, and still not know…

You are old, kine: your body weak, your spirit tired. It is time to rest, time to let go.

The warrior that still remained in William wanted to fight to the very end. But the man in him was weary of struggling, weary of the endless battle.

William still couldn't speak, but the Green Man sensed his assent and nodded.

William felt his life leaving him, being drained through the roots the Green Man had sunk into his flesh. It didn't hurt; in fact, the release felt rather pleasant in a distant, numbing fashion. He felt himself relaxing, letting go; he watched as his vision grew gray, then black. And then he was falling, down, down into a warm, welcoming darkness.

But awareness didn't desert him altogether. From a great distance, he felt the sated Green Man withdraw his finger-roots, felt the empty vessel that had been his mortal shell collapse to the forest floor. Sensed the pack move forward to worry his corpse, to get at what little liquid remained in his desiccated husk.

When they had finished with him, the dark ones departed, merging back into the forest shadow that had birthed them. Eventually smaller, more timid predators ventured forth and took their turn, and, when they were done, the insects.

Days passed. Days of sun and rain, of night and cold. Days which gave way to weeks, then months. Until finally time ceased having any meaning for the spark of consciousness that had once been William, and there was only the inevitable, unwavering progression of the seasons. Only the grandeur of the Wood, the glory of the Green, and William, a part of it all.

The Red Elixir

BY KEVIN ANDREW MURPHY

ereon tipped the crucible, pouring the glass across the tray as the chains of the rigging chimed in protest. "It is strange to think that what is so red would be so blue." The molten sand flowed to the far edges of the frame, melting the wax lining with a scent of charcoal and burnt honey. "And yet, by Art, what is now the closest we mortals know of the fires of Hell, will tomorrow be nearest we can see of the color of Heaven's firmament."

"Do you think you hold Heaven and Hell prisoner in your powders and elixirs, glassmaker?" Gereon's guest sat in the corner of his workshop, still shrouded in his scholar's robe and tippet.

Gereon shrugged, releasing the crucible to swing free and laying the tongs to one side. "I know the colors that men ascribe to them. I know the tints and shades which the Greeks have set forth, that if one wears emerald spectacles, the resonance of that shade will induce thoughts of serenity; and that cobalt, when mixed with base sand and the ashes of marsh reed, will produce a blue so pure as to inspire one's thoughts to Heaven. Just the same as bloody crimson incites lust, anger, and the sins of the flesh...yet can only be obtained with powders of noble gold." He adjusted the tray, raising it on one of its supports so the glass did not pool too thickly to one side. "As for the true peace of Heaven or the torments of Hell...what can any man know of such things?"

The scholar sat silent in the corner, head bowed, and Gereon finished the last touches upon the tray. "There," he said, reining the crucible back into its place in the eaves and placing the tongs on their hook, "barring the displeasure of God, tomorrow the Church will have its glass, and I will have my gold. Until then, we may discuss what we might."

Gereon went to the mantle, where the phoenix decanter sat. One of his finer pieces, truly, with a lovely golden shimmer to the glass, though he was more partial to the elixir it contained. "Might I interest you in a formula I have recreated? The ancients know it as the Seeds of Gold, and while hardly the Water of Life, I find it health-giving and invigorating all the same." He poured a glass, gold flakes dancing in the cordial as the aroma of caraway wafted up.

"Thank you, no." The shadowed figure glanced towards the firelight. "I'm certain it would not agree with me."

Gereon set down the glass, then poured another. "What manner of man are you, friend?" He placed the goblets before the fire to warm, gold flake swirling in the cordial. "You come to my home, you ask for my time, then you refuse my hospitality and do not even give me the honor of your name. Come, all I know of you is that you are some nameless scholar, that you purport to have interest in my art, and you still have not allowed me to see your face or let me know what I might call you."

The figure glanced to the glasses before the fire, the gold dancing in each. "You may call me Bonsanguinius."

"That is a scholar's name." Gereon retrieved his glass, watching the flecks of gold dance at the slight movement. "If we are to go by such, you should rightly call me Master Ignatius." He gestured grandly to his surroundings, the bowl of the goblet nestled in his palm. "But we are in my home, and my workshop, and all the apprentices are sent home for the day. I am now simply Gereon, and Master does not apply. Not till tomorrow when I meet with the Bishop and give him the replacement glass which his fumble-fingered monks need to finish the windows." He took a sip of the tonic, warm with fire and spice. "So, now, tell me your name, and allow me to see your face. Otherwise, I have nothing more to say to you."

The scholar glanced to the fire, then to the shop, dark but for the glowing tray of glass. "I had heard you sought the Stone. The Stone of the Philosophers...." He spoke in hardly more than a whisper.

Gereon shrugged and took another sip of cordial. "That is the past. I have since learned that the Bishop will pay me far more gold than I can make at the hearth. And if I can turn sand and marsh reeds into gold, well, then, who's to quibble about an extra step with a Bishop and a church in between?" Gereon laughed, pleased, since it had been a while since he had had opportunity to use that jest, then remembered the situation that had prompted it. "Yet I fear that Nature will more easily reveal her secrets than you will yours."

The scholar paused, then looked up. "Not quite so impossible as that." He tugged upon the end of his tippet, the silken hood falling back to reveal his face, young, but wan, drawn and pale as only an ascetic's could be, a man who cared more for books than human company, and more for knowledge than the sun. "My mother called me Ernhardt. It has been a long while since anyone has called me that, though I will not object if you do."

Gereon smiled. "Very well then, Ernhardt. Welcome to my home. Will you drink with me, or must we philosophize more before you will?" Before he could object, Gereon swept up the glass of warmed cordial and placed it in the scholar's pale hands. "As the song says, 'Come, let us drink it while we have breath, for there's no drinking after death!'" Gereon raised his glass.

Something in this must have touched the young scholar as funny, for he laughed dryly, then clinked his glass against Gereon's. "'And he who will this health deny, down among the dead men let him lie!'"

Gereon drank, though he noticed that "Bonsanguinius" did nothing more than touch the cordial to his lips. Gereon shrugged. Odd little bird, that one. Scrawny, scarcely more than twenty. He reminded Gereon of himself when he had first reached journeyman in the Glassmakers' Guild, the proudest guild in all of Cologne, and when he'd started his quest for the Stone, the most costly and ridiculed task in all of Hansa's League.

KEVIN ANDREW MURPHY

But he could forgive youth its follies; it was a way of forgiving himself. "And so do you now quest for the Stone, young Ernhardt? Do you wish to ask a master where he has gone, and what paths he has taken, so you might profit by his folly? Well then, let me tell you this—there's more gold in the Bishop's purse than there are fishing bobs at the docks, and even if you were to transmute bushels of lead, it would hardly equal the coffers of the church. *That* is what I have learned."

"Yet, what of immortality?" The words fell, pure and brittle as glass, to the floor of the shop, and Gereon felt his finger tense around the delicate bowl of the goblet. "Immortality," Ernhardt said again. "Isn't that the quest of the alchemist? The true prize of the philosophers? The gold, or so I have heard, is merely a sign of the purification of base mortal flesh into the ichor of the gods."

Gereon took a sip of his elixir, then lowered the glass slowly. "You speak blasphemy, Ernhardt. Do not let the Bishop hear you talk in that manner." Then he smiled. "With God's grace, I'll have my immortality in the next world. As for this one, well, I leave two fine sons and a daughter, and a bit of Sappho's legacy, at least in material form. The glass I have poured this evening will be placed in the *Tempelhaus*, and will shine in the sun long after I crumble to dust, and the same with my children, and my children's children. It is prideful enough for me to think of that. Anything else would be presumptuous."

The young scholar looked into his glass of gold-flecked cordial, the level unchanged. "Then you have abandoned your quest?"

Only the young could speak with such disbelief, or such dismal lack of understanding. "Look at me, Ernhardt," Gereon said. "What do you see? I am an old man. My tonics may aid my longevity, with the grace of God, but I have marked forty-seven years this spring. How many more might I expect?" He took another draught of the Seeds of Gold. "Were I a man of twenty, immortality might be a fine thing. But as I am? I've grown nearly as fat and slow as the Bishop, and what hair still remains upon my head is grey as driftwood. My Sylvia, whom I cherished, is dead, and even if I were to take another to wife—for I am certainly rich enough—how could I expect her to share the love and devotion which can only come when two are young together?" He paused, wistful, remembering how beautiful she had

THE RED ELIXIR

been when he was young, then shook his head and took another sip. "No, no. Immortality is nothing without youth, and the only proven way to preserve that is to end it. Persephone's beauty is nothing more than early death, and I am too old to have even that as an option."

Ernhardt nodded sagely, as if in agreement, but then said, "I had been told that the alchemists also knew the secret of returning the aged to youth."

"And are you in need of that?" Gereon grimaced wryly, and was glad to coax even a reluctant smile from the dour young scholar. "Ernhardt, let me explain a bit more of the alchemist's quest, and then you will know of the scope of the folly you contemplate." He drained the last flecks of gold leaf from his glass, then set it on one of the tables. "If you wish to proceed upon the Path to the Great Work, you will need some place to begin. But where? The ancients all agree upon the steps—sublimation, exhalation, calcination, putrefaction—but what base matter do you start with? Antimony? Bismuth? Perhaps lead, for it is so very popular, or quicksilver, since it magically alloys with anything? Or do we tire of mineral matter and proceed to vegetable? Shall we be literal in how base we wish our material to be and start with dung and offal? Believe me, I've tried. You won't even begin to comprehend the subtle bouquets of stench you can coax from a mere horse apple. But at least those seldom explode like the salts of mercury or the compounds to be made from sulfur. I've tried those as well, and it was a lucky thing I had very little of the substances and only lost an oven to the concussive force."

The scholar sat there, dour and serious, and Gereon felt a twinge of pity, as much for himself as for the boy. Not one more laugh or smile could he coax from the waxy face, even with the heights of his own folly. "Truthfully, Ernhardt, I have tried them all. I have tried combinations. And in the end, I must say that the lore of the ancients is correct—the only ones who will discover the Stone of the Philosophers, the Flower of the Quintessence, are those who are destined to find it, and who have already been accepted into the society of the True Adepts, who have judged them worthy."

Ernhardt sat there in the firelight, pale and serious. "What is required for that?"

Gereon shrugged. "Merely an Adept, one who has achieved the Flower of Immortality. And a bit of the Quintessence. The *Lapis Potensimus* itself, or perhaps just one of the Elixirs that comes before, the White, or even the

Red. It hardly matters. Any of them will do." He waved his fingers dismissively, doing his best to make light of his failure.

Ernhardt stood. "Very well then, alchemist. I give you the Red Elixir." He held up the goblet then, and the golden cordial had transmuted to crimson, red as blood. "If you speak the truth, then this is all that you will have need of from me."

Gereon paused, looking at the goblet, his phoenix glass, then at the young man with the burning eyes who held it. "You jest, boy. Tell me, who has put you up to this? Who in the Guild? Trust me, I'll pay you well, and your secret will be safe with me."

The youth's eyes blazed in the firelight. "I am no member of the Glassmakers' Guild, Master Ignatius. I come only on my own business, and yours, prompted by rumors some twenty years old of a worthy candidate, one Gereon of Cologne who inquired deeply into the mysteries of Life and Death and Quintessential perfection." He paused. "I am sorry. If I have found the wrong man, I can simply pour this into the fire, then leave you to your glass and your bishops, to remain content with your gold and whatever immortality Sappho and God in their mercy grant you."

Gereon stood stricken, then raised a trembling hand and pointed to the glass. "It is...the Red Elixir?"

"It is a Red Elixir," the scholar once known as Ernhardt said. "It was given to me, and I achieved my measure of immortality, as it was given to one before me, and one before him. That is all." He glanced to it, then back again. "Do you desire it, Master Ignatius?"

Gereon did not know whether to cry or curse, whether dead Hope had returned to life, let free from Pandora's Box where it had been buried, or if this were merely some cruel joke played by his fellow Guildsmen. "Yes," he said at last, then laughed uneasily. "Place it on the mantle, young Master Bonsanguinius. The steps are simple. I've done them many times before, and I'm fat and old and can indulge in a hobby. And if I fail, well, then, the least I can expect is a glass of wine from whoever set you to this jest, and a good laugh from the Guild."

"And if you do not fail?" The young man held the cup as if it were the Lord's chalice itself.

THE RED ELIXIR

"Well then," Gereon said, "I suppose I shall have all of eternity to contemplate that very question."

✜

"I see the old fever has troubled your brow again, Master Ignatius." The Bishop padded about the shop, his golden slippers silent as cats' paws, his attendants holding the hem of his vestments clear of the sand which strewed the floor. "I thought you had forsworn the quest of the Philosophers."

"I have not forsworn the Sciences, nor my Art." Gereon fit tubes together and placed the cucurbit over the burner. "Matters of philosophic inquiry can only reveal more wonders of God's creation, your Holiness."

"I see," said the Bishop, peering at the vessel in the center of the apparatus. Bonsanguinius's gift of the Red Elixir had gone through many stages, all the colors of the peacock's tail, but now sat in the fluid in the bottom of the vessel, a blackened lump. "Be careful that your inquiries do not lead you to damnation. Tomorrow is the Sabbath, let me remind you, and the Lord commands that all work be set aside. Even the Great Work."

"No trouble there." Gereon adjusted one of the flames, sheathing the wick of the alcohol burner. "The Philosopher's Work mirrors that of God. What was begun on a Monday can be resolved by Saturday."

"You will miss evening services."

Gereon looked to Bishop Hatto. "Can you absolve me of that?"

The Bishop smiled fondly. "I believe I can grant special dispensation, considering the fine work you have done for the church. But perhaps you might make a gift of this latest bit of glass? God would look kindly upon it."

"Alas, your Holiness," Gereon said, "my sons are both at university, and the lining of my daughter's dowry chest is still quite thin. To give more glass to the *Tempelhaus*...I know what I must do for God, but what must I do for my children?"

The Bishop wandered over to the latest sheet of glass, propped up and polished for his inspection. "Such a beautiful blue. Heavenly, in truth. I am certain that any bride would be proud to be married under a window crafted from such fine materials."

Gereon looked at the black lump in the middle of the alembic. Bubbles were beginning to form around it. "I'm afraid Gretchen will not marry that high. The *Tempelhaus* is reserved for the nobility."

"And friends of the church," the Bishop added, counting the pearls upon his rosary. "I know cobalt glass does not come cheap, but for such a lavish gift... Well, special dispensation can be made for a great number of things. A fine marriage in the *Tempelhaus* will more than make up for shortcomings in a dowry...and such a favor is a gift that money cannot buy."

Gereon nodded. "Such a gift would be only too kind. Gretchen will be thrilled once she hears the news."

"Very good," the Bishop said. "Bless you, my son." He then looked to one of his attendants, who passed off his half of the Bishop's vestments to his fellow, then bowed and quickly went outside the shop.

A moment later he returned with five sturdy monks, who placed the topmost sheet of glass in the wood shavings, then lifted the crate by its rope handles and set out the door. "Careful, Brothers." The Bishop raised a hand in caution. "God would be most displeased were we to lose another such crate. Master Ignatius has been only too kind to give us these replacements as a gift, but I'm sure he cannot afford such generosity again."

Bishop Hatto looked back to Gereon and smiled. "So very kind of you, Master Ignatius. Your Gretchen will have a lovely wedding once her time comes, and you have only to tell me once she has selected the young man and I will post the banns myself." He then placed a hand on Gereon's shoulder. "But I expect to see you in church tomorrow. The Lord declared the Seventh Day as a day of rest, and you are in need of it, my friend. You have been neglecting your sleep and your health, and you are not a young man anymore."

"I know," Gereon said. "Thank you, Your Grace."

"Bless you, my son." Bishop Hatto extended his hand, allowing Gereon to kiss his ring.

Gereon bent and touched his lips to the pigeon's blood star ruby, glowing in the dark of the workshop.

❖

Stage turned by stage. The black egg in the belly of the alembic cracked, releasing white light, glowing and swirling as the Red Elixir transmuted to the White, the Quintessential purity of Aristotle's Fifth Essence.

Now all that was left was to produce the Flower, and the Stone at its center.

Gereon had read the manuscripts, followed all the steps before, but had never progressed this far. Never but in his wildest imaginings. Yet while the alchemists' riddles and the writings of the Philosophers had revealed many things, they had not explained everything, and he was at a loss to know what must be done to produce the Flower, now that the Red Elixir had been transfigured to the White.

He looked about the workshop, empty now that all the apprentices had gone home for the day and the Bishop and his retinue had taken their glass and left, and then his gaze came to rest on the mantle and the phoenix flask.

The cordial. His ancient formula. The Seeds of Gold.

All flowers began with a seed, and while his tonic had not been the Elixir Vitæ itself, perhaps all that it needed was the Quintessence to nourish it, the Quintessence he had been gifted with.

Hesitantly, Gereon retrieved the flask, then swirled it, mixing the flakes of gold into the elixir so they hung in suspension. But how much? How much to add?

God had worked his miracle in seven days. A seventh should be enough. Carefully, so as not to lose the suspension, he poured a measure in, then set down the phoenix flask and watched.

The Seeds of Gold washed down through the tubing he had crafted, around the waxen seals, and then poured into the main vessel, disturbing the milky purity of the White Elixir. Then the two mixed together, the luminescent white with the liquid crystal, the gold collecting together with the luminous precipitate, like iron filings to a magnet, and then the tree began to grow.

Slowly, at first, it formed, a heap of golden sand at the base of the vessel,

KEVIN ANDREW MURPHY

but then it began to put up shoots and branches, reaching out like a spray of coral, until at the end of each twig a blossom of white opened, glowing at the tips, like a spray of elderflowers caught in the morning sun. The Flower of the Quintessence.

Gereon then watched as the flower grew dim, the lights going out one by one, like stars at the approach of dawn, until the fantastic spray of the golden tree melted and congealed again, becoming not a black egg, but a golden-yellow one, the *Lapis Potensimus*, the Philosopher's Stone.

He watched, knowing that there was one last step left, one step which would transform the Philosopher's Stone into the *Elixir Vitæ*, the Water of Life. Slowly, Gereon raised the heat, searing the bottom of the flask until it glowed like a phoenix's egg, all but molten. He pumped the bellows, maintaining the temperature, sweating with the effort and exhaustion as he watched the last transformation take place.

Like an egg, the Philosopher's Stone split in two, the golden contents exalted to the top of the vessel like the legendary phoenix rising from its ashes, spreading out its flaming wings until it enveloped the contents of the vessel. Then it dissolved into sparkles and fire, the vessel glowing gold. The *Elixir Vitæ*, the Water of Life.

Gereon ceased to stoke the fire, and watched as the flames died, but the radiance continued. He sheathed the wicks of the burner, but still the Elixir maintained its radiance.

He had done it. He had succeeded. He, Gereon of Cologne, had been admitted into the society of the Philosophers, the immortal Adepts who guarded the secret of eternal life, youth, and wealth.

Sylvia had said he was mad. He'd been mad to continue his quest, mad to follow the alchemist's dream while he had a wife and child to look after. And so he had set it aside, and then one child had become two, and two had become three. A small family, truly, but one which he could care for, and provide what advantages diligence and prosperity could.

The Elixir glowed, yellow as a shadowed sun. Sylvia had died. Died before she could see this. Dead. And with her death he had forgotten the meaning of his quest, and why he'd been on it.

Gereon held his hand up, testing to feel the radiant heat of the glass, but felt nothing more than residual warmth. Hesitantly, delicately, he touched

THE RED ELIXIR

his finger to the side of the cucurbit, and while it was warm to the touch still, it was hardly burning, though glowing from within all the while.

The Philosophers had not written of this, but Gereon was familiar with the phenomenon. Some liquids caught fire, burning with an inner demon when mixed together, even when both had been cool to the touch before, while others drank in heat, pulling it within or transmuting it to light, as it seemed did the *Elixir Vitæ*.

He could not wait. If he were to hesitate, the liquor might lose its potency, the Water of Life could turn to ice, or turn to vinegar like wine left exposed to the air. Quickly, Gereon took the cucurbit down from its stand and poured a large measure of it into the phoenix glass which had stood empty since the beginning of this work.

The Elixir glowed, and Gereon took it up, feeling it beginning to chill his fingers now that it was no longer trapped within the superheated glass. Hesitant at first, he took a sip, and then a greater draught.

It tasted of winter snows and cool ice, honey and amber, crystallized violets and dried rose petals. All things cold and perfect and immortal, forever young and frozen in their flush of beauty. Like Persephone.

He drank more, then poured another glass, feeling the cooling fire flow through his veins with the touch of winter. Gray hair fell to the counter as he picked up the second glass, and he saw the withered back of his hands, spotted, with the fat melted away.

The Philosophers had mentioned this. That to regain one's youth, one first had to experience old age and death. The dance of the hours ran only forward, and even though the sun would come back full circle, night would still have to fall in between.

The second draught of the Elixir caught in his throat as if the icy claws of Winter were choking him, but he forced himself to swallow. His hand convulsed, the glass shattering, and then he fell to the floor as a violent tremor came over him.

Death. It was the Dance of Death. The curse of St. Vitus. He lay there feebly, expecting the Reaper to take him, or the Angels, or even Hell itself, but none came. Only Winter and the touch of ice, numbing first one part, then another, until at last he felt no more.

KEVIN ANDREW MURPHY

❖

Gereon woke to the crack of fire in the hearth, a log popping as the flame found some knot of sap, and he sat up to find his clothes hanging loose. He touched his hand in wonder, feeling the smooth skin of youth, then shook his head to move aside the long hair hanging across his face.

He brushed it back, feeling the ease of movement in his joints and the freedom from the aches and pains that the flesh was heir to, then stood up, grasping very quickly at his belt as his pants nearly fell down.

"Congratulations, Ignatius," said a voice from the shadows, and Gereon looked and saw the Adept Bonsanguinius sitting there in the nook beside the fire. "You have done what many immortals would give their eyeteeth for—you have returned to youth at the moment of your rebirth. Congratulations, I will say it again."

Gereon cinched his belt tighter, amazed by how far it went as much as by anything else, then shivered involuntarily. "I'm very cold."

"That is a thing you will get used to." Bonsanguinius poked up the fire with the poker, stirring the ashes until more of the coals were exposed. "Come, warm yourself. But do not look into the flames too closely. You will find that our kind have an unreasoning dread of them." He shrugged. "I suppose that is simply the way that Nature would have it; swallows hate crows and crows in turn hate hawks, just the same as any creature hates that which can destroy it. So, it is to reason, the dead hate pyres, and all that is related to them."

"Dead?" Gereon echoed.

"Dead." Bonsanguinius shrugged. "Come, sit down and warm yourself. You are dead. But you have the beauty of Persephone, and we walk in her footsteps, perfect and immortal."

Gereon sat down beside the fire, drinking in its warmth, but hesitant to look at it, for it now stirred some primal fear, as the other Adept had said. "I do not understand..."

"Do not worry, Ignatius. You will soon enough. You are a clever man." He stirred the fire, his skin waxy in its light. "The immortality of the Adepts was not as true as we would have liked. True, we lived for centuries, many

THE RED ELIXIR

of us, but even the power of the *Lapis Potensimus* began to pale, and we looked elsewhere for that which could extend our existence. One named Tremere peered into the dark corners of the world, and hidden in them, he found the Damned, and with them the box of Persephone's beauty, which Venus had Psyche fetch up from the Underworld."

Gereon shivered. "Psyche perished."

"True," the dead man said, "but she returned to life. And Psyche is the Soul, which is both beautiful and immortal, and all the more so for death."

Gereon looked to the fire and recoiled in fear, seeing in its depths the flames of Hell and the torments of the pit. "So it is true. I am damned."

"For meddling with pagan things?" the dead man asked, then laughed with dry humor. "I suppose so. But if it salves your conscience any, you may consider the Bible to be the source of your state. Indeed, many immortals believe it was neither Persephone nor Psyche who were the authors of the Damned, but instead that the Red Elixir is the blood of Abel, which Caine spilt and which God then took and marked him with upon his brow, damning him to walk the earth and display his shame until Judgment Day. The first victim and the first murderer, the first death and the first curse." He grinned. "Unless you are among those blasphemers who favor Lilith, numbering her as the first of our kind?"

"I am Damned," Gereon said, looking down at the floor.

"Damned, and welcomed," Ernhardt said. "Come, brother. You have all of eternity to reflect on what that might mean, and all of those who have followed the Path of Tremere to discuss it with you. And when Judgment Day comes, and God sits on his throne, you may come before him, truthfully, and tell him what you have learned." Bonsanguinius waved to the darkness and fire. "After all, you have all the nighttimes from now until then to make your inquiries."

FINI

KEVIN ANDREW MURPHY

The Winged Child

BY RICHARD LEE BYERS

The newborn was pleasant to look upon in the common manner of babies, with tiny hands, a round, ruddy face, and wide brown eyes. She smelled of tears and her mother's milk. But the small wings—all but invisible when she lay on her back, covered with a fine down that was nonetheless a little coarser, more feather-like, than the hair on her head—set her apart from her fellows. Many Romans had debated the significance of her deformity. A few thought it a token of heavenly grace, while others, unable to imagine that God would bestow any such favor on a Jewish household, deemed it a punishment. But everyone agreed that the child's birth was a sign. And I'd broken into her home under cover of darkness to discover how the blood of an omen tasted.

I'd never fed on an infant before. Since they were too frail to survive the ordeal, my scruples had forbidden it. But now I was living in an age of miracles and portents. A gigantic torch had fallen from the sky. An image of Christ had wept crimson tears, and a wolf had slunk into the church to worship it. It had rained blood, and stones, and fiery armies had fought among the clouds. Not that I'd witnessed these prodigies myself, nor had anyone I knew, but we believed the reports. How could we not? It was the autumn of 998. The eve of the millennium. According to countless prophets, doomsday was less than a year and a half away.

One might have expected the imminence of the Last Judgment to inspire repentance, and in a handful of souls, it did. But generally speaking, the world seemed to become more depraved than ever. Nobles waged war with exceptional savagery, butchering their enemies' serfs and laying waste to the countryside, abbots and bishops contending for land and gold as viciously as the counts and princes. In times of famine, which were all but constant, parents ate their children, and certain butchers vended human meat. In Rome, we had, if rumor spoke true, an ailing lunatic for an emperor and a devil-worshipping sorcerer for a pope. Presumably our patricians were scheming to overthrow them—less because of their infirmity or necromancy than because they were foreigners, Saxon and French respectively—but they spent most of their time pursuing their endless feuds with one another, waylaying their foes in the twisting alleys.

And if the threat of the Day of Wrath drove mortals to terror and madness, imagine how it affected us vampires. According to Mother Church, even the wickedest mortals had some hope of salvation, but we Cainites were already judged and damned. Thus it seemed only sensible to seize every pleasure and indulge every whim, even the cruelest, in what little time remained.

Drawing out the moment, savoring it, I leaned over the crib, pulled back the linsey-woolsey covers, and put my scaly, twisted Nosferatu finger in the palm of the baby's hand. Her skin was very soft. Too young to distinguish between fair and foul, or between wholesome and unnatural, she cooed and gripped my digit in her own. Abruptly I heard her heart thumping, smelled the blood pulsing through her veins, and my fangs slid out of their sockets. I picked her up.

Someone gasped.

I turned. A smoky, pungent candle in her hand, a young woman with long black hair stood in the doorway to the next room. She'd drawn on a linen chemise against the chill. She too smelled of milk, and I surmised she was the baby's mother.

With only her taper and the moonlight leaking through the oiled-parchment window to illuminate it, the room was dark. Even so, given my hunch, crooked limbs, leprous snout, and mismatched, gleaming yellow eyes, I should have been a terrifying sight. Yet she advanced on me calmly, hands outstretched. "Please, give her to me," she said. There was only the subtlest quaver in her musical alto voice.

Bemused, with a bit of difficulty—the blood thirst, once awakened, was not easily denied—I retracted my fangs to facilitate speech. "Don't you know what I am?" I asked in my grating rasp. The infant gurgled and squirmed, the tip of one wing tickling my chest. I shifted my hands to hold her more securely.

"You're one of the Night People," the woman said. "The blood drinkers who haunt the old ruins and catacombs."

"Yes," I said. "So why didn't you run away?"

"I knew I'd never find help and get back in time," said the Jewess. She was only a stride or two away now. With my apish arms, I could easily have clawed her to shreds. "I beg you, spare my daughter. If you must have blood, take mine."

I shook my head. "Yours won't do. I came to sample the life of a harbinger of the apocalypse." When I heard the sneer in my voice, I realized just how angry I was at God. I'd worshipped Him when I was a mortal clerk, three centuries before. Yet He hadn't seen fit to save me from the curse of my sire's taint, nor would He deliver me from perdition when the stars fell and the rivers turned to blood. Perhaps I hoped to nettle Him by slaughtering one of His works.

"Please," the woman said, "whatever else she may be, she's a *baby*. I see by the way you're holding her that you've cradled infants before, when you were alive. If you ever cherished any child, spare mine in memory of that other."

Like many of my hideous bloodline, deemed monsters and pariahs by even our fellow undead, I flinched at any reference to my lost humanity, and wanted to punish the Hebrew woman's presumption. I imagined myself pretending to give her the baby, then snatching the child back and plunging my fangs into her throat. I wanted to see the horror in the mother's face, and to hear her scream.

RICHARD LEE BYERS

Yet simultaneously, and against my will, I remembered the day my own mother had given birth to my little brother. How proud I'd been when my parents had trusted me to hold him, and what an outpouring of love I'd felt when he goggled up at me.

A sudden spasm of shame smothered my malice and thirst alike. I thrust the winged child at her mother. "Take her," I said.

The Jewess did so with alacrity. "Thank you," she babbled. "Thank you—"

I veiled myself in darkness. Her words catching in her throat, she peered wildly about. I slipped from the chamber, and then from the house.

My return to reason and mercy, if one can dignify my forbearance with such words, was fleeting. In the months that followed, I prowled the city, giving my thirst free rein and playing pranks.

Up on the Caelian hill, workmen were demolishing a graceful pagan temple for building stone, part of the ongoing desecration of the glories of the past. No doubt they wanted the material to erect a new church, some nobleman's lumpish, squalid keep, or just a row of paupers' hovels. I rigged a pediment to collapse on top of the laborers, and several were crushed.

Several weeks later, I myself vandalized a grotto sacred to Priapus, down by the Tiber in the very shadow of the Lateran. I snapped off the god's *membrum virilis*, garlanded with flowers by matrons wishing to conceive, just as it must have been in Julius Caesar's time, then threw the remainder of the statue in the river. I carried the stone phallus away with me, and when an unfortunate Cluniac monk crossed my path, I sodomized him with it until he died.

Cloaked in darkness, I spied on noble families, divined their schemes and secrets, and then anonymously divulged these to their bitterest rivals. Such intelligence tempted them to strike at one another. Most nights the city echoed to the clangor of steel.

Curious to see what would happen, I tainted the cakes at a St. Catherine's Day feast with the spores of a phosphorescent fungus I found growing deep underground. Those who partook beheld terrible visions. One woman slashed her tablemate's throat, and a falconer clawed his own eyes out.

It was as if I was doing all I could to injure Rome. Which was perverse, because I loved the place despite its corruption and decline. It was the only

THE WINGED CHILD

home I'd ever known. Perhaps I imagined that by damaging it myself, I could cheat God of some of the pleasure He would otherwise derive from its demolition.

But my nights weren't entirely devoted to mischief. Occasionally I returned to the home of the Hebrews, to hover about them unseen. I learned that the mother's name was Judith, and that she'd called her daughter Sarah. Judith was the wife of a trader obliged to travel as far afield as Burgundy, the Lombard lands, and even the Caliphate in pursuit of his living. In his absence, she managed both his household and various business matters with a competence which I, who had once tended to ledgers and correspondence myself, could only admire. The winged infant was still the talk of the town, and Christians often came to gawk at her. Frequently they attempted to proselytize Judith as well. Such intrusions vexed her, but she bore them with courtesy and patience.

I didn't fully comprehend the impulse that drew me back. But for some reason, it soothed me to watch Judith chopping onions for a stew, blinking away tears, or listen to her singing lullabies to Sarah. Even when such homely spectacles filled me with sorrow instead of joy, it was a *calm* melancholy, uncontaminated by the rage which was ordinarily an integral part of my grief, and that made me prize it.

And sometimes, when Judith left the room, I dissolved my cloak of shadow and revealed myself to her baby. Sarah always greeted me as happily as she had at our first encounter, smiling when I picked her up and crooned nonsense to her, chortling when I made faces or tickled her. Her affection suffused me with a warmth which the fellowship of my fellow undead had never evoked. I reckoned that the child must indeed be a saintly or angelic being, if she even had love to spare for a monstrosity like me.

Having no wish to alarm Judith, I never intended to appear to her again. But fate amended my plans.

One February evening I awoke in my cubiculum, a snug crypt littered with my belongings and decorated with a fresco of Daniel and the lions. I pushed aside the lid of my sarcophagus, a massive, ornately carved marble box I'd plundered from the tomb of one of the Theophilacts, and began my ascent to the city above, casually avoiding the myriad traps with which we

Nosferatu defended the approaches to our lairs. Near the surface I met Octavian, scuttling down from above. With a left profile that was largely bare bone crisscrossed by a few strands of festering flesh, and empty eye sockets that somehow still possessed the power of sight, he was notably grotesque, even for a member of our breed.

"Don't go up there!" he said. His voice had a buzzing undertone that always reminded me of a swarm of flies. His breath smelled like a bloating corpse.

"Why not?" I asked.

"There are devils," he said, "killing the humans and setting fires! I saw them myself!"

"Then the last days are here," I said, nor did I question that the apocalypse had arrived ten months early. Not everyone expected it to come at midnight on the final night of the year, though that was, perhaps, the commonest belief. Some visionaries had prophesied that the world would perish on the summer or winter solstice, or on the eve of the nativity.

Now that the end was nigh, I found myself affrighted, but with a strange, hypnotic sort of fear which urged me closer to the source of my dread. Hindered by the narrowness of the tunnel, I tried to maneuver around Octavian. "I have to see," I said.

"You don't understand!" he wailed. "Everything's burning!" Belatedly I recalled that he had a horror of conflagrations dating from a misadventure two hundred years before, when a pack of werewolves had set him ablaze.

Feeling a pang of pity, I put my hand on his shoulder. "It's pointless to try to hide," I told him. "God's angels will still find us and cast us into the Pit. So we might as well face the end bravely, and witness what there is to see. Perhaps we'll get a chance to bow to Lucifer, or to spit at Jesus."

Octavian shoved me backward. "Get away from me!" he screamed, and then ran deeper into the catacombs. I watched him for a moment, then climbed on.

When I reached the streets, I found a scene which, if not quite as hellish as my fellow Nosferatu had predicted, was nonetheless ghastly enough. The air reeked of blood and smoke, and firelight flickered against the sky. Rome echoed with screams, the crackle of flames, and the crunch of breaking

THE WINGED CHILD

timbers. Shadowy figures blundered through the darkness, staggering, sobbing, bleeding, pleading. Or else smashing any object in reach, raping the weak and wounded, and striking people down. Though none of the aggressors in my immediate view sported horns or tails, their contorted features and bestial howls were sufficient to suggest they were devils who'd taken on human form, or at the very least, mortals possessed by imps.

Beholding the carnage, I went berserk myself. I drew my *patula*—my short sword—and joined the fray, lashing out at one victim after another, indulging my baser nature for what I assumed would be the final time. After a time I found myself slaying in concert with two brawny fellows swinging axes. My deformities didn't seem to trouble them. I was wrapped in a cloak and my hood shadowed my features, so perhaps, in the darkness and frenzied confusion, they didn't notice. Or perhaps, I thought murkily, being demons, they were accustomed to monstrosity.

I don't know how long I spent wreaking havoc, or how, demented as I was, I yet managed to notice petty details of the world around me. But eventually it occurred to me that, though scattered fires were burning throughout the city, the sky was particularly bright off to the west. I could even feel pulsations of heat throbbing from that direction. Which meant that the Hebrew Quarter was well and truly ablaze. And as soon as I realized that, I thought of Judith and Sarah.

It was the apocalypse. Everyone on earth was about to die in one fashion or another. Still, my mental picture of mother and child trapped behind a wall of flame, choking on smoke, their flesh charring, was intolerable. I turned to go to their aid. Perceiving that I was about to abandon our shared butchery, one of the axemen struck at me. I sidestepped, avoiding the blow, and slashed his face open. I shoved him into his comrade, knocking the other murderer backward, then started to run.

My gnarled, mismated legs were better suited for endurance than speed, and as I pounded along, I cursed their clumsiness as never before. Finally they conveyed me to Judith's narrow street.

The houses surrounding the cul-de-sac at the far end were burning fiercely. Silhouetted against the amber glow was a rabble armed with knives and cudgels. I perceived instantly that they were humans, not devils, probably because, unlike my erstwhile comrades the axemen, their violence wasn't random. No doubt believing the act would endear them to God, and that He might then shield them from the demons running rampant through the city, they'd gathered for the specific purpose of burning out the Jews. And to kill Sarah, whom they had evidently decided was an abomination. A ranting Benedictine held the squalling infant over his head, displaying the sacrifice to God. Forced to kneel, Judith struggled impotently to throw off the hands which were holding her down.

I hurriedly considered my options. I could mask myself in illusion, assuming the appearance of some cardinal or lord, but I suspected the mob was too hysterical to heed the commands of any such authority. Shrouded in shadow, I could conceivably attempt to snatch Judith and Sarah from their captors' grasps, but since I had no way of sharing my invisibility with them, their tormentors would simply grab them again. The only viable strategy was to attack.

I plunged into the mass of humans, striking left and right, carving a path to those I hoped to rescue. Two of the Christians fell beneath my blade before the rest realized anything was amiss. Then the shouting and screaming began. Many of the rabble recoiled before me. Either they'd gotten a good look at my features, or they simply lacked the stomach for a fight. But others lunged at me with weapons raised.

It didn't matter. I was as strong as any ten of them, and whenever I cut or punched one, he went down. They battered and slashed me in turn, but, equipped as they were with weapons of ordinary wood and steel, they would have needed an extraordinarily deft or powerful stroke to incapacitate me.

In half a minute I came face to face with the friar, a paunchy little fellow in a stained habit. Had he been courageous, and strong in his faith, he might have caused me more trouble than all his minions put together. But he yelped, hurled Sarah at me, and took to his heels. Though caught by surprise, I managed to snatch the baby from the air and fumble her up against my chest.

An instant later all my adversaries were running, no doubt demoralized by the flight of their spiritual captain. Disheveled, her green kirtle torn at the shoulder and a bruise mottling her jaw, Judith climbed unsteadily to

THE WINGED CHILD

her feet, and I handed the shrieking Sarah to her. She dandled her and crooned nonsense to her, and, rather to my amazement, the baby soon stopped crying.

"Come with me," I said. "It still isn't safe here."

"All right," Judith said.

As I led her away from the nearest fires, I pondered where we might seek shelter from the general mayhem. I was loath to escort my charges into the catacombs. The law of my people forbade it, and in any case, the tunnels were by no means a salubrious environment for mortals. Eventually it occurred to me that if we couldn't descend, we might do well to rise.

A twist in the road brought us close to a square brick tower. "Can you hold on to Sarah and cling to my back at the same time?" I asked.

"I think so," Judith said. "If I wrap my legs around you."

She climbed onto my hump and then I scaled the tower, digging my fingers into the cracks between the bricks. As was true of most of Rome's modern buildings, the stones were so poorly fitted that the gaps provided deep handholds, and the ascent was relatively easy.

When we reached the flat roof, Judith dismounted, and I turned to look out over the city. I suppose that attending to the practical business of rescuing mother and child had cooled the fever of dread which had consumed me earlier. In any case, I surveyed the scene below with saner, more critical eyes than I had before.

And I perceived that *all* the figures rampaging through the streets and alleys were human. Deranged and wicked, but mortals nonetheless, not demons. Moreover, I saw no angels opening seals, nor grim Horsemen thundering across the heavens. No crimson dragon, and no Great Whore of Babylon astride a hydra-headed Beast. This despite the fact that I was in Rome, which, even more than Jerusalem, was the spiritual heart of the world. If the visions of St. John were about to come true, then why hadn't the principal players appeared?

"My god," I muttered, "this is just a common riot."

Judith hesitated before replying. Rescuer or no, I was still a monster, and she couldn't be certain of my ultimate intentions. "Yes," she said at last. "What did you think it was?"

RICHARD LEE BYERS

"I thought it was the beginning of the apocalypse," I said sheepishly. "Someone claimed to have sighted the hordes of Hell invading the city. That's what's driven everyone mad. I imagined I saw them myself."

She burst out laughing.

"What's wrong?" I asked.

"Forgive me," she gasped. "I don't know why, but it's just funny. A creature like you, cowering in fear of other horrors."

For a moment I glared at her. Then it seemed ridiculous to me as well, and I laughed along with her, my mirth like the bray of an ass. And as I guffawed, the delusions which had tormented me for so long dissolved like mist in the morning sun. Somehow I simply *knew* that all the portents I'd heard tell of, the giant torch, the rain of blood, and all the rest of it, had been as fictitious as tonight's infernal incursion. That Sarah's wings were merely a sport of nature, and not an omen of anything. In short, that the world *wasn't* about to end. It would weather the current year and go on the same as always.

I thought of all the needless harm I'd done, enraged by the notion that my ultimate damnation was at hand, and cringed in shame and revulsion. Now laughing and sobbing at the same time, tears of blood streaming from my eyes, I crumpled to my knees.

Judith hovered behind me. I sensed that she wanted to rest a comforting hand on my shoulder, but didn't quite dare. Then she gasped and cried, "Oh, no!"

Lifting my head, I looked where she was looking, and immediately understood the cause of her dismay. One of the arsonists roaming about had set fire to the city's largest granary. Thanks to the recurrent famines, the poor were already on short rations. Now it was certain that many were going to starve.

As I watched the flames licking up the walls of the storehouse, I realized that while the earth was bound to survive the year, Rome very well might not. Frenzied with the alleged approach of doomsday, the mortals were likely to keep rioting, slaying, and destroying until they'd ravaged the city beyond repair.

THE WINGED CHILD

The thought was like a blade twisting in my breast. At that instant I vowed that, come what may, I'd keep Rome from murdering itself.

A worthy intention to be sure, but how was I to manage it? It was easy to kill and maim, but how could a loathsome monster like me cure the cankerous despair gnawing in thousands of mortal breasts?

Suddenly a scheme came to me, and I smiled up at Judith. Not recognizing my expression for what it was, she paled. "Don't worry," I told her. "Everything is going to be all right."

Eventually the emperor's troops marched out and restored some semblance of order to the city. Afterwards Judith and I discovered that not every Hebrew had lost his home, and that those who still possessed walls and a roof were sheltering those who didn't. I left her and Sarah in the care of their own folk, then hastened to the catacombs, reaching their sheltering darkness just before sunrise.

As soon as I could convene a council, I advised my fellow vampires of my intentions. Many, as certain as most of the humans that the apocalypse was at hand, thought my plan pointless. Some deemed it foolish for other reasons, or so perilous it was bound to result in my destruction. A few regarded it as an impudent jape at Heaven and Hell alike, which would surely elicit supernatural retribution. But a smattering were game; enough, I hoped, to carry off the final movement.

The next night, cloaked in shadow, I slipped into the Castle of St. Angelo.

In my three centuries of existence, I'd explored Rome rather thoroughly, but I'd never ventured there before. Immense and forbidding, it had been built to serve as the mausoleum of the emperor Hadrian, but for a long while now it had been the stronghold of the popes. It was a fortress, not a basilica, and no doubt the orgies and atrocities of recent residents— Theodora the She-Wolf, Alberic the Serpent Child, John the raper of nuns, and the rest of their ilk—had polluted it. Still, countless masses had been celebrated there, and sacred relics abided within the walls. A pale shadow of holiness clung to the place, wracking my flesh with cramps and twinges, clouding my thoughts with a dull, amorphous dread. Bearing these discomforts as best I could, skulking past sentries and slumbering servants, I finally located the sickroom of Otto III.

RICHARD LEE BYERS

The Saxon emperor stank of sweat and illness, and he was twitching and jerking in his sleep. Gently, so as not to wake him, I pulled down his tangled linen sheets and fur blankets. The naked form beneath was gaunt with fasting, scarred with scourging and the chafing of a hair shirt, and some of the galls were infected. Evidently, terrified of the millennium like everyone else, he'd been mortifying his flesh. Quite possibly he'd rendered himself sick thereby, after which his physicians had weakened him further with cupping and bleeding.

I clawed open the tip of my finger, then insinuated it into his mouth. After a moment, still without waking, he began to suckle my blood like a babe at its mother's breast. I gave him a good long draft, then slunk away.

The following midnight his color was better and he was resting more easily, and his pus-filled wounds had begun to heal. The unnatural vigor in my blood was mending him. When I returned yet again, he looked all but fully recovered, but I gave him a third drink anyway. I had to, to bind him to my will.

Afterwards I placed my lips to his ear and whispered suggestions. He wouldn't remember them, not consciously, but he'd carry them out when the time came. Then, aching and weary but feeling smug, I withdrew.

The brazen man was waiting for me in the antechamber. The automaton was taller and bulkier than any mortal, and its contours were a radically simplified version of the human form. It had sculpted eyes and ears, but no hair, nose, mouth, neck, nipples, nails, navel, or genitalia. Pivots and hinges, stinking of olive oil, linked its gleaming parts together.

I'd heard the tale that Pope Sylvester had animated a metal figure with his magic, but I hadn't encountered the thing on my previous incursions into the fortress. Now, startled, I froze, and the automaton lunged at me, not clanking and rattling as one might have expected, but silently as a ghost. It threw its arms around me, pinning my arms to my sides, and began to squeeze.

I could tell instantly that the thing was strong enough to crush my torso and snap my spine. Even that grievous harm wouldn't destroy me, but it would incapacitate me, and then the creature could pick me apart at its

THE WINGED CHILD

leisure. I butted its face, denting it, but my attacker didn't falter. The terrible pressure of its embrace increased. Blind with agony, I thrashed.

Something snapped, and then my right arm was flopping around, loose but ablaze with pain, and bending in the wrong places. Somehow, in my frenzy, I'd torn it free of the brass man's grasp in the only way possible, by breaking it.

I willed a surge of my blood into the afflicted limb. With a fresh burst of pain, the shattered bones knit. I punched the automaton's dome of a head.

At first the blows didn't seem to damage the creature, but then its polished yellow skull flew from its shoulders. It collapsed with a hideous clangor, half pinning me beneath its weight.

With considerable effort, I dragged myself clear. I desperately wanted to sit and rest, but I didn't dare. Someone had surely heard the noise and would come to investigate. Drawing on the dregs of my strength, I wrapped myself in darkness, then shambled away.

As I made my way back to the catacombs, I pondered what had happened. Apparently Sylvester had somehow discovered I was visiting the emperor's bedside, and dispatched the brazen man to trap me. But why had the automaton waylaid me on the way out rather than going in? Perhaps the sorcerer pope comprehended exactly what I'd been up to. Perhaps he'd wanted Otto to enjoy the benefits of a final measure of my blood, but also meant to ensure that I'd never have the opportunity to compel my newly made slave to do my bidding.

It was disturbing to think that any mortal, even a mage, might understand the ways of us Cainites as well as that. But I had more pressing concerns. I'd managed my three forays into the castle and survived to tell the tale. Now it was time for the climax of my plan.

The following night, the night of St. Simeon's day, I led my vampire comrades up into the city. I only had a dozen helpers, but most of them, like me, knew how to commune with animals, and they augmented our numbers with gigantic rats, spiders, ants, fleas, lizards, and serpents, the pets we Nosferatu grew to unnatural size by feeding them our blood. With such monsters swelling our ranks, I hoped we might pass for a credible host of Hell.

RICHARD LEE BYERS

I stole a magnificent black destrier from a nobleman's stable. The horse, sensibly enough, didn't like my looks or those of my companions, but, using my powers, I bound him to my will. Then I masked myself in illusion. Whenever I'd played the trick before, I'd used it to pass for mortal. This time, however, I endeavored to become a grander monster than before.

I gave myself the heroic chest and perfect alabaster features of a statue of Apollo I'd seen in the Forum of Augustus. Still, no one was going mistake me for a god or a seraph. Long, fantastically curling horns sprouted from my brow, while my eyes were orbs of crimson flame. Immense black bat wings unfurled from my shoulder blades. My *patula* grew into a sword five feet long, the blade surrounded by crackling hellfire, and my mail shirt glowed as if it were red hot. My hairy goat legs and cloven hooves were naked, the better to display their satyrish deformities. In short, I resembled Satan himself, or at least one of his more impressive lieutenants.

When my disguise was in place, my friends and I began our rampage. Momentarily possessed by their vampiric thirst, some of the Nosferatu slew the occasional mortal. Scenting blood, excited by our bizarre procession, a few of the giant animals forgot the commands we'd given them and did the same. But by and large, things went according to plan, and we drove the humans before us, shrieking the grim tidings that this time, devils truly had invaded Rome.

In order to sow as much terror as possible, we followed a winding course. It was well after midnight when we reached the Piazza of St. Peter. As I'd hoped, a huge crowd jammed the square in front of the basilica, wailing to God and Mother Church for deliverance. At our entrance, they screamed and cringed back against the high, gray, oval walls, trampling and crushing one another.

We Nosferatu roared, gibbered, and struck menacing postures. Then the gate to the Court of St. Damaso swung open, and, as per my instructions, Otto rode out on a snow-white destrier to meet us.

His face was calm and resolute, without a trace of fear. Instead of a helm, he wore the diadem of Charlemagne, and he'd eschewed gauntlets to display the gold ring Sylvester had placed on his finger on his coronation day. A cloak of shining, gilt-trimmed imperial purple streamed from his shoulders.

THE WINGED CHILD

The mob stopped shrieking and cringing. They gazed up at the emperor with desperate hope in their eyes. Suddenly it didn't matter that he was a foreigner. He was their monarch, duly anointed by the Church and miraculously risen from his sickbed to defend them in their darkest hour, and, for that moment at least, they loved him.

They were reacting exactly as I'd hoped, and I wished I could feel glad. But I was too dismayed at the sight of the lance in Otto's hand. To my eyes, it shone with a hurtful silvery light.

It was my fault he'd brought the wretched thing. I was the one who'd instructed him to clothe himself in his regalia, to look as impressive and kingly as possible. Accordingly, he'd armed himself with the *Dominica Hasta*, the Sacred Lance. A Saxon treasure, not a Roman one, which is probably why I'd forgotten he possessed it. It was the weapon Constantine had used to overthrow Maxentius, and so supersede paganism with Christianity. Supposedly the spear contained one of the nails that had bound the Savior to the cross. In any case, it was clearly a genuine relic, and deadly to creatures like myself.

One of my friends whispered to me, urging me to flee. I wanted to, but stood my ground anyway. Perhaps, in the final analysis, I didn't prize my monster's existence all that much, or perhaps I simply felt I'd come too far and put my comrades to too much bother to turn tail now.

Otto shouted the bellicose yet pious speech I'd composed for him, challenging me to single combat to decide whether God or Beelzebub would possess the city. Lightheaded with fear, I accepted the invitation with the sneering arrogance appropriate for an archfiend. The mortal leveled the spear, and we charged one another.

I hadn't told Otto to hold back in the battle for fear that he'd move as if he were in a trance, and in so doing render the fraudulent nature of the combat obvious. He was really going to try to destroy me, and thus my scheme had always had an element of risk. But given my vampire powers and skill with a blade, I'd thought the chances of his beheading or crippling me were slim. I'd imagined that after a suitably thrilling engagement, I could undertake to sustain a lesser wound, which would nonetheless look mortal to the spectators. As I toppled from my steed, I'd veil myself in shadow, leaving the mortals to infer that when I perished, my body had melted away.

The presence of the *Dominica Hasta* altered everything. It was at least conceivable, albeit unlikely, that one tiny nick from the weapon might destroy me, and in any case, it was excruciating just being near to the thing. Its radiance all but blinded me. Pain stabbed through my limbs, and panic yammered through my mind. Resisting the desperate urge to fly, telling myself again and again that Rome, Judith, and Sarah needed me, that it didn't matter if I perished so long as they were saved, I struggled to control my mount, to parry or dodge the thrusts of the spear, and to lash out with dangerous-looking but harmless strokes of my own. Fortunately, even with my vision clouded, it wasn't too difficult to avoid inadvertently cutting Otto, considering that my blade was two feet shorter than it appeared.

Somehow I kept the spectacle going for several minutes, until the Sacred Lance had stolen all but a shadow of my strength. Then, squinting against the weapon's glare, guiding my destrier backward, I dropped my guard, inviting Otto to thrust at me. He did.

I'd attempted to place myself at the very edge of Otto's striking range, hoping that if I then swayed away at the instant he attacked, I could keep the lance from penetrating deeply. But either I'd misjudged the distance, or else, enervated as I was, I simply moved too slowly. The spearhead slammed between my ribs.

Agony blasted through my entire body. Octavian may have felt something similar when his form was enveloped in flame. The pain was so overwhelming that I couldn't even scream, let alone maintain my illusory mask. The onlookers beheld the winged paladin of Hell wither into a meaner sort of horror.

I toppled from my destrier, pulling myself off the lance in the process, and thudded to the ground. After a few seconds the fire in my flesh abated slightly.

I tried to become invisible, but I still didn't have the strength. A dazzling radiance shone above me. On foot now, Otto poised the lance for another thrust.

I tried to scream that I was his master. To command him to spare me, and never mind my idiot plan. Before I could gasp the words out, the weapon hurtled down and drove into my heart.

This time the pain was so terrible that it became my entire world. I barely heard the mortals cheer. I never sensed my fellow Nosferatu making their retreat, or felt the wary hands lifting me and carrying me into the Vatican, nor would I have cared if I had. I just wanted the *Dominica Hasta* to complete my destruction, and in so doing, bring my torment to an end.

I was certain that it would, too, for I could feel its holy fire corroding my substance away. But after a while—eons later, it seemed to me—someone pressed down on my chest, immobilizing me, and, with a series of grunts and tugs, some other fellow laboriously extracted the weapon.

When I was able to focus my eyes, I saw that I was lying in one of the deaconries established to minister to the poor. It was a good thing, too. Weak as I was, if my captors had borne me into one of the churches, the aura of sanctity might have killed me. Here in this long, dark chamber the air smelled faintly of sickness, of pus and phlegm, but none of the other cots was occupied. Two monks in Benedictine habits were backing quickly away from me. A third man, tall and gaunt, studied me from farther off. He wore the same robe and rope belt as the others, only with the cowl up, shadowing his features. But when, groaning, I managed to sit up, he involuntarily lifted his arms as if to fend me off. His long sleeves fell away from his hands, revealing the ruby on his finger, a jewel which ecclesiastical protocol reserved for the pope.

"It's all right, Your Holiness," I croaked. "At the moment I lack the strength to harm you, even if I wished to."

"I must compliment you," Sylvester said calmly. "It was a clever notion. The people have been going mad in expectation of an Armageddon, so you gave them one. Not quite the end of the world, but a gaudy clash between Good and Evil nonetheless. And miraculously, their champion prevailed, and saved them from the jaws of Hell. I pray the mummery will prove as cathartic as you hoped, and purge them of their fear."

"Amen," I said. "Now, what do you mean to do with me?"

"You willingly subjected yourself to the *Dominica Hasta*," Sylvester said. "Was it because you *want* to die?"

RICHARD LEE BYERS

"Not yet," I replied. "To tell you the truth, I wasn't expecting the spear."

Sylvester smiled as if I'd said something funny. "In that case, yonder door"—he pointed—"leads to the gardens. Head east and you'll find a postern, unguarded and unlocked." This, then, was the reason for his disguise. It would scarcely be politic for the Vicar of Christ to be seen liberating one of the Night People to resume his predations.

I hastily hobbled out of his presence before he could repent of his mercy.

In the months that followed, people remained obsessed with the millennium, but they seemed somewhat less hysterical than before. Perhaps my efforts had made the difference, though of course there was no way to know for certain. In any event, Rome endured till December 31st. As midnight approached, a hush fell over the city. When the bells of St. Peter's rang out the old year, a number of mortals simply dropped dead, their hearts stilled by terror, while vampires moaned and shuddered in their lairs.

But the earth didn't open to swallow us, nor did fire rain from the sky. Soon afterwards all the bells in the city began to peal in jubilation at the world's survival. People wept, laughed, embraced, and danced in the streets.

For some years afterward I kept watch over Judith and Sarah, though only the latter knew it. On one occasion my vigil required me to protect all the Hebrews from another mob, and a legend grew up of a hunchbacked goblin with the brawn of Samson, who appeared to defend the ghetto in times of need. Sarah wed in 1015, and bore a daughter the following year. It was probably just as well that the baby had no wings, but I thought it rather a pity even so.

THE END

THE WINGED CHILD

FREE BOOKS FROM WHITE WOLF PUBLISHING!

We at White Wolf are constantly striving to bring you revolutionary fiction from the hottest new writers and the legendary voices of the past. Filling out this form will help us better to deliver our unique stories to the places where you go for books. And if our undying gratitude is not enough to get you to respond, we will send a **FREE WHITE WOLF NOVEL OR ANTHOLOGY** to everyone who returns this form.

But enough about us, tell us a little about yourself...

Name

_____

Address_____

_____

Where do you go to buy new books? Check the type of store you shop. If your answer is a chain store, please list your favorite chains.

__ Chain
stores_____
__ Independent bookseller
__ Comic or hobby stores
__ Mail order from publisher
__ Mail Order House
__ Internet bookstore

How do you find out about new book releases that you want to read?

__ Published reviews
   __ In magazines (please list)
   __ In newspapers (please list)
__ Advertisements in magazines
__ Recommendations by a friend
__ Look of cover
__ Back cover text/review quotes on cover

That's it. Send completed form to—   White Wolf Publishing
      Attn: FREE BOOK
      735 Park North Blvd.
      Suite 128
      Clarkston, GA 30021

One response per customer, please. Allow 4-6 weeks for delivery.

A Vampire:

THE MASQUERADE EVENT

FROM THE SHADOWS OF THE DARK AGES, TO THE MODERN VAMPIRE UNDERWORLD, THESE TWO CROSSOVER TRILOGIES WILL SHOW YOU THE SWEEPING GLORY AND THE TERROR OF THE LORDS OF THE NIGHT.

TO SIFT THROUGH BITTER ASHES
BOOK ONE OF THE GRAILS COVENANT,

AVAILABLE IN JULY.

OBSESSION TAKES A 12TH-CENTURY VAMPIRE ON A QUEST THROUGH THE DESERTS OF THE HOLY LAND. HE MUST RACE AGAINST TIME, THE CHURCH, AND ANCIENT DARK FORCES IN HIS BID FOR THE MOST COVETED TREASURE OF ALL.

THE DEVIL'S ADVOCATE

BOOK ONE OF THE TRILOGY OF THE BLOOD CURSE,

AVIALBLE IN OCTOBER.

THE THIRST FOR BLOOD BECOMES UNQUENCHABLE IN THE VAMPIRES OF THE MODERN WORLD. THEY FEED ENDLESSLY, AND STILL THEY STARVE. WILL PANIC DESTROY THE MASQUERADE, OR IS THERE OPPORUNITY IN THE CHAOS?

WHITE WOLF PUBLISHING

WORLD OF DARKNESS